Where There's a Will

By Richard Gilbert

Copyright © 2006 by Richard Gilbert

ISBN 0-7414-3116-5

Cover photo by R. Gilbert.

Published by:

PUBLISHING.COM

1094 New DeHaven Street, Suite 100
West Conshohocken, PA 19428-2713
Info@buybooksontheweb.com
www.buybooksontheweb.com
Toll-free (877) BUY BOOK
Local Phone (610) 941-9999
Fax (610) 941-9959

Printed in the United States of America

Printed on Recycled Paper

Published September 2006

Many have helped and influenced me in the development of this novel. To them I offer my thanks and gratitude. To name a few: Denise Wallace & Crew, Amoy Allen, David Gilbert, David and Kathy Biddle, Bill and Cheryl Hopmann, Barry and Paula Wicks, Roger Hamm, Bonnie Magee, Jorge R. Guzman, M.D., Tom Berry, Jan, the kids and grandkids.

For Jan: I hope the wait was worth it. Thank you my love.

The Beginning of the End...

The world was black. The world was red. The world was pain. I kept slipping back into the void, unable to reclaim full wakefulness. There were brief instances of half awareness, kind of jumbled together, not making any particular sense. At one point a bright light seemed to be burning in front of (above?) me, the heat of its rays felt on my face. My eyes were closed and for the life of me I couldn't open them. There were subdued voices talking nonsense in matter-of-fact tones. At another point I had the sensation of smooth movement through cool air. Everything seemed fantastic, like the lyrics from some old psychedelic rock music.

There was the reassuring touch of Jenna's hands, wiping my brow and rubbing my arms. I knew her touch. I knew her caressing voice. I couldn't make out the words but I knew the voice. At times I'd become aware of warmth beside me and I knew that warmth to be Jenna's body, pressed close to mine.

I heard other voices, familiar though not quite identifiable, yet comforting nonetheless. I sometimes wondered what had happened to me. Had I crossed over? Was I in a staging area, waiting to emerge into the afterlife? Or was this the afterlife, this dim region of uncertainty? Would I spend eternity in this black and gray tunnel of despair and pain? Between periods of unaware existence and time spent in the gray area, the pain became more real but less threatening, if that makes any sense.

Slowly I became more aware of my surroundings. At last, as I was listening to voices that I'd decided were those of Jenna, my mother and Aunt Chili, I managed to open my eyes. The searing intensity of the lighting caused my ocular neurons to scream with pain and I closed my eyes and bellowed my discomfort. It came out something like "Glumph." Not loud enough to startle a three year old waiting for a monster from the closet to devour her on the spot. But Jenna heard me. I sensed her leaning over me as the others in the room wanted to know what was wrong.

"He's waking up!" Jenna exclaimed. I wanted to tell her to turn the lights down but my mouth seemed to be in need of

lubrication, like the Tin Man's in The Wizard of Oz. *My eyes, still stinging from the light, were gummed together with sleep crud and I tried to reach them with my right hand to wipe the grit away but couldn't. I felt a warm and wet presence on my face accompanied by a soft cooing sound from Jenna.*

"What's happenin', is he wakin' up?" My mother's voice had come closer. She sounded fearful yet full of hope.

I continued to struggle with my eyelids and finally was able to open them again. The light assaulted me once more but with superhuman effort I managed to keep my eyes open. As they adjusted I could see that it wasn't a brightly lit environment as I'd first thought. In fact, the lighting was subdued, provided by hidden low wattage track lights and a small lamp on a table between two chairs at the far end of the room. I was in a hospital bed in a hospital room, a private room, and Jenna's lovely face was peering down at me with concern. The faces of my mother and Aunt Chili floated above the foot of the bed.

I tried to speak to them but made only a dry rasping noise. My head was somewhat elevated and Jenna placed a sliver of ice from a Styrofoam cup on my lips. As it melted, the shockingly cool liquid poured over my cracked lips and traced a path of near ecstasy through my mouth and down my throat. The sensation was wonderful. I never wanted to stop drinking in the sweet nectar of life but Jenna put the cup on a table after but a few ice chips.

"Wha..." I tried but Jenna shushed me.

"Don't try to talk right now," she admonished. "There will be plenty of time for that later. Right now, you need to rest and gather your strength." My mother leaned over me from the other side of the bed and took my hand and smothered it with both of hers.

"That's right, Roy-Roy." I hated when she called me that. But I couldn't object, could I? I mean, I was alive, right? And surrounded by three women who loved me? I knew they all loved me, even Jenna. Still.

"Ya need to get your strength back," my mother continued. I wanted to tell her that I was fine, aside from a little pain and wooziness, but I fell asleep first...

Chapter One

I was close. I could feel it. Soon I'd have him. I'd been searching for a long time and I was finally closing in. My fingers rotated the knurled knob, the steel slightly cool to the touch. I allowed myself a small smile as I swiftly brought him into focus. Suddenly, my fingers were still, my breathing halted. There he was. Henry J. Siner, Jr. I gazed for a moment, transfixed, then in one swift motion I slapped the green button and he was mine! The machine whirred and clicked and I allowed myself to relax a bit. As I leaned back in the chair, I wished for a cigarette. I'd quit some two years before, but it seemed the craving would never go completely away.

I ejected the cartridge from the machine and placed it in its rack. Then I headed for the front to retrieve my copy of the deed recorded in 1947. They're public records, but I always feel a bit like a detective, tracking down long ago events, reconstructing the past through a trail of documents. I know I'm romanticizing, but, hey, it's one way to keep the job from boring me silly. Besides, I'm good at what I do. At least, *I* think so. Those two claims a few years ago could have happened to anybody.

I sauntered to the counter and slapped my dollar down like a cowboy ordering a drink in an old John Ford western. But the paper bill didn't provide the satisfying clunk of a silver dollar.

"I always get my man," I drawled, hoping Gladys wouldn't notice the lack of a clunk.

"Roy, you always make my day when you come in here." She plucked my copy from the tray in the laser printer. "Yep," she said. "You always make my day with your funnyisms." I wasn't sure what a funnyism was but I smiled and gathered up my deed and the receipt.

"Listen here, shweetheart. I'll cover you up in funnyisms." I did that Bogart thing with my lips and teeth and Gladys giggled as I walked down the corridor toward the elevator.

Where There's a Will

My name is Elroy Sebastian Dixon. I don't know how I got those names. No one else in my family has those particular monikers, except for Dixon, of course. That's my mother's name. I've asked my mother about it almost as many times as I've asked her who my father was. She couldn't answer on either account. Said she couldn't even remember Dad's name, really. She'd been a hippie, one of the first in the early sixties. She gave birth to me, her 'love child,' in '65, and some areas of her recollection were hazy. At least I wasn't named Moon Spirit or something.

I grew up here in Southwest Florida. The only time I got farther north than Tampa for any length of time was the two summers I spent in my youth as a barker with the Great Smokey Mountain and Eastern Seaboard Traveling Carnival. I mostly worked the games and slept under a truck but I developed a keen insight into human nature. Everyone is looking for something for nothing. It's true: you can't con an honest man. I'd seen it over and over while with the carnival. The marks thinking they're going to win big at games obviously stacked against them. I've seen in it in real estate transactions, the closing and insuring of which I've made my life's work. Well, it's how I make a living, anyway. And real estate transactions in Southwest Florida have been particularly notorious for involving hustlers and marks.

I'd tried several forms of gainful employment in my life, including commercial net fishing. My family had a long history in the business until the net ban legislation of the mid '90s sent them madly scrambling to find other income streams, such as drug smuggling and welfare. I'd given up on the way of life much sooner than that, say, about two months after I first gave it a try.

I'd also tried tomato growing and packing. My ex-wife's family had been in the business for three generations until the North American Free Trade Agreement pretty much forced them out. I'd given up on the agricultural approach somewhat earlier, about seven weeks after my ex-wife's uncle Creighton Mullis had put me in charge of stacking 25-pound boxes of tomatoes on pallets to ready them for shipping.

I exited the Courthouse and was struck by how beautiful the day had become. Earlier, the sky had been a leaden gray, the wind brisk. The palm trees lining the streets of old Ft. Myers had whipped to and fro. Broken fronds scuttled along like large,

2

whispery insects. It looked like it might rain. We sure needed it. It hadn't rained at all so far this month and we were already nine inches behind for the year. We were under mandatory water use restrictions and the fire index was high.

Now, the sun was shining in all its radiant glory, its warmth and brightness enveloping the city. Another perfect, though dry, winter day had arrived. In the parking lot I let down the top of my 1976 Cadillac El Dorado. It was a gorgeous thing, a classic. White to reflect the heat. It was large, roomy, powerful, and sexy. So I told myself each time that I bought gas.

The big engine turned over and caught smoothly and I goosed it a little as I left the parking lot. When I reached US 41 southbound, I put my mind in cruise mode and relaxed, enjoying the sunshine and the warm breeze in my face. I reached up on the dash where I kept my aviator style sunglasses and put them on. I slouched in the seat and thanked the fate that had placed me here rather than on some chilly tundra far to the north. True, I had to filter out the six lanes of roaring, rushing traffic darting in all directions around me. I also had to ignore the caustic fumes of exhaust and the bleating horns. All things considered, though, I was happy to be where I was. I tuned the radio to a classic rock station and settled back to enjoy, as much as I could, the thirty mile, 90 minute drive to Mangrove Springs.

Traffic was bumper-to-bumper, stop and start. It took nearly 20 minutes to go from the river to Page Field, the airport that was once the main, make that only, commercial airport in the county. It was also once south of town. Out in the boonies. Not any more. A bustling metro area had grown up around and beyond the small airport, though the city limits had not moved past it. Congestion and development had taken over the entire unincorporated county to the south, even beyond, into the next county of Collier. All the way to Naples. And Naples was about as far south as you could go before you had to turn east.

US 41, or Tamiami Trail, once mostly a two-lane country road carved at great expense and significant human toll from the unyielding Florida landscape, was now four lanes, and sometimes six lanes, from Tampa to Naples. It was hard to tell where one community ended and another began if you missed the signs. Lee County had metamorphosed in my lifetime from a rural, farming county with only a couple of significant settlements, into a sprawling, booming area that was beginning to resemble the greater Miami/Dade megalopoplex. I made up that last word but it seemed to express the sheer, unnerving size of the growth better than any real word I could think of.

Driving down the road I daydreamed a bit about the way it had been, lamented a bit about the way it was, and worried a bit about the way it would become. I also was nearly rear-ended three times, was forced to the verge twice, was cursed several times and did the cursing myself a half dozen times more. A typical, stress filled travail that I had come to know and expect.

I pulled into the parking lot of the Mason Dixon Title Insurance Agency, wiped my sweaty palms on the knees of my Bugle Boys, threw my sunglasses on the dash and gathered my keys, papers and other effects. I glanced skyward but all traces of the early morning grayness were gone. The sky was clear blue with puffy, brilliant white clouds floating about and looking like various sorts of animals. Well, they did! I left the top down.

I went up four steps to the veranda of the building that housed our office. It was a one story modern interpretation of what they call Key West, Olde Florida, or Cracker architecture. High-pitched tin roof, frame construction, up on short stilts with a wide veranda along the front, and painted in pretty pastel colors. It had a wooden ramp at one end of the veranda for wheelchair access. Inside was a little over 3,000 square feet of office space. My partner, Ollie Mason, owned the building, and the company leased it from him at what amounted to a sweetheart rate, given the market in Mangrove Springs.

Just inside the entrance was a small lobby with a vaulted ceiling and ceramic tile floor. Sigrid Holtz, our secretary/receptionist, sat at a desk facing the door, with computer and phone conveniently placed on her work surface. Sigrid was from Germany, as were a good many Mangrovians. Mangrovites? We'd lost our receptionist to pregnancy and Sigrid answered the ad we'd placed in the Mangrove Messenger. Her English was pretty good, if a bit fractured at times, and her German, of course, was perfect. Also, her Green Card was in order. Since there were so many Germans coming to our area, we figured that having someone who speaks German on our staff would be a plus and help generate more business. And her secretarial skills were more than adequate, even in English. We made her an offer immediately and she'd been with us for two years.

"Good morning!" she barked. It sounded more like 'Goot Moornin.' I glanced at my watch and saw that it was 11:58 am. Sigrid was precise, as always.

"Morning, Sigrid. What's up?" I stepped around her to the left and headed down a small corridor toward the offices in the rear.

"You have two messages," she called after me. "One is from the bank about overdrafts again." I could detect faint disapproval in her voice. " And the other is from Jack Muncie. He wants you to call him at your convenience." The phone rang and I could hear her answer it crisply: "Mason Dixon Title. How may I help you?" We were lucky to have her and her Teutonic efficiency.

On the way to my office I had to pass one of our two closing rooms. It was empty. The corridor turned right in front of my office and passed two offices and a small kitchen and break room. Then, right again past the bathroom and our other closing room. I suspected it was empty, also. Then on to the lobby on the other side of Sigrid's desk from the way I'd come, like a horseshoe.

I went into my office and left the door open. Walking around the desk, I glanced at the seat of my chair. Messages, files and anything that needed my attention were usually placed on the seat so that I would be sure to notice them. Papers and files could easily be lost or go unnoticed amid the clutter on my desk. The two messages Sigrid had mentioned were there, along with a file folder with a hand-written notation on the cover. I picked them up and slid into the big leather executive chair. I'm a rather large man, 6'2" and 200 lbs. Well, maybe 210. Okay, 220. The chair, like the Cadillac, just seemed to fit me.

I placed the message slips under the corner of the desk blotter and tossed the items I was carrying on the desk before I looked at the file folder. It was the one for which I had gone to Ft. Myers that morning, the one in need of Mr. Siner's deed. Hey, poetry! I put the deed in the folder and set it aside. Now that I had a complete chain of title I could examine it for flaws before issuing the title insurance commitment. I would do that after lunch.

I briefly considered returning Jack Muncie's call. He was an attorney in town specializing in Real Estate. We were competitors, both selling title insurance and closing services, and a call from him usually meant some sort of headache for me. Or, I thought, maybe he's calling about the election. Mangrove Springs had just recently been incorporated by referendum in a general election and now a race for Mayor and a five member City Council was raging. A special election was to be held in a couple of weeks and politicking had become the areas new pastime. Jack hadn't declared a candidacy but he was lobbying for a position as City Attorney. It was an appointment to be made by the Council and he knew my cousin Evan Muster was favored to win a Council seat. He probably wanted me to put in a good word with Evan. He could wait until the afternoon as well.

I got up and followed the corridor past the kitchen and one office and on to the other corner office. I stopped in the doorway and leaned upon the doorjamb. I had a good three-quarter profile view but she didn't seem to notice me. She was bent over her computer keyboard, a look of concentration on her face. Her brows were knitted slightly, her eyes squinting at the LCD display. Her auburn hair was cut fashionably short, but then it had been cut the same way over fifteen years ago, when it was definitely unfashionable. Her figure was full and robust. Not fat, mind you, but exuding health and vitality. And she had these really amazing breasts that I just had to ogle as I stood there.

Eventually, she sensed my presence and looked up, laugh lines crinkling her eyes as her face lit up a bit upon seeing me. I thought she was the most gorgeous woman I'd ever seen.

"Hi," I said. " Had lunch yet?"

"No. Is that an invitation?" She leaned back in her chair and tilted her head in a questioning way.

"Sure is. If you'll let me, I'll buy you the biggest, juiciest hamburger Burger Baron sells. *And* fries. *And* a shake. What do you say?"

She reached down and grabbed her purse from under the desk.

"What are we waiting for," she said, rising and coming around the desk to join me.

"After you," I said, bowing and pointing the way. After all, I could take my ex-wife to lunch, couldn't I?

6

Chapter Two

I didn't take her to the Burger Baron. Actually we went to Boyd's Shanty. It's a nifty little place right on the Gulf of Mexico, where Sunset Drive turns north to become Tarpon Boulevard, which runs along the beach and across several barrier islands, finally arriving at Ft. Myers Beach. Boyd's Shanty was a three-story restaurant sitting 100 feet from mean high tide. The higher up in the restaurant you were seated the more spectacular the view. I was acquainted with the owner and we were ushered into the elevator and whisked to the rooftop. Plastic patio tables, chairs and umbrellas were scattered about and the view was just breath taking. We sat with our backs to the east and gazed out over the broad expanse of the Gulf. The beach below was peppered with scantily clad sun worshippers of all ages, sexes and proportions. A Chickee hut housed the attendants who'd rent you a lounge chair, a beach umbrella, a paddleboat or a wave runner. They'd also sell you a Para-sail ride 600 feet above the water. A customer was gliding, as we were seated, being pulled south to north by a modified cigarette boat about 1000 yards off shore.

We ordered conch chowder, grouper fingers, Cole slaw and fries. We'd spent nineteen years together, and though we'd grown apart and divorced, we were still quietly comfortable in each other's company. In a strange sort of way my regard for her had been re-awakened by the divorce. Before, I'd been taking her for granted, our existence together actually boring. It had become difficult to keep our lovemaking vibrant and vital. Since the divorce, I found myself thinking about her in a new and fresh way. We were both dating others. She was seeing Vern Otto, someone we had grown up with from childhood, but whom I'd never considered might someday replace me in her affections. She and I still shared the same house with our son and two daughters, though I'd moved to a separate bedroom. And I sometimes would see my old high school sweetheart, Lila Clay. Lila was a travel agent and was on a twenty-one-day cruise through the Panama Canal and up the western coast of Mexico. One of the perks of her trade was a super low price on cruises and other travel. She was gone almost as much as she was in town. I found that to be convenient.

Complicated, huh? And who knew what effect the whole situation was having upon the children, who, thank God, were nearly grown. I'd read that children are mostly formed by the age of six and I hoped this was true.

Back at the office after lunch I found myself in the big chair behind my desk, sliding into a somnolent haze brought on, no doubt, by the sun and the food. I nodded off once or twice as I considered the lunchtime conversation with Jenna. We'd chitchatted about this and that but the talk eventually turned to business. Or, to be more precise, the lack of it.

We'd been in business for ourselves about fourteen years and had gone through downturns before. But the good cycle had lasted so long that it became easy to forget that a slowdown was inevitable and natural. Don't get me wrong. Mangrove Springs was booming, to be sure, but the segment of the real estate market that we serviced was the first to tighten up.

The big gated or waterfront communities were doing just fine, thank you. There apparently were still plenty of multi-millionaires coming in from up north to absorb the product being produced by the major builders. A lot of them even paid cash. Most of the big builders had their own title insurance divisions, which they enticed the buyer to use by offering a discount on the purchase price of the home being sold. A price that was artificially inflated to provide room for the discount. Maybe I'm just a cynic. I suppose that discounts of a few thousand dollars when you're speaking of properties selling for a million and up, way up, probably didn't make a difference, and using their title division was just a matter of convenience. At any rate, that's the cream at the top of the market. What the title divisions of the large developers didn't get generally went to lawyers.

Lawyers could also offer discounts in their legal fees. Independent Title Agents couldn't even provide Realtors with three dollars worth of mailing labels to make it easier for them to obtain listings. The piece of legislation known as RESPA, the Real Estate Settlement Procedures Act, had set up the guidelines in a professed effort to level the playing field so that the bigger players did not unfairly force Independent Title Agents from the market. Right. It seemed to be having the opposite effect. Was it coincidence, I'd often wondered, that many, if not most, legislators were also lawyers? Hmm.

We, Mason Dixon Title, could best be described as bottom feeders in the market. We served the retirees with more modest means, the working class families, and the lower tier of foreign buyers. And then there was the re-finance market. People were constantly re-financing their home mortgages when interest rates were favorable. But the Federal Reserve Board had raised interest rates eight times in the previous nine months and was threatening more raises in the face of inflationary trends. The stock markets were experiencing roller coaster ups and downs and gas prices had nearly doubled in six months. These thoughts made me wake up a bit and I reached into the drawer where I kept some antacid tablets. I chewed two of the chalky things.

Jenna, who kept the books as well as processed the files and conducted closings, had pointed out at lunch that we were closing about thirty percent fewer deals than we had during the same period the year before. And the forecast was for an even bigger drop off in the near future. Our cash flow wasn't critical yet but it might be in intensive care by the time the non-season summer months arrived. And they'd be on us before we knew it.

We'd survived some tough times and we'd probably survive once more. But thinking about it could sure ruin how a man's lunch digested. To calm down a bit I did what I always did when things were tough: I thought of some of the sayings handed down by generations of the Dixon and Mullis clans. Cousin Evan liked to say, "Don't worry it so, boy. Ain't nobody gonna kick ya outta the world." And he'd laugh that big, hearty laugh of his and you'd somehow feel better. And Jenna's dad said something similar when he counseled, "They can't eat ya." That one in particular was reassuring.

I figured that was about all the cheering up I could stand and I cast my eyes over the desk in search of something to do. My gaze caught the file folder with the unexamined chain of title, but that was a little too tedious to appeal to me. Then I noticed my phone message slips and the name Jack Muncie caught my eye. I wrinkled my nose. Not too appealing either. But definitely better than a boring title exam. I picked up the phone and punched up an outside line. I dialed Jack's law firm and told his receptionist, Beverly, who I was and what I wanted.

"Oh, yes, Mr. Muncie's been expecting your call. Will you hold one moment, please?" Before I could tell her that I didn't want to hold one moment, she'd placed me on hold, where I had to listen to one of those nauseating custom advertisements on an endless tape loop. A syrupy female voice informed me that Jack Muncie was indeed the lawyer for me because he specialized in every sort of law there was and, in addition, was the absolute best at all of them. Then I was told that my call was important to the Muncie firm and someone would be with me in a moment. Then I got to listen to some synthesized imitation music before the voice was back. I was going through my fifth cycle of imitation music when it abruptly stopped and Jack's voice came through the line.

"ROY, HOW ARE YOU," he boomed. Of course, he didn't speak in capitals but that's as good a way as any to describe what he sounded like.

"I'm fine, Jack. How's it with you."

"Never better, Roy, never better. The real estate part of my practice is off the charts. Closings are up 166% over last year!" I gritted my teeth and managed a feeble 'great, that's great.'

"Listen, Roy, that's what I wanted to talk to you about. I'm so jammed up that I can't do it all myself. And I'd like to ask a big favor of you, though," he chuckled a bit in what I suppose he thought was a good-ole-boy kind of way. "I don't think you'll find that helping me out will be exactly distasteful." What did he mean by that? Of course it would be distasteful.

"Exactly what is it you'd like me to do?" I was already yearning to be done with this so I could move on to that enticing title exam.

"Well, you know the widow Chastain died last summer."

"Yes, the Dixon's were well represented at the funeral. I was there myself."

"Yes, yes," he said, somewhat impatiently. "Well, after Ralph Rennegar passed away I represented Alma. When she passed away I immediately began the long process of probating her estate. You can imagine how complicated it was, what with her vast holdings and far-flung progeny." He actually said progeny.

"Well, probate's not closed yet, you know, you have to wait two years for creditors, blah, blah, blah." He actually said blah, blah, blah. "But I've got the will admitted to probate and Toby, her grandson, is the executor and successor trustee of her trust which holds all of the major assets. Now comes," God, spare me lawyerly language, "a buyer for one of the parcels and time is of the essence and I HAVE to be out of town for the next ten days or so and, well, that's where I need a favor. Will you do the commitment and write the policy for me and I'll conduct the closing when I get back?" I sat up straight and started paying closer attention.

"I suppose," I drawled, hoping he couldn't hear the saliva dripping onto my desk. "Let's see, I'll need a copy of the contract, a copy of the trust, at least the pertinent part about the powers to convey real property, a copy of the will and the probate case number."

"No problem. I'll have Beverly fax everything to you. If you need anything else, just let her know. I'll be back about, make that the, um, 24[th,] and I'll need everything by then." I was stunned.

"I don't see any problem as long as the chain of title is clean and the will and probate are in order. I assume there will be an order to sell?" I was referring to a probate judge's order to sell property, necessary because probate wasn't closed yet.

"Everything's as it should be,"

"Uh, by the way, what's the purchase price of the parcel being sold?" I asked. "So I know how much to write the commitment for," I added lamely. I'd get that information from the contract. I thought I heard a chuckle from his end.

"Twenty million." I closed my eyes and quickly calculated: a very hefty premium, seventy percent of which would stay with Mason Dixon. We'd make no closing fees, but big deal. Time to welcome in the off-season summer months.

"Okay, Jack. I think we can cover you on this one." Like we were doing HIM a favor.

"Good, good, I thought you might. I'll talk to you when I get back in town. Like I said, Beverly will fax everything to you."

"Righto. See you then." I started to hang up.

"Oh, by the way," he said, drawing my ear back to the phone. "I'd appreciate it if you'd put in a good word with Evan for me. Scuttlebutt has it that he's going to win that council seat and I'd make a damn fine city attorney." I was too elated to feel any revulsion. Maybe Jack Muncie wasn't such a bad sort after all.

"I'll see what I can do."

After I hung up I sat back in that big chair and blew 30 or 40 cubic feet of air through my pursed lips. I recalled another family saying, this one handed down by my Great Aunt Minnie Dixon: "The good Lord only lets you fall so far." My summer safety net had arrived.

Chapter Three

Let me tell you about the Chastain family.

Florida had experienced a land boom before, just after the turn of the century. That's the 20th Century. Land prices were highly inflated. Farsighted visionaries, dreamers, and con artists painted a picture of paradise to flush investors, much as today, but without the controls and sanctions. Then came the Crash of '29. Prices plummeted. And even then there were few takers.

Walker Chastain came to southwest Florida from Chicago during the thirties, and he had a problem. He'd made a lot of money during the twenties from bootleg whisky and he needed a place to put it. When he traveled to Florida they said he carried two suitcases, among his other luggage, which he allowed no one to handle but himself. The story was that the two suitcases were full of large denomination bank notes and that old Walker was looking for a place to invest it. He found it in SW Florida.

Walker Chastain was not formally educated but he had an innate cunning that served him well in dealings involving money. He saw the vision and he was content to wait for it to develop into reality. At those prices he could afford to buy big, dig in, and wait. Land values had nowhere to go but up. So he began buying. He was shrewd. He was a hard bargainer. He was patient. The smell of his money began to circulate.

He took rooms in The Montford Arms Hotel in Ft. Myers, long since demolished, but then a headquarters for the cattle trade. Located on a dirt thoroughfare in the three block downtown area, The Montford Arms had a wide veranda that sported a number of large rocking chairs for the comfort of its guests. And there he held court for the local landowners eager to be rid of their holdings and for the local agents of those far away investors who were likewise inclined.

He never culminated a deal, however, before personally walking the perimeter of the land in question, with forays into the interior at frustratingly irregular and thus unpredictable intervals. He carried two firearms at all times and wore big hip boots. He hired several locals, who'd never owned land but had lived and worked in the area all their lives, to guide him. They walked the land and killed snakes, alligators, bobcats, panthers, and anything else that threatened them. Or just came too close. Or would make an interesting dinner or piece of apparel. Rumors circulated that the group did away with at least one, possibly two, men, squatters who didn't agree with Walker's acquisitive ways.

Once satisfied that the piece of land he was buying wasn't worthless swampland, he'd pay for his purchase with cash and send one of his assistants to the courthouse to record the deed. He purchased land by the acre, by the quarter section and even by the section, which is a piece of land, a mile square, containing 640 acres.

After a full seven months in the area, Walker Chastain returned to Chicago with the two suitcases that had held money now filled with deeds. He'd spent a fortune and now owned 87,650 acres of southwest Florida real estate, much of it close to or along the Gulf of Mexico. It took him two years to tie up the loose ends of his business affairs in Chicago and move his family to Florida. The family resided in a suite of rooms at The Montford Arms until a new, palatial home could be built on one of his prime holdings along the picturesque Royal River, in Mangrove Springs, seven miles inland from the Gulf of Mexico.

In 1956, Walker Chastain passed away at the age of sixty-two. His wife, Thelma, had died the previous year from a bout of influenza. Walker still owned over 20,000 acres. The rest had been lost to con men who took advantage of his reduced mental acumen due to early senility, and to the escapades of his four sons. Three were scoundrels, always in trouble of one sort or another, trouble which required large sums of money to rectify. Not to mention their prodigious spending habits. But Walker loved his sons and denied them nothing. There were bad marriages and messy divorces. Paternity issues were raised several times. Eventually, the three had all left the state in an effort to create new lives for themselves, or, at least, to avoid the law: one in Texas, another in Montana, and the last in golden California. They took large chunks of the family's dwindling fortune with them.

Clive, the remaining son, tried to manage the remnants of the estate after Walker passed on. After a further division of the property via Walker's will, Clive and his wife Alma were left with just under ten thousand acres and less than a hundred thousand dollars. And the family estate.

Clive was not a brilliant man. He was steady, plodding, hard working, friendly and generous with his neighbors. He and Alma had three children. They were involved with their small community and the Calvary Baptist Church. When Clive's congenitally bad heart quit beating in the mid 70s and after the kids and the government got their share, Alma was left with the family estate, a small monthly income and 2560 additional acres of prime Southwest Florida real estate. Her children quickly disposed of their land holdings and fled to new lives elsewhere.

They didn't care for the backward ways of the little rural community. They didn't see the coming storm. The land they sold brought a good amount of money but would have fetched much more if they'd waited a few years.

Eight years before Alma's death, her son Andrew and his wife were killed when their car left the road on a curve and slammed into a tree two miles from their home in Gaithersburg, Maryland. They had one child, 13-year-old Toby, who hadn't accompanied them on the fateful trip. He came to live with his grandmother Alma in the increasingly fast paced environment that Mangrove Springs had become. Toward the end of her life, when she grew so ill, Toby took over and became her sole caregiver. Locals marveled at the selfless actions of the boy, tending to her needs day and night for several long months until the end.

Chapter Four

He was parked in the most remote, and darkest, corner of the parking lot, farthest from the street. The car was running, quietly adding to the pollution. The windows were open so that he might hear the slightest sound above the occasional hum of traffic from Fowler Street, and the muted, bass-heavy strains of the stripper music coming from the girlie joint to which the parking lot belonged.

He felt a little extra thrill whenever he hunted this close to home. He had long ago decided that it was in his best interest to range far a-field in his conquests, to make it harder for anyone to tie him to the events of the evening. But tonight he couldn't help it. His need was great and his time was limited. If it had been at all possible he would have worked one of the larger cities to the north or east, losing himself in the increased hustle and bustle. But the need called him, not allowing him the luxury of time, asking him to hurry, please hurry. He would be as careful as possible under the circumstances, but the need must be met.

He heard noises from the alley that ran behind the strip club and responded by slipping low in his seat, just his eyes above the padded door of the luxury car. A brawny, tattooed man appeared, dragging a protesting young woman by the arm. They stopped under the naked bulb of a security light and the woman raked her long fingernails across the left cheek of the man. He dropped her arm and protested loudly.

"What the hell ya doin', Angel?" You know I wouldn't hurt ya for anythin' in the world." She tugged at her tube top before she lashed out at him.

"I don't know nothin' of the sort, you big jerk! All I know is, you're tryin' to make me do somethin' against my will." She drew herself up to her full height. "And that ain't gonna happen!"

The guy threw up his hands and, head bowed, said, "all right, all right. I get the picture." He peeked at her from behind his raised arms.

"Will you promise me you'll come home tonight?" A smug look of satisfaction crept over her features and her tongue slyly licked her lips.

"You go on home," she said. "I'll be along soon as I make some money so we can pay the rent." He turned, utterly defeated, and headed back in the direction they had come from. She watched for a moment before patting her hair back in place and, clicking along in her high-heels, headed for the entrance to the strip joint.

On her way to the club she passed within several feet of his car. He leaned out the window and appraised the situation: The boyfriend was gone around the other side of the building, there was no traffic in the parking lot at the moment, no people entering or leaving the strip joint, and no traffic on Fowler. He made a decision.

"Hey, sweet thing, you're the one I been waitin' for all night. I was about to give up and go home and do all of this lovely blow by myself. Where ya been?" She stopped and looked at him and he tried to present as non-threatening an image as he could. The smile felt positively goofy on his face. That was good. She made up her mind and moved toward him, smiling seductively, a welcome wiggle on her hips.

"Goodness gracious, you been waitin' for little ole me?" He grinned. They both had their parts to play in this little drama. He didn't reply, just reached over and opened the passenger door, all the while grinning at her and scanning the area at the same time.

Later, after he'd had his fun and was deciding the exact symmetry he would try to achieve in the disposition of her parts, he allowed his thoughts to linger on the pleasures he had derived from her. There had been the cocaine, as he had promised her, he was a man of his word, after all, and the slippery, teasing sex, for which she thought he was going to pay her a ridiculous sum. Then came the surprise as he stole her breath with clenched arms and fists, as his whole body joined the effort to subdue her, his weight atop her, smothering her panicked efforts to dislodge him. Her lungs finally failed under the assault but he waited a few more minutes before releasing his death grip.

Eventually he felt the peace that always came when things fit together, and he decided that her limbs belonged in the Garden while her torso and head needed to go into the Cemetery. He laughed out loud as he realized he couldn't justify the decision to dispose of her in that particular fashion, but somehow it just seemed right. He began working with the shovel, sweating in the moonlight, feeling the ancient thrill once again.

Chapter Five

I checked the fax machine. Nothing. Sigrid gave me an odd look; probably because it was the fourth time I'd checked the fax in half an hour. It was against the wall behind her desk, next to the laser network printer.

"Look," I said, "I'm expecting some materials to be faxed over from Jack Muncie's office. It seems silly for me to keep coming out here when you're right here all the time. I mean, not all the time, but most of the time." I was rambling, and I knew it. "So, could you please notify me when they come in?" Any other time, I would have considered the look of consternation on her face comical.

"Yah. That is what I would do anyway. It is my job." Her spine stiffened and a look of firm resolve accompanied her comments. I chuckled and began retreating down the hall toward my office.

"I know it is, Sigrid, I know it is. And you do your job in a most excellent fashion. I've told Jenna several times, 'that Sigrid really does her job.' I'm sure you'll let me know the moment that fax arrives." I scurried down the hall and into my office feeling somewhat silly. I could hear her talking to no one in particular.

"I ALWAYS do my job. Always. I have not had any complaints about NOT doing my job." I closed the door to my office and her voice faded away.

I decided to put the Chastain deal out of my mind until the paperwork was in my hands. Muncie had probably instructed Beverly to take her time just to make me quiver. I sent that cynical thought packing as fast as it had come. After all, it hadn't been long since I'd revised my opinion of the man. The fax would arrive shortly.

I picked up the file that I had to examine before Jenna could conduct the closing scheduled for the following week. Usually, as per MARTA, the Marketable Records Title Act, I only had to search a property back for thirty years. There were some exceptions, but not many. But Mr. Siner owned the property in question from 1947 until 1986, when he'd sold to the current owners. To satisfy MARTA, I had to find the deed that conveyed title to Mr. Siner even though it was more than thirty years ago. Get it? Don't feel bad if you don't. That's why there are professionals, such as myself, on the job.

Mr. Siner's curious relationship with MARTA was the reason I had been to the courthouse in Ft. Myers earlier. Lee County had a nifty web site up and running, but it would be some time before all recorded documents could be viewed online. Currently they only went back to 1970. For documents prior to that there was always the courthouse, where every document was available for viewing.

I assembled the papers in the file in reverse chronological order and began perusing them. I was looking to make sure they conformed to the legal standards for each type: deed, mortgage, satisfaction of mortgage, etc. I was also looking for any ownership interest that had been created anywhere in the chain of title which had not been satisfied. After careful examination, I scribbled some notes for Jenna concerning which documents needed to be executed at the closing, and by whom. The deal was clean and could close on time.

The product we deal in is known as title insurance, but I don't think it's really insurance at all. Rather than providing protection against what may happen in the future, we're providing a warranty of what's taken place in the past. Anything that occurs after the date of issue of our policies isn't covered. In addition, we get to search for defects, and implement a cure or write an exception to the coverage, before we issue the policy. Claims still happen. But mostly they arise out of sloppy search and examination techniques.

Sigrid buzzed me at a little after three to inform me that the fax had arrived. I took the Siner file with me and headed to the lobby. Sigrid was grinning and holding out a sheaf of papers for me.

"Now I know why you were in such a hurry to receive this." I didn't think it was proper syntax to be in a hurry to receive something, but I didn't mention it to Sigrid. "It is a good one, yah?"

I raised my eyebrows and nodded. "Yah!" I gave her the Siner file. "Prepare the documents I've outlined on the search sheet and pass this along to Jenna. It's closing next week."

It was difficult to reach calmly for the papers in her hand. I wanted to snatch them and run back to my office. Sigrid grinned at me. When I was out of her sight, I increased my pace and started to eyeball the papers in my hand.

The top sheets were the contract for sale and I peered at them as I negotiated my way around my desk and plopped into the chair. I reared back and placed my size 12 Doc Martens' on the desk. The contract called for VH of Florida, Inc., to purchase a tract of land, further identified in exhibit A, hereunto attached, from the Alma C. Chastain Revocable Trust, Tobias Walker Chastain, Trustee, and Personal Representative of the Alma C. Chastain Estate, for the sum of twenty million dollars, with no financing contingency. The due diligence period of three months had expired. Due diligence was the length of time usually stipulated in commercial contracts to allow prospective buyers to make sure that they could legally do with the land what they wanted to do. The amount of time allowed varied from deal to deal.

You could tell that lawyers had been involved. Realtors, whom we mostly dealt with, would never be so verbose. And, they would use the standardized Florida Association of Realtors contract form. They weren't being paid by the hour and thus didn't need to spend their time writing language that was so confusing to everyone else involved that they would need a lawyer too.

Valhalla Homes, huh? They were the third or fourth largest builder operating in the state, in company with such behemoths as US Homes, Arvida, WCI, and the like. Their bread and butter project was one in which they designated a site on the development property as a borrow pit, that is, a place where the County allows the developer to dig fill dirt to build the elevation of the rest of the property. This pit, in turn, fills with water, due to SW Florida's unique topography and geology, and thus creates instant waterfront property. Allow a few alligators to migrate in and use some of the water as hazards for a golf course, and the desirability of the property soared, even if it really wasn't close to the Gulf of Mexico, which is where the really desirable property was still located. The strategy had been successful over and over for Valhalla. The resulting projects were well known and spread throughout Florida.

I carried the contract into the office between Jenna's and mine. On one wall was a computer workstation. Along the opposite wall were filing cabinets to house the sub-sheets: Information on a subdivisions history so that when we closed a property within that subdivision we only had to search back to the developer. There was also a long oaken table, with two chairs, that provided a place to open and peruse various tax maps and plat books. The tops of the file cabinets supported piles of those and the tabletop was a-litter with pencils, a protractor, a compass, and a magnifying glass that I'd been finding it necessary to use more and more as time went on.

The west wall was almost entirely tinted glass, giving a spectacular view of the traffic on Donovan Drive. A bookshelf filled with reference works graced the other wall.

I'd decided to take a preliminary look at the property, become familiar with it, before I made a full search and examination the next day. The legal description of the property was contained in exhibit A, a long and involved bit of legalese. It was a metes and bounds description, born out of the Geodetic Survey that had mapped Florida from the wilderness. That told me that the property had not previously been sub-divided.

The strap, or ID, number on the deed contained the property's Range, Township and Section, all designations derived from the Survey. I grabbed the appropriate tax map and looked it up.

Sometime in the next hour or so I heard Sigrid call from the front of the building that she was leaving for the day. A bit later Jenna stuck her head into the plant to advise me that she was leaving and that she would see me at home. Just like old times. I distractedly waved to her, thoroughly immersed in my study of the Chastain property.

Later, I leaned back and glanced at my watch. It was almost six p.m. If the chain of title was clean, and I had no doubt that it would be, then all I had to concern myself with were the three Ms: MARTA, Muncie and Money!

Chapter Six

It was almost six thirty when I walked through the door at The Grouper Hole. The name came from the fact that local fishermen referred to their favorite grouper fishing spot as a 'grouper hole' and not from an anatomical feature, as many snowbirds thought at first.

The restaurant was located in a marina on the bay. It had been a watering hole and gathering place for over forty years. Always a popular hangout for locals, it now also attracted a mixed bag of snowbirds, transplants and tourists. It's gastronomic claim to fame was a fried grouper sandwich, what else? It consisted of an immense portion of fried grouper fillet caught fresh daily by one of the proprietor's own commercial fishing vessels. Lightly dusted with cornmeal and spiced to perfection, it was served on a seeded bun along with a mound of hand-cut french-fries, skin on, cooked in peanut oil. The peanut oil allowed for a higher cooking temperature and the result was divine. Add to that the cold, crisp, slightly sweet and delicious house Cole slaw, and a signature 22-ounce schooner of the coldest draft beer in three counties, and you could see why the place was so popular.

I'd arrived in the middle of that American phenomenon known as happy hour. The drinks were two for one and finger food was gratis. Wings were a given but today the cook had added a chafing dish of what appeared to be scallops primavera. I couldn't really tell because there was a crowd four deep, as usual, around the table offering the freebies.

I worked my way to the bar, insinuating myself into an unoccupied space approximately eight inches wide, and hollered for a vodka martini on the rocks, hold the vermouth, with an olive. The bartender, Dan, a man I'd known casually for years, gave me a wink and a smile as he set two draft beers a 'sloshing on the bar, where a harried looking waitress, well, waited.

I elbowed my way a bit closer to the bar and looked around at the animated, noisy crowd. The barroom, with a large carved cypress bar in the shape of a C that was finished with urethane to protect against the nightly onset of spills, and ten or twelve small tables, along with a postage stamp sized dance floor, was filled to overflowing. At the far end from the entrance door was a small, elevated stage area that contained a couple of amplifiers, drum set and a PA system.

On the other side of the wall that ran parallel to the side of the bar that I was on, I knew, though I couldn't see it, was a cavernous room with seating for more than two hundred. It was the main dining room, added after Mangrove Springs had been "discovered." It would steadily fill from five, when the early-bird specials were big with retirees and snowbirds, until about eight o'clock, when the dinner hour was in full swing. At nine o'clock the band would start to play, currently a three-piece group named Tabby Catz that didn't offend anyone while managing to be completely forgettable.

As Dan delivered my drink and placed a cardboard record of my tab in front of me I reminded myself that I was working. This was not a pleasure visit. It was a carefully planned marketing effort. Distasteful as it was, I'd have to endure it in the interests of furthering our business. That's what I fervently hoped the IRS would believe when I attempted to deduct the bar tab. So far, I'd been lucky.

I was sipping my drink and pondering how I could effectively advance my business interests when my back was roughly slapped and then kneaded by a large, warm hand. I turned to see the alcohol-reddened face of Lonzo Dixon, a cousin and a fisherman laid low by the net-fishing ban, working odd jobs and drinking himself to death.

"My boy Elroy," he sang, badly, in homage to that cultural staple of our childhood, *The Jetsons*. His sun-crinkled face was stretched wide by a grin, his breath redolent of beer and tobacco.

"Hey, Lonzo," I replied. "How you doing?" As children we had spent a lot of time together in that long ago, sleepier world. We'd fished and swam and gathered bugs and snakes. Generally, we comported ourselves like two young, healthy boys growing up in a semi-tropical paradise, with nary a care in the world. And I guess that's just what we were. Boy, things sure had changed since then. Lonzo and I hardly saw each other anymore.

"Roy, muh man, I's doing poorly 'til I saw you. Now I'm happy as a milk fed kitten in a fat lap!" I wondered just how long Lonzo had been at The Grouper Hole. I had to admit, though, he did turn a charming phrase. His glassy eyes slid over and past my face and he spied another long lost friend.

"Now Roy, you just keep a pluggin', and it'll turn out right, sure as shit. Scuse me now, I gotta see a man 'bout a dog." I sipped my martini and continued my scrutiny of the lounge.

I saw mostly anonymous faces, but here and there was a familiar countenance. I saw Rita Muncie, Jack's young trophy wife, sitting at one of the small round tables, two full drinks in front of her and a partial one in her hand. Two gentlemen were seated with her and I wasn't that surprised to note that neither was Jack Muncie. There'd been rumors, but far be it from me to repeat, nor lend any credence to, unsubstantiated whisperings.

I spied Delbert Hinley, a local Realtor who directed a good bit of business our way. I caught his eye and lifted my drink. He nodded and held up a forefinger before returning his attention to the sixty-ish blue haired lady with whom he was speaking. Delbert was a long time resident of Mangrove Springs, one of the areas most successful Realtors, and was among the field of candidates for Mayor.

Rick Palomino walked by without seeing me and I reached out and tugged his arm to get his attention. Rick was the son of Jesus Palomino, the Mexican labor gang boss who had provided Jenna's family and the other tomato growers with the crews to plant and pick their crops, back when they still had crops to pick.

Rick was a handsome young man with the firm, clean lines of his Mayan and Spanish ancestors. But he was thoroughly American. Educated at the University of Florida, he owned and operated a trio of businesses involved with the hot housing market. He had an air conditioning installation and repair outfit, a wholesale appliance outlet and a home inspection concern. The last was of particular use to us since most homebuyers these days insist on a satisfactory home inspection as a pre-requisite to the purchase of a home, as well they should. Mason Dixon used his services on a regular basis and we'd yet to be dissatisfied.

"Hey, mi amigo, que pasa?" Rick liked to affect a good ol' migrant pose with the gringos but he was anything but. He was hard working, ambitious, educated and smart.

"We did that place on Rainbow Lane over by the beach today," he continued. "You know, that one that's about eighty years old? Just about falling down? I don't think the buyer's gonna like our report. Just want to let you know, man, so you can be, like, prepared for the deal to go south."

"Actually, I think the buyer will be pleased. He'll use your report to try to get repair allowances or negotiate a lower purchase price. But it doesn't matter. He's going to do a tear down and build a new home from the ground up," I told him.

"Hey, that's good, man. Maybe it won't fall through and we'll both get paid. By the way, that's the last one a yours on my list. What's wrong, you mad at me?" As closing agent, we generally placed the orders for surveys, termite inspections and home inspections, so Rick expected a steady stream of business from us.

"I wish it were that simple. The basic problem is we're not all that busy."

"I hear ya, man. Things are cranking down across the board. You ain't the only one that's off. Re-finance and re-sales are starting to do a serious fade. Thank Dios I got three oars in the water, know what I mean?"

I did. And I told him so. We commiserated a few more minutes, he offered to buy me a drink and I let him. Finally he gave me the Sammy Sosa chest thump, finger kiss and peace sign and left, cutting nimbly between the bar patrons, leaving not a ripple in the sea of heads.

I turned back to the bar and Dan was standing across from me, plunging glasses into the four sinks under the bar-top, each with a different solution, from cleaning agent to rinsing agent. He looked up at me, his head bobbing in time to the motion of his hands and arms.

"You eating with us tonight, Roy?" Sometimes, when Jenna had a Chamber of Commerce or Board of Realtors function to attend, or she was meeting Vern or I was seeing Lila, I'd sup at The Grouper Hole, usually taking my nourishment like a man, standing at the bar. Jenna generally drew the official side of the marketing duties, such as Board and Chamber functions, while I got the grittier assignments, like tonight, known in the business as street level marketing. Always ready to sacrifice for the good of the company.

"Nah, I'm gonna maybe have this one and one more then I'm headed home, where all virile male stud types should be of an evening." He grinned and shook his head at me. People do that a lot, I've noticed.

I'd finished the second martini and Dan had just set my third and final one before me when I heard Delbert Hinley saying 'scuse me, scuse me," as he pushed his way to the bar. I turned toward him, drink in one hand, and leaned my opposite elbow on the bar. Like Dean Martin in that cowboy movie with John Wayne where he played a gunfighter gone to drink. I realized that both those guys were dead. I suddenly felt ancient.

"Roy, Roy, Roy," Delbert said. "This Mayor thing ain't all it's cracked up to be. Don't know when's the last time I pressed so much flesh. Not just shaking hands, mind ya. It's the hugs and the pats and the up close views of the wrinkles and the fats. Hey, I'm a poet and don't know it! Seriously, a fella could catch somethin'." He paused to pull a Marlboro Light 100 from a crumpled pack and he ignited the infernal tube of weed with a BIC lighter. I recoiled from the cloud of noxious blue smoke until I suddenly recalled my pledge not to be one of those preachy reformed smokers.

I'd known Delbert since grade school. His folks lived east of Mangrove Springs, virtually in the swamp, in a trailer on ten acres. You needed a four-wheel drive vehicle to visit them nine months of the year.

"So, anyways Roy, what's new?"

I just smiled, not knowing where to start.

Chapter Seven

I turned off my lights and put the transmission in neutral. The big Caddy coasted the last few yards to its usual parking spot. Moonlight reflected from the waters of Mangrove Bay about a hundred yards away, at the end of a narrow channel with boat slips on either side. Directly in front of me and to my left, was a concrete boat-launching ramp.

A dirt road made its way out to the bay and turned south to follow the shoreline for about a hundred and fifty feet. At its end was a weathered tin-roofed building that had been the Dixon Fish House for as long as I could remember. Boats could pull up to the dock and unload their catches to be 'weighed and paid on the spot,' as the faded words painted upon the tin roof proclaimed. Lights hung from the high, bare ceiling. Walk-in freezers and ice making machines were grouped together in the center of the concrete floor. Rollers and conveyors snaked about the perimeter where the fish were processed. The Fish House remained open but few boats visited on any given day.

About halfway to the bay on the left side of the channel a light flickered and I saw a couple of men loading a small runabout with assorted rods, tackle boxes and coolers. My cousin Charley Dixon, who ran the tackle and bait shop at the bay end of the small channel, had told me that the red-fish action was beginning to heat up, especially on a high tide.

I put the top up and locked the Caddy, something we'd never have done before the spurt in development of the last few years. Not so long ago this little point of land on which Dixon's Fish Camp sat was a four mile journey down a dirt road from US 41, past palmetto scrub and pine trees, with only a few cracker houses scattered along the way. The view across the bay had been unobstructed by any evidence of human habitation. How times had changed. Now, the road back to US 41 was wide and smoothly paved with a mixture of gated and non-gated communities built, being built or planned to be built along the entire length of it, right up to the edge of the Dixon land.

From there to the bay was pretty much unchanged, except for the abandoned and rotting paraphernalia of net fishing. There was the bait house, the boat ramp and the enclave of over twenty-five residential dwellings of indeterminate age and varying states of repair. There were also several trailers strewn about the eastern edge of the Dixon land. We Dixon's have had all we could do to pay the ever-rising taxes, let alone always provide proper upkeep.

Looking out across the bay you could see the impact of all the growth. Residences lined much of the shoreline. Tall condo buildings were dotted here and there, with more sprouting up all the time. Currently there were five under construction that could be viewed from our place. Ugly cranes perched atop the skeletal structures like malevolent birds of prey. And far across the bay, on the long, narrow barrier island that formed Mangrove Beach, all was high-rise condos and multi-million dollar beach houses with only a few more than twenty years old.

I walked past the ramshackle spread that was Uncle Lemuel's and Aunt Chilicothe's (we called her aunt Chili), the unofficial leaders of the Dixon clan, around the gently curving path, past boats in need of various repairs resting on trestles. There were at least seven mullet skiffs, those odd looking boats with the outboard protruding through a well in the middle of the craft. This design allowed the gill nets to be deployed over the stern without fear of fouling the propeller and destroying the netting. Gill nets had been among those banned.

On past the row of houses and gallery of memories to the cracker classic that Jenna and I shared. The house that we'd moved into the day we returned from our wedding trip to Big Pine Key and had molded into our home. Where we'd lived, laughed, loved and made babies for the better part of two decades. And where we lived still, no longer tied together by that rope with the legal knot, but still connected by the flesh and blood of our children, whom we had created together. And by the ghostly echoes of laughter and tears, joy and despair, all the stuff from which the fabric of our lives had been woven. Also, by the very powerful economic need for two incomes and one set of bills in today's fast paced, high-pressure world.

I stood in the darkness a moment and gazed at the house. The upper story was dark, moonlight reflecting from the glazed panes of the windows. The lower story, in contrast, was awash with light, and the noisy ambience of a family at home could be heard through the opened windows. Jenna was there. I had seen her business-like Ford Taurus parked in its usual spot. All around the semi-circular shell pathway could be heard the sounds of families, young and old, settling into the evening routine.

A cool breeze blew in off the bay and it entered the house with me, rippling curtains and disturbing the sheet music that Rae, our middle child, had propped on a music stand before her. She stopped sawing the violin with her bow and looked at me in exasperation.

"Daddy!" she said. Then she bent over with an exaggerated groan and plucked up the offending pieces of paper.

"Sorry." I walked on, giving her and the violin an awkward hug, as I continued into the kitchen. Jenna was there, hard at work in front of the microwave. She was preparing tonight's dinner, which appeared to be the remnants of last night's dinner. Most people would call it leftovers but we, in an effort to bestow some panache on the re-heated affair, termed it PSF: Previously Served Food.

Actually, evenings that we cooked a full meal had become rare, as we all had our own schedules to attend to, making it difficult to co-ordinate meal times. Tonight was one of those times, when band, swim, soccer, baseball, field hockey, photography, boxing, roller skating, ice skating, Debate Club, 4H, DECCA, Chess club, movies, concerts, the library, or any one of numerous activities didn't intrude to the point of making it impossible to perform the simple act of eating together. When Jenna or I did cook (I was at LEAST as good a cook as she, though we each had our own specialties) we still tended to cook in amounts that would do any large family proud. Jenna called it Army Pot Cooking. Thus, the frequent appearance of leftovers on our table. Excuse me. Previously Served Food. Other times we grazed. We tried to make sure that healthful items were available, such as fresh fruits, juices, cereals, and the like. But frozen dinners and entrees had taken on an important role in our dietary affairs. I suspect it's the same with every family not able to afford a personal nutritionist and accompanying chef.

Jenna had her back to me and I took a moment to stand and contemplate. She had a faint perspiration line visible on her neck. She had changed to shorts, flip-flops, and a sleeveless blouse. She looked sturdy, competent and vibrant, and I wanted to pull her to me and hold her, just hold her.

Later, as we bowed our heads and thanked our non-denominational God for our blessings, I reviewed our menu and assured myself that Rae could eat a nutritionally correct meal. Under the guidelines of her modified vegetarianism, she was allowed to eat poultry, fish and eggs, but no red meat. Unless she felt an overwhelming need to eat a hamburger. Or a Philly cheese steak.

Bobby Jane, our youngest, sat to my right, a bright, athletic girl, large for her thirteen years. She was already an accomplished swimmer and a member of the Mangrove Springs chapter of Swim Florida.

I thought Bobby Jane had adjusted really well to the fact that her best and closest friend had been snatched, taken from a group of children with whom they'd been playing in the community park, by person or persons unknown, as they like to say. Patrick Kelly had never been heard from again and it was finally assumed that he was dead. There'd been a series of child abductions in Mangrove Springs over a period of two or three years. No one had been sure when they'd begun or how many there were. Until Patrick, all had been the children of migrant laborers, people working long hours toiling in the fields and the packinghouses.

Because of the transient nature of the victim's parents, their reluctance to deal with governmental authorities, and the slight indifference to their plight shown by the more permanent residents, an intense investigation was slow to get under way. At least until Patrick disappeared. Then a special Task Force had been formed and the Sheriff's Office went into overdrive. Four or five detectives worked full time on the investigation and manpower with special expertise was loaned from other areas in Florida, places that had more experience with this sort of horror. Press conferences were held and Deputies spoke to concerned civic groups. Parents wouldn't let their children out of their sight. After Patrick disappeared no more children were taken. It was theorized that the perpetrator had died, moved away or simply quit in the face of the increased public response. No one was ever charged or even seriously suspected. Eventually people forgot about those scary times.

The Kelly's didn't forget. They were casual friends of ours who operated a U-Pick on thirty acres just down the road from the fish camp. They grew tomatoes, sweet onions, green peppers and strawberries that people paid a reduced price per pound for, provided they pick their own. If you didn't want to pick your own you could purchase those items for slightly more money at a large Chickee hut at the front of the property, where you could also select other fresh vegetables, cold drinks, ice and baked goods made daily by Sheila Kelly and her mother. Kevin Kelly did the planting and weeding and spraying and such. He and Sheila were active in their church and had three children, all boys. Patrick was the youngest. The others helped out where they were needed in the family enterprise when they weren't in school or attending church functions. Sheila's father had passed away and the Kelly's, along with Sheila's mother, lived in a ramshackle Cracker style house on the southwest corner of the property. Two years after Patrick vanished, when they could no longer entertain any real hope, and looking thirty years older, Kevin and Sheila sold the farm and gathered the remaining kids and Grandma and moved to Arkansas. The property now sported a sixteen-story condominium and a single-family subdivision called Tropic Breeze Estates.

Bobby Jane didn't forget, either. She and Patrick were close and they had started school together. We lived close enough to the Kelly's that it was easy to drop one off for a visit at the other's home.

The Mangrove Springs grade school was adjacent to the community park and the school made use of the parks playground for recess and other activities. Patrick and Bobby Jane were eight years old and in the third grade when Patrick disappeared from the park while they were attending the after school program. The two had been climbing on the jungle gym and Patrick had gone to the drinking fountain at the recreation hall about fifty feet away. The fountain was on the other side of the building and he turned and waved an arm at Bobby Jane as he rounded the corner of the building. No one ever saw him again, at least no one who was willing to talk about it.

After that, Bobby Jane would have nightmares, waking herself with her screams until she refused to sleep anywhere but in the big bed with us. Jenna and I discussed it and decided to take her for counseling. We tried three therapists before we found one who seemed to connect with her. It took two years of weekly and then bi-weekly sessions for Mrs. Clark to declare that Bobby Jane would no longer need her. The nightmares had gone and Bobby Jane appeared to be nearly returned to her cheerful self. Only once in a while did I see a shadow cross her face whenever something reminded her of Patrick or disappearing children in general.

Cleve was last to the table, as usual. Cleveland Titus was our eldest, 16 years old, and thank you very much. So, of course he was allowed certain behavioral latitude that the others didn't share as yet. And believe me, we heard many a 'He does, why can't I?' I stressed to the girls that there always had to be a pecking order in life and it's best learned young enough so that one may deal with it in "real life." I don't think that this explanation was to their liking but it quieted them somewhat when I used it. The fact that I was bigger than they were helped.

We sat there, spooning up globs of PSF, and chattering away like a family of precocious primates, which is what we were, anthropologically speaking. We heard about Rae's run-in with a palmetto bug the size of the Taco Bell dog, in a corridor at school on the way to photography class. An amused senior, just GEAR and A'right (hope I caught the vernacular there) came to the rescue and squashed the offending vermin. Rae confessed she'd been giggly and dreamy eyed the rest of the afternoon.

Jenna related the story of our lunch at Boyd's and got sounds of envy from the others as she described the setting and the food.

Cleve told us of a sparring match he'd had in boxing club in which he'd delivered a fierce blow to his opponent's nose, which had resulted in a heavy nosebleed. The girls pressed him for more on his manly deed while Jenna hastened to steer the conversation in another direction. I enjoyed the story.

Bobby Jane was persuaded to tell of her victory in a butterfly stroke race at swim practice.

Later, after the kids had gone to bed, Jenna and I shared a glass of diet Coke. Mmm!

"So," she said. "What was your day like? Anything you want to tell me?" She peered at me with one eyebrow raised to the stratosphere. I figured Sigrid had told her about Jack Muncie's fax.

"Well not much, really," I said, drawing it out as much as my ego would let me. "Oh, Jack Muncie called. Said that since I was the best title examiner in these here parts, he wanted me to examine a small deal for him, one that he felt positively incompetent to do." I paused for effect, absently polishing the nails of one hand on my shirt, as I waited for the expected response. We'd been playing these types of games for years and I knew my part just as well as Jenna knew hers.

"Oh? Just how small a deal was it?"

"Twenty million." We nattered on for a while about what the deal would mean for us, for Mason Dixon, and how we were pretty much assured of surviving the slow summer real estate market and next season things would be back to normal. I reminded her of Great Aunt Minnie's aphorism: "The good Lord only lets you fall so far." After awhile our conversation turned to the instrument of our salvation, Jack Muncie, and his young wife.

"They say she spends money like it's going out of style." I shrugged.

"Well, I guess he can afford it."

"What do you mean?"

"Jack told me his real estate closings are up and off the charts for the year. Seems like the market's not down for everybody." Jenna squinted at me.

"Hmm. Beverly, you know, his secretary?" I nodded. "She's been quietly asking about job openings around town. Pat, over at Third National, told me. Says she's worried about her job, business is way off. Says he's in big money trouble, bad investments and such."

I felt a little flash of alarm in the section of my brain that is charged with the task of looking out for my well-being. But after a moment I disregarded the warning. After all, Jack's financial problems weren't any of my concern. The seller was paying us and that was the estate of Alma Chastain. And that entity was most assuredly solvent.

Still later, when we walked down the upstairs hall on the way to our separate bedrooms, Jenna stopped at the door to hers. She hesitated with her head down and her hand on the doorknob. My heart seemed lodged at the base of my throat. I stood still, afraid to breathe, for what seemed an eternity. Just as I was about to say something, anything, she pushed open the door and disappeared into the room beyond. The door closed behind her with a finality that jerked my head upright with the force of a physical blow.

Chapter Eight

The next morning, after I dropped Bobby Jane off at her school, I spent a half-hour cruising around town. I do this at least twice a month to keep current on the rapidly changing face of real estate sales and development in town. New buildings are constantly being started, lots cleared, for sale signs raised and sale pending riders attached to them. I liked to keep up to speed on our business. I also liked cruising around southwest Florida with the top down.

When I reached the office I plopped down in my chair after removing a couple of message slips, which I threw on the desk. I thought of the previous nights closeness, then awkwardness, with Jenna. When she'd returned that morning from taking Cleve and Rae to school I couldn't read her; she had closed herself off to me again. I sat there, head back, eyes closed, feeling sorry for myself for a while. I decided that a good therapy would be to immerse myself in the Chastain deal, to remind myself of the nice payday ahead.

I went into the title plant and searched the property back far enough to satisfy MARTA. Because all remaining Chastain land had been deeded into the trust in the '70s I wouldn't need to go to Ft. Myers. I assembled the documents in reverse chronological order and glanced at the clock: ten to twelve. The examination would have to wait. It was noon on Wednesday; time for the weekly lunch gathering of the Mangrove Native Men's Club Plus Two.

The MNMC+2 was an informal association of four native Mangrove men and two transplants. We had few members and fewer rules. Each Wednesday we met for lunch, the location determined at the meeting the week before. If it was Wednesday, you could find me at the MNMC+2 meeting. Unless I had something elsc to do. Same with the other guys.

I drove to the Red S, a greasy spoon out in an area east of Interstate 75 that was known as Mobile Home Heaven. It was a broad stretch of wetlands and semi-wetlands east of the Interstate where trailers sat on five or ten acre tracts that were connected by dirt and shell roads. The land was mostly under water half the year and the vehicles tended to be four-wheel drive pick-ups and ATVs. So far the Water Control District had bought out about half of the residents in the area, over their objection, and the rest were targeted. The goal was to make a huge retention area east of the Interstate to hold the summer rains in order to correct flooding problems caused by development west of the interstate. The problem was that developers were already moving into the area east of 75 to the north and south of MHH, and plans were under way for a four-lane road, running north and south and east of 75 to connect the areas of development. There would be heavy pressure to develop everything in between.

The Red S was located in a double wide set on a huge mound of fill dirt with a wide, dusty parking lot full of big wheeled pick-up trucks. Because of the recent lack of rain the lot was dustier than usual and a fine film had settled onto the vehicles parked there. Dust still billowed and roiled from the disturbance the Caddy had made pulling in. I put the top up and climbed out of the car. In the distance to the east a line of gray smoke smudged the horizon. This was the time of year for wildfires and the longer we went without rain the worse the fires would become.

As I walked to the door of the Red S I noticed two black Explorers parked side by side. They belonged to Harry and Barry Oatman, identical twins with red hair and the greatest abundance of freckles I'd ever seen. They were natives about my age and I'd known them all my life. Locals referred to them as Pete and Repeat.

I also saw the bright red Dodge Ram pick-up with matching topper that belonged to Don Stone, a non-native. He'd put the topper on his truck to fool his neighbors into thinking it was an SUV. Pick-ups weren't allowed in his subdivision. So far it had worked.

Inside was jammed with the Dickees and work boots crowd, mostly truck drivers and construction types. Here and there was an occasional farmer, a remnant of the formerly flourishing agricultural industry of the area. I saw Pete and Repeat at a large table toward the rear and I headed toward them. The screened windows were open and dust motes swirled in shafts of sunlight. It was warm, with no air conditioning. Several fans on pedestals stirred the grease-laden air. All walls, except those around the bathrooms, had been removed and the place was filled with tables and a counter with stools. The kitchen was in full view. It was all bustling activity, with much opening and closing of upright coolers and the sizzling of frying meat. Which was why we occasionally chose the Red S. The Country fried steak was like manna from heaven; fork tender, drenched in rich white gravy, and served with mashed potatoes, two fresh vegetables and big, fluffy biscuits. To die for. Literally. A heart attack on a plate, but irresistible to someone who'd grown up in the south.

I nodded to Pete and Repeat as I pulled out one of the mismatched chairs and sat at the scarred wooden table.

"I thought I saw Don's truck outside. Is he here?" Pete, or was it Repeat, looked up from the menu he'd been studying. Then I saw the scar under his chin that told me it was Pete. He'd been bitten, while on a fishing trip to the Keys, by a barracuda. It had been following a yellowtail he'd hooked and when he pulled the fish into the boat the barracuda had leaped after it, sinking it's long and numerous teeth into his neck. They'd been fishing about ten miles out and Repeat had had to cut the fish loose with a fillet knife, leaving the elongated jaws and teeth still embedded in Pete's flesh. Then Repeat had to apply pressure to the wound to stem the flow of blood as the guide headed for land. Each time he let up a bit blood spurted anew. There was a light chop and each time the boat smacked down after jumping a crest a frightened Pete screamed at Repeat; "Don't you let go, you son of a bitch! Don't you let go!" They'd finally made it to Fisherman's Hospital on Islamorada and it had taken over sixty stitches in two layers to repair the damage. The doctors said that Repeat had saved Pete's life. Repeat complained of cramping in his hands for several weeks.

"He went to the john. You gonna have the Country fried steak?"

"Of course. Aren't you? That's why we come here."

" I was just thinkin' I might try somethin' else this time. You know, be adventurous." Repeat looked up from his menu.

"Yeah? Like what?" he asked. Pete squinted at his menu.

"Don't know. Maybe smoked mullet. Or the vegetable plate. Or, how bout this?" He placed his finger on the stained menu. "Farm raised catfish fillet," he read, "smothered with creamed sweet potatoes. Says here it's a house specialty."

"This is no house," I said. "It's a trailer."

"Huh?"

"You'd best be careful about anything they claim is a house specialty," Repeat said.

"What house specialty?" Don had returned from the restroom and was settling into his chair.

"They got this catfish slathered with creamed sweet potatoes," Repeat told him. "Pete here wants to have an adventure." Don flicked his menu away.

"Not me. I come for the steak. That's what I'm gonna have."

"Me too," I said.

"I have enough adventures, what with Donna and the kids," Repeat informed us.

"Well, I just thought, you know, I'd like somethin' different. I don't care for ruts." Pete picked up his menu and studied it some more. A waitress came and asked if we were ready to order.

"I guess Marcus and Jim ain't gonna make it. What ya think?" Don looked around the table.

"I'll have country fried steak and sweet tea," I told the waitress.

"Me too," said Don.

"Me too," Repeat, well, repeated.

"I'll take the catfish fillet smothered with creamed sweet potatoes," Pete said. He made a show of looking left and right over the menu. "And raspberry iced tea." The waitress wrote that down and left.

Don leaned back and fished a cigarette from his shirt pocket and lit it with a cheap plastic lighter. He inhaled deeply and blew smoke toward the ceiling. A look of pleasure swathed his face.

"I thought you quit," Pete said.

"Did. For three days. Figured I'd be better off trying to ease out of it, you know. Now I keep it to ten a day." Something in the way we looked at him made him sit up a bit.

"Used to be two packs a day," he said, a bit defensively. "Forty cigarettes! Now, it's one before and one after I eat. Then, in the evenin', I have three drinks so I smoke one with each drink. Then one at bedtime. That's ten. Not too bad, huh?" He looked around the table for approval.

"Not bad," I said. It was an improvement over two packs a day, wasn't it? Pete and Repeat stared at him. They were both reformed smokers, but a bit preachy, if you ask me. Pete put his chin in the palm of his hand, with his elbow on the table.

"What if you have more than three?" he asked slyly.

"What?"

"What if you have more than three drinks? Hell, happens all the time with me!" He snorted with mirth and looked about for approval of his bon mot. Repeat chuckled and I smiled. Don blew more smoke.

"Well, then, you got more of a problem with drinkin' than I have with smokin'." He grinned to take the sting out of his words.

"No, really. We've all been out together. It happens. What then?"

Don leaned his head back and contemplated the problem. "I guess I'd just hafta cut back on cigarettes earlier in the day to make it come out right." Pete did a long take before he joined the rest of us in laughter. I do believe he had been serious.

The waitress came with our drinks and a basket of big buttermilk biscuits that you just knew hadn't come out of a can, and a bowl full of ice chips covered with individually wrapped pats of butter. All talk ceased as we each grabbed a hot biscuit, fork split it, and covered it's flaky center with gobs of butter that melted rapidly into pools of a lovely, artery clogging, viscous yellow.

Not much later the waitress brought our entrees. She had to ask who got the catfish and we all pointed at Pete, who seemed proudly defiant. She wanted to know if everything was all right and I was tempted to tell her we didn't know yet, we'd just received our food, but instead I just grinned at her with buttery lips and nodded my head.

The steak was positively wonderful. The flour coating was perfectly seasoned, with more than a hint of black pepper, and the meat was pounded to a delicious tenderness. The gravy was smooth and creamy and you could tell that the huge mound of mashed potatoes didn't come out of a box by the occasional lump and the scattered pieces of potato peel.

The vegetables of the day were mustard greens and fresh corn on the cob. The corn was white, sweet, with small kernels. Silver Queen, I think. It required more of the artery choking sweet cream butter.

After the first adventurous mouthfuls, Pete resorted to poking at his catfish and sweet potato with a dissatisfied look of long suffering on his face. The rest of us felt a need to point out to him that that's what an adventure is, to see if you like a certain thing. We urged him to place another order, or to share our bounty, but he stoically maintained that his fare was just what he wanted. All the while he was pushing the unappetizing mess about on his plate and taking tiny sips of his raspberry tea, which he seemed not to enjoy, either.

Don was already smoking his after meal cigarette when I pushed my plate away with a contented sigh. All that was left on the plate was a well-stripped corncob, some traces of gravy and a small fork full of greens.

"What's the matter, Bubba? Couldn't finish?" Don grinned through a cloud of blue smoke.

"Nope, just couldn't do it." I leaned back in my chair and rubbed my belly contentedly. "Man!" A moment later Repeat threw down his napkin with an air of finality. Pete had already given up on the Catfish Supreme. He was hungrily eyeing the last biscuit. Don noticed and shoved the basket in Pete's direction.

"Go ahead, hoss. I think the rest of us are pretty much belly up." Pete looked around the table and then reached for the biscuit.

"Well, I hate to do it, but I have to get back to good ole Mason Dixon." I looked at my watch with a frown.

"Why's that? You never do anything there of an afternoon 'cept put your head on your desk and nap." The Petes laughed.

"Usually that would be true," I said. "But not today. I've got to examine a deal where we're writing the insurance but Jack Muncie is doing the closing. Promised him that I'd have it done when he got back to town. It's large and a bit complicated so I need to get to it." I stretched and patted my belly. "Hope I can stay awake."

"Sounds commercial to me, Bubba. What is it?"

"A parcel of Chastain land that Toby's moving. Twenty million dollars worth."

"To a developer?" Repeat wanted to know.

"Yeah. Valhalla Homes." I heard a quick intake of breath.

"Wow." Repeat looked surprised.

"Why wow?" Don wanted to know. "Valhalla's all over the place. Why not here?" Repeat slowly shook his head.

"Well, she swore it wouldn't never happen."

"Who?" I asked. Pete looked across the table at me.

"Alma Chastain, that's who. Donna and my wife are members of that darned Control The Growth In Mangrove. They call it Cit-Gim." He and Repeat leaned on their elbows, looking earnestly at first Don and then me, in unison, like a pair of identical meat puppets. Twins could be downright freaky sometimes.

"Alma was a founding father, or mother, or whatever. She always said she was sick and tired of the willy-nilly growth and she was gonna take steps so that no more Chastain land would be developed up."

"Yeah," Repeat added. "Donna told me she had it all fixed, in her will. She was giving most of her land to the county to be used for parks and the county could never use it for nothin' else."

Don was lighting his after meal cigarette. Hey, wait a minute, I thought. That was two after meal cigarettes!

"Well, I doubt Muncie got it wrong. I mean, he's a jerk but not totally incompetent." Pete said.

"Never fear, that's but one of the things I will verify in my complete examination of the documents," I said with my professional voice. I changed the subject. "How about Luchese's next week?" I said. I loved Italian food.

Chapter Nine

Back at the ranch I checked in with Sigrid, who informed me that Jenna was at a Realtor luncheon. I headed for my office. I was feeling extremely stuffed and needed to reach my chair as quickly as possible. I thought forty winks might restore my natural vigor.

I settled back and put my feet on the desk. I closed my eyes and tried to relax. I fully believed, given my post feast condition, that it wouldn't take long to slip into a dream state. I was wrong.

After twenty minutes or so of futilely waiting for that totally relaxed state known as napping to overcome me, I opened my eyes.

The problem, as I saw it, was the difference between what Alma had told Cit-Gim and the terms of the will. I would have to pass judgment on whether the deal was properly executed and write a policy in the amount of twenty million dollars if I deemed everything to be in order. Of course, a nice payday would ensue should I decide that everything was kosher. But my personal integrity would be on the line. And the consequences for me, to my personal and professional life, would be significant should I be wrong. And to complicate matters, there were those two claims previously made against policies I'd written. I'd weathered the storm, reaching an out of court settlement paid for by my Errors and Omissions insurance. My rates had gone up and my reputation had suffered. But I still truly believed I'd reached the proper conclusions in each case, though it turned out that the information I'd acted upon had been faulty. I'd vowed that it would never happen again.

I grabbed the Chastain folder and spread it on the desk. Working carefully and methodically I examined each document. I was looking for proper form and execution. I looked closely at the faxed copy of the will. If Alma had meant to protect her property from development, that was likely where she would have made certain provisions. I noticed right away that the law offices of Ralph Rennegar had prepared the will. I recalled Muncie mentioning on the phone that he'd taken care of Alma's legal affairs after Ralph had passed on. Ralph had been dead four, no, five years.

He did good legal work and as I scrutinized the will I could find nothing wrong, though I'm not a lawyer. The will was properly signed, witnessed and notarized. Besides, Judge Bifferato had admitted the will to probate. I looked again at the acknowledgement section. The notary and her signature were well known to me. Linda Wong had been Ralph's secretary cum legal assistant for thirty years before Ralph's death and I'd seen her signature a thousand times on documents in the public records over the years. It was widely believed that she had been Ralph's mistress as well. I'd called on her at Ralph's office dozens of times to check on documents. I thought that she still lived in Mangrove Springs, having retired after closing up the office and attending to Ralph's last professional affairs after he passed on.

The witnesses were unknown to me but that wasn't unusual. However, one witness signature did catch my eye. Dent Billie. Billie was the surname of a large family of the Seminole Indian Tribe, so I was pretty sure Dent was Native American, though that wasn't what attracted my attention. There'd been an Indian family of caretakers who'd lived in an old house on the eastern end of the Chastain property, tending the garden, washing the cars, making repairs around the house and outbuildings. I didn't know whether they were still living there or not. At any rate, it was something about the signature itself that caught my eye.

I'd once read a book on graphology, or handwriting analysis. I didn't recall a whole lot about it but one thing had stayed with me. When an ascending line to the right of the stem formed the crossbar of a small letter "t" without lifting the pen from the paper, where the t is at the end of a word, as in the 'Dent' of Dent Billie's signature, it revealed certain personality traits. The person possessed the desirable attribute of "initiative." I could close my eyes and recall the description in the book on graphology almost verbatim:

"The person who exhibits this characteristic has an abundance of common sense. He has a natural sense of responsibility. She is a self-starter with little need for supervision. He will remain aware and fully capable, especially in stressful situations. Reliable, resourceful and able are words to describe her. He is adaptable and pragmatic, able to make swift, rational decisions."

That one passage had cemented my firm belief in the accuracy and dependability of handwriting analysis, though I'd never had occasion to rely on it for anything of import. I was sure of the accuracy of this one trait, at least, for I, myself, formed end-of-the-word t's in this manner. And I knew myself to be accurately described by that passage. That's why I found myself imagining this Dent Billie to be a sturdy and solid type, with a glint in his intelligent brown eyes. He was a man who could hunt and fish with his bare hands, who always won out over adversity, and yet exhibited unparalleled kindness and understanding to those less talented and wise than he.

I roused myself and returned my attention to what I'd discovered. Ralph Rennegar had prepared the will several years before. It was properly executed and acknowledged. The judge had admitted it to probate. Toby Chastain was indeed the executor and personal representative. The judge had issued an order to sell. The will was not contested.

I went back into the room that housed the title plant. Fifteen minutes of careful searching convinced me that I'd missed nothing.

It was, all in all, a clean deal. Pete and Repeat's wives, and Cit-Gim, would have to accept the fact that Alma had not followed through on her pledge to them about setting up some sort of protective device to keep her property from becoming fodder for the developers.

Back in my chair I found that my thoughts were eased enough to allow a nap, which was ended some time later by the buzzing of the intercom. I fumbled for the button.

"Yeah," I mumbled thickly.

"Roy?" It was Jenna. I dropped my feet to the floor and straightened in the chair. I cleared my throat.

"Yeah?"

"I wanted to remind you that I'm going to dinner with Vern. Your mother said she'd sit with the kids 'til one of us gets home. I left her money to order in a pizza." My mother? How sick was that? My mother watching Jenna's and my children while she went out with another man!

"Okay," was all I could manage. I looked at my watch. It was a little after four.

"Guess I'll do a little marketing down at The Grouper Hole. I'll get something to eat while I'm there." I tried to keep my voice pitched normally.

"Okay. I shouldn't be too late. I'm going to take off now. I'm all caught up and I want to stop by the house and change clothes. I did three closings today. Pretty good, huh? See you later."

I sat and thought about my miserable life and the bizarre situation Jenna, our children and I were trapped in and I thought that a stiff vodka martini would taste good right about then. I looked at my watch again. Four-thirty. I realized that I was all caught up, too, so I decided I'd get right to my marketing duties. I threw a quick wave and a 'see you in the morning' to Sigrid as I rushed out the door.

The Grouper Hole was just beginning to fill with Happy Hour patrons as I pulled into a spot at the rear of the property in the shade of a live oak. This parking lot was almost as dusty as the lot at the Red S. I couldn't see the smoke of the wildfires on the horizon but it seemed as if I could detect the faintest whiff of it on the breeze. I hurried toward the entrance. An elderly gentleman and a short, blue-haired lady arrived at the door just as I did and I opened it and waved them ahead. They smiled and blue-hair said 'thank you.' I hurried to the bar.

Dan came right over as I pulled up one of the tall wooden stools. Happy Hour was just under way and I looked forward to three hours of two-for-one vodka martinis. A thought crossed my mind that perhaps I should just go home but I quickly shushed it.

"Usual?" Dan said, smiling. In fact, I couldn't recall a time when Dan wasn't smiling. What, I wondered, could make a man so happy with his lot. Or was it put on? I eyed him suspiciously.

"Vodka martini, my friend. And refill the glass as needed." Dan smiled an even bigger smile.

"Uh oh," was all he said. He brought my drink in about thirty seconds flat and stood smiling as I nearly drained it in one swallow. He brought another a few moments later as I finished off the first. I relaxed a bit as my stomach glowed with the heat of the vodka.

About a third of the barstools and tables were occupied and here and there were small clumps of people standing, smoking and chatting, with an occasional belly laugh erupting forth. Servers were busy unfolding linen and preparing the free buffet. Several people had lined up though no food had yet made an appearance. Every now and then I would spy an acquaintance and I would smile and wave to them. I was friendly in my manner but gave no gestures that would encourage anyone to come over and begin a conversation. I wasn't ready for that yet. Maybe after another drink or two. Dan got busier and busier but he was right there with a fresh drink every time I emptied my glass.

The food finally appeared from the kitchen and people began heaping those ridiculously small plates with ridiculously large helpings of chicken wings, fried cheese sticks and the evening's feature, toasted ravioli. The Grouper Hole had a chef of Italian lineage and he found ways to show off his heritage despite the fact the The Grouper Hole was primarily a Florida seafood palace. I'd turned back to the bar to give my undivided attention to the most recent incarnation of vodka martini that Dan had placed before me when a ridiculously large helping of toasted ravioli, wings and fried cheese sticks on a ridiculously small plate was set in front of me by a delicate, bejeweled, long-nailed and fish-belly white hand. I turned toward the hand's owner and came eye to eye with a smiling and intricately coiffed Rita Muncie. My surprise must have been apparent.

"You may need this, judging by the speed with which you're polishing those off." She nodded at the vodka in front of me. With her other hand she set a fork rolled in a napkin by my elbow. She turned and walked away. I watched her backside sway above her long, slim legs and felt a swelling of desire. I quickly turned back to the bar, not sure what to make of the encounter. I knew Jack's wife, of course, but not that well. Her husband and I were both involved with the Realtors in town. We attended many of the same social functions, including the Annual Realtor Installation Banquet. I'd spoken with her on several occasions, but only to discuss, in general terms, the functions and the people involved. Always polite but innocuous conversation. I was totally surprised by her overture. But I had to admit eating something might be a good idea. The vodka was already causing everything to be viewed as if through a thick pane of glass. I smiled at Dan, who was removing my depleted libation and replacing it with a fresh one, and picked up the fork and napkin, having only slight trouble separating the two. I began shoveling the bite size deep-fried cheese sticks and the toasted raviolis into my mouth with much relish. The chicken wings, which required more concentration and were messier, because of the hot, greasy sauce, would come later.

I was seriously engaged in the demolition of the food and nearly missed the plate being placed on the bar to my left. I glanced that way and was surprised to see Rita Muncie sliding onto a stool, napkin rolled fork in hand, purse clasped under her left arm, eyes and lips smiling at me. I liked it when a person smiled with their eyes. I straightened a bit and raised my napkin to my greasy lips.

"You're back," I said. Not the most gracious words ever to leave my lips, but she didn't seem to mind.

"Yes. I thought I'd join you." She leaned close and whispered conspiratorially, " I was feeling the alcohol, too." I nodded sagely and continued to fork food into my craw. I nearly choked on a ravioli when I felt the gentle pressure of her delicate hand upon my thigh. Dan chose that moment to appear and ask Rita if she would like a drink. She glanced in my direction before answering.

"Vodka on the rocks." She turned my way again and smiled. I saw how attractive she really was. I smiled back at her.

A little while later, food eaten and the plates cleared away by Dan, Rita suggested we go somewhere else, somewhere we could really kick up our heels. I agreed.

Rita left first, at my direction, waving goodnight to several people on the way out. I sat at the bar for another ten minutes by my watch before paying my tab, a clumsy effort to conceal my shenanigans. I made my way to the door, through a crowd that was much larger than when I'd come in, saying hi-bye to several faces that I thought might belong to someone I knew.

She was waiting in her car at the dark end of the parking lot, engine running and lights out. I slid in the passenger door, trying not to feel guilty about the whole thing, the alcohol talking to me, telling me it was okay. Rita leaned over and kissed me before switching on the lights, putting the car in gear and rocketing out of the lot. Her window was down and her hair was whipping about her head and she was laughing out loud. I leaned back in the soft leather of the Lexus and grinned.

Rita drove us to a lounge that was located in a chain motel out by the interstate. The wildfires glowed red in the distance. Traveling salesmen and long distance truckers dominated the clientele. We took a table near the back of the dimly lit room and ordered drinks from a bored looking cocktail waitress. A three-piece band gamely played classic rock tunes, more than making up for a lack of talent with high-energy exuberance and sheer volume.

We danced nearly every dance of each set, using the time between sets to recover, to talk and to drink vodka. Some time after the band had quit for the night, the servers went into clean-up mode and the bartender declared last call. I was having trouble seeing and closed my left eye in an attempt to focus my right. Rita was all over me. Her lily-white hands, all seven of them, adorned with several articles of jewelry, had found their way, at one time or another, underneath the waistband of my Hagar's. The hands excited. The jewelry sometimes caused discomfort. I had inserted my hand beneath the waistband of her slacks several times. Her flesh was marble-cool and hot at the same time.

We staggered from the lounge to the lobby of the motel where Rita rented us a room while I tried to remain upright. Rita led me by the hand to the second floor and we fell together onto a king sized bed. Somehow we got naked and under the covers.

As near as I can recall, I fell asleep with Rita trying to manually arouse me. I thought I heard her whisper, "No wonder it was you." But that made no sense, I thought, as I dropped into an alcohol induced coma.

Chapter Ten

Over the course of a lifetime many things change. But one change, I think, that comes to us all equally as we grow older, is that hangovers hurt more.

As I slowly regained consciousness, I became increasingly aware of the painful pulse of a humongous, diesel-powered machine, driving pilings inside my head. The tremendous blows reverberated through my skull in cadence with the beat of my heart. Now, I'm not an expert on hangovers, that wild portion of my youth notwithstanding, but I believed that I was experiencing the single most debilitating hangover ever to afflict a modern day non-military person.

A new pounding began, in counterpoint to the pile-driving racket. Just when I thought I would scream from the sheer pain, the counterpoint ceased and I could make out a far away voice.

"Maid service." It took a moment to fully understand the meaning behind that phrase. I recalled portions of the night: Rita and the motel and oceans of vodka. I strained to open my eyes but the lids seemed cemented together. With great effort I managed to tear them apart only to find I was blind! Panic began to devour my heart and I broke out in a cold sweat. I was opening my lips to scream when I heard a rattling sound and then there was a burst of white pain that made me immediately forget the machine in my head.

I thought of the accounts of near death experiences that I'd read in *Reader's Digest* and the white light that everyone always seemed to be drawn toward. I didn't remember, however, any of those accounts mentioning pain. Those people always seemed to describe great feelings of joy and happiness as they were drawn to the light.

Within the great rectangle of pain appeared the silhouette of an angel of heaven, her otherworldly chariot a-waiting behind. As my eyes adjusted to the hideous brightness, I realized that it was a motel cleaning lady, and behind her the cart containing cleaning supplies and linens.

"Oh, 'scuse me sir. I'll be comin' back later." She could obviously tell from my fetal position on the bed that I was not ready for maid service.

"Hornph," I said. The silhouette disappeared along with the rectangle of brightness as she closed the door. The complete darkness that had fooled me into thinking I was blind returned. I realized that the motel provided blackout curtains so guests could get a good night sleep.

The panic subsided as I began to understand my environment and to remember the events of the previous evening. I groped over my left flank, searching for the comforting bulk of Rita Muncie. Nothing. Slowly, some sight was returning as my eyes adjusted to the dim light. A faint red glow from a digital alarm clock / radio illuminated the room enough for me to make out shapes. I rolled over. An acre of bed stretched away into the red tinged gloom. No Rita. I looked toward where I supposed the bathroom to be. No light peeking from underneath a door. I glanced again in the direction of the glowing red numerals on the clock. Assuming that the clock was correct, it was now 10:47. I further assumed that it was a.m. Thus, the blinding light at the open door.

Vern Otto. He was the catalyst of the chain of events that had led me to this place and time. I remembered that. I remembered the feelings of inadequacy and the sense of futility that Jenna's date with Vern had engendered.

I hadn't intended to compound matters by ending up at a motel with Rita Muncie, of all people, but when massive amounts of alcohol are involved, anything can, and will, happen. I remembered with some embarrassment that I hadn't been able to perform sexually, despite Rita's best efforts. Oh, good, I thought. I cheated on my ex-wife and Lila, my official girlfriend, with the wife of a man I held in low esteem, and I didn't even manage to get laid in the process. And my ex-wife probably had a swell time that culminated in a bout of sexual acrobatics with one of my friends. And Lila was probably playing house with one of her shipmates. Only I could pull that one off!

Rita had probably awakened earlier than I had and I assumed that she'd gone home. Maybe she'd tried to wake me and failed. But she was gone and my car was still in The Grouper Hole parking lot.

I needed to get out of the room before checkout time, which was probably 11:00, or I would owe another nights rent. I glanced again at the red-eyed LED. I had eight minutes to find my clothes, put them on, and get out. The room was visible now and I spied my Hagar slacks draped over the back of a sled chair. My Polo shirt was on the floor at its base. My Jockey's were lying about three feet away, crumpled into a ball of red.

I made use of the bathroom, relieving myself noisily, and proceeded to dress. I splashed water on my face and into my mouth to slake a raging thirst before peering at my reflection in the mirror. My face was creased here and there with those marks you get from lying on a wrinkle in the bedding. My eyes were rheumy and reddened and I needed a shave. I had no comb so I smoothed my hair as best I could with my fingers. Unruly clumps stuck out at angles, real bed head. I looked like Harrison Ford.

The room key was lying on the dresser and I left it there for the maid. I consulted the phone book for the number of Mangrove's only cab company and punched it into my cell phone, which had been clipped to the waistband of my slacks. I didn't want to incur extra charges on the room phone. After ordering a taxi I opened the door, wincing as the sunlight bit into my eyes, and stepped out onto the second floor walkway. I passed by a maid's cart on my way to the stairs but no maid was in sight. The mid-morning air smelled of diesel fumes and wood-smoke. There was a slight haze diffusing the suns rays. I waited for the taxi under the large motel sign.

After I retrieved my car I phoned the office and told Sigrid that I was hard at work, calling on several clients, but that I'd be in the office in about an hour. She didn't seem impressed. She started relaying several messages but after the third or fourth my cell phone chirped and died. Battery. I had a charger plugged into the cigarette lighter and plugged the other end into the phone and tossed it on the seat next to me.

At home I started a pot of coffee dripping and headed for the shower, stripping on the way. The fine needles of hot water did wonders for the aches and tightness in my shoulders and back. A quick shave and I almost felt human again. Downstairs, the coffee was ready and I sat at the kitchen table and let the hot, black liquid rejuvenate me even further.

My stomach was grumbling, asking my backbone if my throat had been cut. On the way to the office I grabbed a bag of burgers at a fast food drive-thru to eat at my desk.

Sigrid seemed a bit agitated when I finally got to the office. As soon as I entered she began barking at me.

"You should always be sure to have a fully charged battery with you at all times!"

"You're right, Sigrid. I'll try to remember." I started down the corridor to my office.

"Wait! You must let me finish delivering your messages to you." She was waving a sheaf of message slips at me. I stopped and faced her. There was no use asking her why she didn't just put the slips on my chair, as usual. I just nodded at her to let her know that I was listening. I waited for her to finish, prayed for her to finish, as I stood, stomach growling, burger smells tantalizing me, saliva pooling in my mouth, causing me to swallow repeatedly. I heard her mention Ollie, our partner in Mason Dixon.

"He said it was very important that you call him as soon as possible," she hissed. I marveled that a depleted battery could cause this animus in her. I took the message slips and smiled at her until she melted a bit.

"Now go," she said. "I have more important things to do than sit here and explain things that happened in the past." I hurried down the hall before she thought of something else.

The familiar contours of my chair welcomed me. I sat and put the messages aside. The aroma from the burgers was causing me to feel light headed and dizzy. I tore open the bag and unwrapped one of the grease bombs, tearing off a huge hunk with my teeth, so huge, in fact, that I couldn't close my mouth all the way as I chewed, grunted and swallowed.

I ate three of the things. No fries, no apple pies. When I was finished I felt the earth move and hurried to the bathroom. Afterward, I settled once more into my chair with an audible sigh. The hangover was nearly gone and it now appeared that I might survive the day. I was feeling rather sated until my wandering eyes came to rest upon the message slips.

I put the message from Ollie aside and looked over the others. There was nothing that couldn't wait. I picked up Ollie's message. Sigrid had checked the important box rather than the urgent box. Ollie always said that whatever matter he wanted to speak about was important. He valued his time and thought each action he took was important even if he was just calling to gossip. Which he occasionally did.

I'd known Ollie as long as I could remember. His full name was Oliver Wendell Holmes Mason. His mother had desperately wanted her son to be a jurist, having read a biography of Oliver Wendell Holmes during her pregnancy. No one knew what name his father would have wanted for his son. His father had not even known that he was to be a father. Otis Barnes and Peggy Mason were to be married when he returned from WW II. Ollie was the product of a final moment of tenderness the night before Otis left to re-join his outfit and ship out. Otis and Peggy were not long out of high school at the time. Peggy was the daughter of a schoolteacher and a homemaker while Otis's parents operated one of Mangrove Spring's two gas stations and his mother worked seasonally in one of the area's packinghouses, grading tomatoes. Otis was killed just seven weeks later. Peggy shelved her plans for college after Ollie arrived and made a life for them by working at the grocery store founded and operated by her brother, Edward. She never married, never even dated. She seemed content to try to nurture Ollie's intellect. During his childhood she constantly read to him from the works of the great writers and poets, having her brother take her to the Lee County Public Library in Fort Myers every two weeks for a new batch of books.

She lived with her parents, eventually taking over all cleaning and cooking duties as her mother began to fail. When her mother died, her father seemed to become a smaller version of himself, somehow much diminished. When her father died, she inherited the small family home. Her parents had long before agreed that their other two children could take care of their families and themselves just fine but that Peggy and Ollie would need the security afforded by the small homestead.

Peggy continued her efforts to prepare Ollie for greatness. He learned easily and was accelerated two grades by the time he graduated high school at fifteen. He was an outgoing person, easily liked and accepted by his peers, though he was obviously superior to most in learning and brainpower. He was also a bit rebellious. In the early sixties he adopted the goatee and sideburns of the beat generation. He was among the first hippies in the area and experimented with all manner of psychedelic drugs. He decided not to pursue higher education, which greatly disappointed his mother and placed a great strain on their relationship that would last until shortly before her death.

For all that, Ollie was, in his own way, hard working and ambitious. He walked the edge sometimes, like when he battled county commissioners over the morality, and legality, of certain ordinances he ran afoul of when he opened a go-go club in Fort Myers Beach in the early 70s. He won that battle and lost some others over the years. I learned this and much more about the life and times of Oliver Wendell Holmes Mason in many conversations, both with Ollie and with area old-timers who were, for the most part, awed and respectful of both his intellect and his business feats. He was now in his early sixties and very comfortable financially. He had his hand in many businesses in the area, including mine, many of them of the more traditional kind than in his earlier years, though he still occasionally invited controversy.

Ollie had never married but he was known to be appreciative of the female form. A prize specimen of that species was almost always on his arm when he appeared at social functions, sometimes two.

My own relationship with Ollie went back over twenty years to a rebellious time in my life, just before I took off with the carnival. Actually, as I found out later, he'd had an impact at various times in my young life; sponsoring a Little League team for which I played; as the benefactor of Mrs. Higgins fifth grade class who provided the funding for a visit to a youth camp in Sebring, Florida, where we canoed, studied native Florida flora and fauna, and did a lot of horseback riding; and as the sponsor of a junior high (now called a middle school) bowling league.

When I struck off on my own to discover and conquer the world I was just out of high school and wondering what to do with my life. I'd already decided that I didn't want to follow in the traditional Dixon shoes and spend my life harvesting the bounty of the deep. I was working with a carpentry crew in the hot, steamy, rainy summer after high school and knew I was meant for something better. But what? College was out. No, more than that, it was unconsidered as an option. People in my social strata didn't even think about it.

Ollie owned, among other things, a bowling alley combined with a poolroom and a lounge located on 41 at the northern edge of Mangrove Springs. I often bowled there and I had become fascinated by the pool tables. I'd been playing for a year or so, tutored by the hustlers and layabouts who took my money at the rate of twenty-five or fifty cents per game of eight ball or nine-ball. I was learning, getting better.

One striking thing about Ollie, he was a hands on type of manager. He was in the house, in the bowling alley, the poolroom or the lounge every night and was many times witness to my growing ability. In fact, when I didn't have the money to play Ollie took to backing me. He would provide the monetary muscle to allow me to play deep into the night, even if I was losing, in a test of long distance wills. I hated to lose; I WOULD not lose, if I could stay in the game long enough to figure a way to win.

A surprising thing began to happen with some regularity: I'd win. It didn't matter if the opponent was a better shot-maker. It didn't matter if the opponent had a flashier style or a really neat custom cue stick. All the hustlers from Fort Myers, Naples, Immokalee, Cape Coral, Lehigh Acres and Golden Gate learned to fear the name of Roy Dixon. There were even a few attempts by lower level hustlers from the Miami and Tampa Bay areas to invade my territory. Through it all Ollie was a steadying influence, constantly telling me that I could achieve anything I wanted, I could be as good as I desired. Thus I was emboldened to strike out with the carnival, much to the chagrin of my mother.

Ollie, though, took it in stride, counseling me on the eve of my departure to keep alert for danger, to take full advantage of any opportunities for romance, and to make some money. He was the father figure that I'd been deprived of, the necessary balancing weight to an overprotective mother who meant well but, in the final analysis, was just too FEMALE to understand the workings of an adolescent male's inner self. I loved my mother but I longed, with all my being, for a father. Ollie almost answered that longing.

Ollie had been responsible for me getting into the title insurance business. After I returned from my second summer on the road I kind of hopped from job to job, a few months here, a few weeks there. I resumed hanging out at the bowling alley though I played a lot less pool than before. I began dating Jenna, a girl who'd attended the same schools I had, but two years behind me. She was working the refreshment counter at the bowling alley in the evenings and taking classes at Edison Community College in Fort Myers during the day. Her wholesome beauty captivated me and things progressed quickly. We were soon to be married. About this time I took her uncle Creighton up on his offer of employment at the family's packinghouse. It didn't take long for me to realize that it wasn't for me. There I was, a groom to be, without gainful employment or any prospects of same. I made a little money shooting pool but that was hardly enough to support a wife and certainly not a family.

A friend of Ollie's owned a small independent title insurance agency in Naples. Ollie arranged for me to take a position as a title examiner trainee. I found that I enjoyed the work, liked the feeling of satisfaction, of closure, that came after I successfully pieced together the paper trail that established a property's pedigree.

Things progressed from there. Jenna earned an Associate's Degree in business and I talked to my employer, for whom I was now a full examiner, and he agreed to hire Jenna and to train her as a closer. When he died several years later and the Agency was closed, Ollie offered to go partners with us in our own agency in Mangrove Springs. Jenna tested for her insurance license and we put up our entire savings, a little over two thousand dollars, which was a small fortune to us at the time. Ollie kicked in a few thousand and we took a small office space next to a television repair shop and furnished it mainly with second hand desks and file cabinets. But Ollie insisted that we get the newest and finest office equipment: calculators, phones, and copier. He told us that the little in extra cash up front would more than be made up for by superior functionality and by the impression these things would make on our clients. He also insisted that we pay cash rather than lease. No payments, he assured us, was an easier nut to make each month than a bunch of equipment lease payments. Many times since we've silently thanked him for that bit of wisdom. Over the years we've had our ups and downs and built a reasonably successful business. Ollie bought the land and erected the building where we were now located and offered it to the agency at a bargain rate.

Sometimes I questioned why he would be so generous with us but then I would feel guilty about doubting him. As with his female companions, his circle of friends was comprised of mostly transitory faces, with few surviving the test of time. People didn't become hostile toward him, they just seemed to realize that you could only get so close to Ollie and they would move on, looking for more in their relationships. Jenna and I accepted Ollie's apparent limited engagement in the relationship not, I hoped, because we profited hugely from the arrangement, but because we sensed and accepted his need to keep people at arms length. Plus, in the good years, Mason Dixon Title Associates, Inc., paid him respectable dividends. We weren't exactly a cash cow but we'd provided him with a reasonable return on his investment. In the poor years, I reasoned, the loss had been useful to him when he filed his tax returns.

Ollie was in many ways a mystery to me but I was glad to accept his friendship and to reciprocate to the extent that he allowed. Over the years he'd always been there when we needed him, whether for moral support, a crucial introduction, influence in places of power, or cash assistance, usually without our asking. And, on the rare occasion that he needed the type of support that friends provide for friends, we tried to be there for him.

Chapter Eleven

I realized that I'd been wool gathering. I'd noticed a growing tendency to do that as I got older. I brought myself out of it by sitting up straight in the chair. I reached for the phone and dialed the number of Ollie's private office line. He answered after the third ring.

"Roy, glad you could return my call." Ollie had caller I.D.

"Hey, Ollie. I've been meaning to call you but it's been hectic. How've you been?"

"Roy, you have NOT been meaning to call me. I know that I am not at the top of your thought processes most days. Don't worry, I'm not offended. I realize that the day to day, indeed, the hour to hour, needs of a virile young male such as yourself far outweigh any responsibility you may feel to your longtime friends and business associates." Ollie's supercilious tone let me know that something was wrong between us, though for the life of me I couldn't imagine what it might be.

"What's wrong, Ollie?" I figured it was best to get it out in the open as soon as possible. He was quiet a moment.

"I imagine that you don't think there will be any consequences, personally or professionally, arising from your illicit tryst with that trollop Rita Muncie." Oh, Christ! How'd he know about that! Just as importantly, who else knew about it? That's all I needed at the moment. I stood and, awkwardly holding the phone to my ear, stepped around the desk until I could nudge the door closed with my foot.

"Look, Ollie, I was drunk. Nothing happened, believe me. I was THAT drunk." My words had a sniveling sound to them, even to me. "Besides," my tone stiffened a bit. "How do you know about that?" I sat down.

"My young friend, have you forgotten that I own a majority position in the franchise arrangement of the very motel and lounge that you chose for your dalliance with Jack Muncie's wife?" I HAD forgotten. "A couple of the staff there are, um, acquaintances of mine. You were seen, recognized, and it was reported to me." The waitress! Or the maid? Ollie was having an affair with one or more of them. My mind was racing, trying to figure out all of the ramifications.

"Who else knows about this," I asked.

"Well, lets see. The lounge staff. The night desk clerk. The housekeepers." I groaned audibly. "The taxi driver." For God's sake, did Ollie have an interest in every business in town? "In case you're wondering, he is betrothed to the sister of my secretary." Like the song said, 'If it wasn't for bad luck, I wouldn't have no luck at all.'

"I am disappointed, Roy. I know that you're divorced, free from the bonds of matrimony, but Rita Muncie is not. And you know that I am very fond of you and Jenna, not to mention the kids. But your living arrangement is a bit unusual to say the least. And there is the added complication that you and Jenna are seeing others while still living together. Now this. I am forced, against my better instincts, to seriously consider the possibility of mental derangement. What were you thinking?"

"It's worse than you think."

"How could it be worse, Roy. Your, OUR, standing in the community may have been seriously eroded, depending upon how many people not under my sway are privy to your indiscretion." My ears pricked up at the mention of 'sway.' That term, I thought, meant that Ollie believed that he could manage damage control, provided that awareness of the incident was contained to those few people that had already been mentioned. Then I sagged a bit.

"It's worse. Jack Muncie's out of town."

"I know," he interrupted.

"He's out of town," I repeated, "and I'm doing a policy for him that needs to be completed before he gets back, that's why he wanted me to do it, and…"

"For God's sake, man, get to the point!"

"Well, it's a twenty million dollar policy and we're heading into the off-season and a softening real estate market. With the interest rate hikes and the clobbering the stock market has taken lately, and higher fuel prices..."

"I get the picture." His voice had taken on a flat tone, one of resignation. I hesitated before continuing.

"And, well, there may be others, a LOT of others, who know about this." I was recalling the crowd that had been present at The Grouper Hole as Rita and I had gotten acquainted. I described it all to Ollie. Surprisingly, his tone lightened a bit.

"I wouldn't worry about that too much. The fact that you had the good sense to wait a full ten minutes after Rita left before you did should have provided sufficient cover. Ten minutes is a long time when you get down to it. The thoughts of most people would have moved on by then, not making the connection." I was surprised at the change in his tone.

"Roy," he said softly. "You don't think for a minute, do you, that this is the first time that she has engaged in such behavior?"

"I don't know, Ollie. I haven't really thought about it. I guess that's the problem, isn't it? I didn't think." His voice kept that soft tone, no longer accusing.

"Look, you are used to being in a stable, monogamous relationship, characterized by tenderness and consideration. Just recently have you been rudely thrust into a far different equation, as has Jenna. I'm not sure what precipitated it but I know that you two are decent people dealing with it as best you can. Don't beat yourself over the head because you were taken advantage of by a female predator. Right now, the only thing we need to worry about is the bartender at The Grouper Hole."

"Dan?"

"Ah yes, a good man."

"You know him, too?" Ollie cleared his throat.

"Acquaintances in all walks of life are important to me, my business ventures being as, er, wide ranging as they are. Dan has been useful to me in the gathering of intelligence, ah, information. People blab when indulging in alcohol and generally regard bartenders as part of the scenery. Or as therapists. Dan's probably not a problem but if anyone put it together it would be him." I didn't follow and told him so.

"Well, bartenders notice a lot, having seen all kinds of she-nanigans in the normal course of doing their job. Besides, he probably noticed your car in the nearly empty parking lot when he went home. Your car is eminently noticeable. Did you tip him well?" I thought about that for a few seconds.

"Sure. I think so. I always tip Dan well, he takes good care of me."

"Good. Even if he put two and two together he'll probably keep quiet about it. A bartender's job security and income depend to a large extent on their discretion. A combination of people, alcohol, low lights and loud music often leads to behavior that the people involved would rather not be reminded of. If Jack Muncie doesn't already suspect his wife of infidelity, I think we're okay." I felt greatly relieved by Ollie's coolly reasoned analysis. He often had a reassuring effect on me. He was so, well, grown up. "Besides," he said, "Dan owes me."

"So," Ollie continued, "tell me about the deal you're doing for Muncie." I explained the sale of Chastain land. I told him about the title search and examination, which had uncovered no blemishes that would interfere with the marketability of the land. He asked me who was buying and why, and I told him.

"Valhalla Homes, huh? Hmm. You say there was a due diligence period?" I said that there was. "Hmm. Alma was quite outspoken about not allowing any more Chastain land to be used for development of any kind. I tried to purchase a tract from her to build a small strip center. It was prime 41 frontage and I was prepared to pay top dollar. She wanted no part of it. In fact, she became quite animated during a heated exchange at a meeting set up by Delbert Hinley at his office. She told me in no uncertain terms that she'd never allow that parcel to be developed for any commercial reason. You know the land, that twelve acres in front of the middle school that she donated to the county school board with the stipulation that it be used for kids to study nature and ecology."

That was Bobby Jane's school. And I did know the land in question. Bobby Jane had been involved in the creation of a butterfly habitat on a small corner of it. Just as her class had created the garden for a school project, I knew that other classes had projects in the works to create eco-spaces on the same land. One class, brilliantly, I thought, had decided to make it their project to maintain a piece of the property in its natural state, thus eliminating the need to do anything to it at all. In addition to being extremely NON-labor intensive, the plan may have also been the most intelligent use of the site.

"Yeah, I've heard about Alma's desire to keep the Chastain land free of development." I told Ollie about Pete and Repeat and what they'd told me of Cit-Gim. "But the will and everything checks out. Maybe she just never got around to making any concrete provisions. Intentions don't count, just legal documents."

"It's odd, that's all. I know for a fact that Alma felt passionately about the issue. That level of passion usually results in action."

I spent the rest of the afternoon responding to all of those messages I'd been putting aside because they 'could wait.' Sigrid buzzed me a couple of times concerning phone calls and I actually spoke to the callers rather than having Sigrid tell them that I 'was in a meeting,' or 'out of the office.' I felt no need to break for lunch due to the absorption of the grease bombs earlier. The hangover was gone, but as the day wore on I became lethargic due to the lack of a proper amount of sleep the night before. I spoke to Jenna a couple of times on matters concerning upcoming closings. I thought I could detect a bit of iciness in her tone. Since the divorce there'd been several times when I hadn't made it home at night but never because I'd spent the night in a motel with another man's wife. I couldn't decide if my guilty feelings were causing me to imagine frostiness or if it was really there. I had to remind myself that we were, indeed, divorced and that, in the final analysis, I'd done nothing wrong. In fact I'd been physically unable to do anything, right or wrong.

That night at home we gathered as a family in front of the tube. We watched some reality TV, a show on which people ate bugs and stabbed pigs to bloody death in an effort to outlast other contestants, who seemed equally willing to do the same ridiculous things. Why? For the promise of a large payday for the eventual winner.

The news came on and the lead story was about the wildfires burning in the Everglades to the east of us. Several hundred acres had been scorched locally and no relief from the dry conditions was in the forecast. Fires were raging in other parts of the state as well.

After that report we started stirring. As Bobby Jane and Cleve made their case to Jenna in support of rounding the evening off with a bowl of butter pecan ice cream, and Rae grabbed the cordless phone and scooted for her bedroom, I turned the TV off in the middle of a breathless report by a junior reporter about the disappearance of several prostitutes. I headed for the stairs, thinking 'another strange evening in the Dixon experience.'

Chapter Twelve

The next day I buried myself in the humdrum of every day life at a title insurance agency. I worked on files and examined title chains and it was after four when I finished the last file. I spent the rest of the afternoon doing some housekeeping chores, end of the week stuff. I cleared my desk of everything I could. I killed the rest of the workday playing Spider solitaire against the computer.

Later, after Jenna and I closed up the office, we drove separately to the Chamber function held at the Pelican Roost clubhouse. Pelican Roost was one of the gated communities that ran from 41 on the east to the bay on the west. Prices in the Roost ranged from $450k for a one-bedroom condo near 41 to $7.5m for a single family bay front home. It was one of the first gated communities in Mangrove Springs and was about 80% built out, including the commercial frontage along 41 that housed supermarkets, restaurants, banks, doctors, lawyers and the other services that kept everything running smoothly. Oh, did I mention the three championship golf courses, the seven man-made lakes and the bay front marina?

Valet parking was offered at the enormous, and, I thought, somewhat gaudy covered entryway. I pulled up behind Jenna, closing the Cadillac's top as I came to a stop, and a buff and tanned twenty-something took my keys and grinned at me.

"Cool ride," he said. I noted the red-eyed form of a fire-breathing dragon coiled about his right forearm. I handed him a couple of ones and he gave me a ticket.

"Treat it with the respect due the elderly." He laughed and slid behind the wheel. As he followed the Taurus to the parking lot I took Jenna by the elbow and we headed for the revolving glass door that led to the lobby of the clubhouse.

The lobby was cavernous, with scattered groupings of sofas, chairs, tables and silk trees. Recessed lighting, a vaulted ceiling and plush dark carpeting contributed to the muted, refined air, befitting such a conclave of affluence. Most of the seating was in use and twenty or thirty other people stood or milled about the large room. These were not residents of the Roost, as the clubhouse was closed to the community for this affair, but members of the Mangrove Springs Chamber of Commerce and their guests. So, the formal gowns, glittering jewels and tuxedoes one might expect to see in a place like this were not in evidence. The people here, for the most part, had, like Jenna and me, come from their workaday worlds and were dressed appropriately. Not shabbily, mind you, but not formally, either. Few jackets and fewer ties were to be seen. The women were mostly in pantsuits or skirts with sensible shoes. Most were 'cocktailing.' Having drinks and eating assorted finger foods from small plates. Those seated had their fare spread out on cocktail tables and end tables while those standing juggled theirs with varying degrees of success.

New arrivals were passing through a super-sized set of open French doors into the main room of the clubhouse where attendants were taking tickets and marking hands with a stamp. Like a high school dance, I thought. Somehow, that didn't fit with the overall ambience of the place. Jenna and I followed. This room was even larger than the first, with at least a dozen huge, glittering chandeliers suspended from the vast gilt ceiling. The room had been set up with two bars, one at each end, and three long buffet tables laden with food and ice sculptures. Along one long wall a small stage supported a string quartet all but unheard over the din created by the two or three hundred people circulating around the bars and the food. A microphone was on a stand at one end of the stage. At the other end, and just off the stage, skirted tables held various objects. I leaned close to Jenna's ear.

"Good Lord, who's paying for this? The Chamber?"

"Naw. The Roost donated the room, the food and the music. They want to keep the Realtors bringing buyers. The rest, the money from tickets and the cash bar, is for the Chamber to raise money." I hadn't known that. "Also, the raffle tickets. Someone will hit on us soon you can bet. You use the tickets to try to win those prizes there by the stage. Put one or more tickets in the basket in front of the prize you'd like to win and later they'll draw for the winners. See that big gift basket near the end? We donated that one. All the prizes are donated."

"We did? How much did that cost?" I hadn't realized that this event would be so expensive. Jenna giggled.

"Nothing. I won it a couple of weeks ago at a Collier County Women's Council of Realtors function. I didn't really want it and that was a different crowd so it won't be recognized."

"Tricky." She smiled up at me.

"Not the first time it's been done. Do you realize how many gifts we're asked to donate in a year?" I didn't. "Lots," she assured me. We headed for one of the bars where we waited in line for a harried bartender to serve us. When our turn came Jenna ordered a white wine and I asked for a Diet Coke. Jenna glanced at me curiously but I ignored it.

"I'm going to get something to eat," Jenna said. "Want me to get you a plate?"

"No thanks, you go ahead. I'll get something in a little bit. I thought I saw Delbert and some other people I know. I think I'll go talk to them. We are working, after all."

"Yeah. I'll get some food and mingle too. I'll find you later."

"Okay." She headed for the food and I began maneuvering my way toward where I'd seen Delbert. I was about halfway there when a hand grabbed my arm and a soft voice spoke my name. I turned toward the owner of the hand.

"Dottie! How are you? I haven't seen you in a while." Dottie Springbridge was a member of the blue-hair set, widowed, a Realtor and recently retired high school principal. She was also a candidate for Mayor of the newly incorporated city of Mangrove Springs.

"I haven't seen YOU. And that's a shame!" She was about five feet, two inches and looked to weigh something less than a hundred pounds. She was wearing a sky-blue pantsuit with some sort of floral design and, of all things, a wide-brimmed straw hat. She looked as if she should be tending her flower garden.

"I know, I know. I've been busy. Besides, you're a politician now. Real Estate is probably the last thing on your mind."

"On the contrary, love. I thought being Mayor would have a positive influence on my Real Estate career. Lord knows I could use some help in that area. You know yourself I don't sell enough for it to qualify as my job. More like an expensive hobby." That was hardly true. She'd been a Multi-Million Dollar Producer ever since joining the Board.

Dottie was standing with several other people but I didn't know any of them. Never a shy one, I offered my hand to the nearest gentleman. I was working, after all. I pasted a big smile on my face.

"Hi. My name's Roy Dixon. I don't believe we've met." Dottie sprang into action.

"Oh, allow me. Roy, this is Ernie LaPointe, a friend of mine visiting from Indiana." Ernie shook my hand and nodded at me. He was razor thin, all elbows and Adam's apple, dressed in beige slacks and a brown jacquard pullover. I guessed he was about Dottie's age, 60 or 65.

"Pleased to meet you," he said. I smiled and nodded.

"And this is his wife, Elaine." Ernie let go of my hand so that I could take the limp fish that Elaine LaPointe offered me. She was even thinner than her husband and wore a purple sweater over a lavender pantsuit. Her hand was damp and she looked cold. She had thin lips and gray, lifeless hair. She nodded, eyes on the floor, and quickly withdrew her hand.

"And this is my pride and joy, my grandson Todd." Todd was a strapping twenty or twenty-one, with an aw-shucks attitude toward the doting way his grandmother's eyes caressed him. The man-boy fidgeted, embarrassed, but managed to proffer his hand. His handshake, in spite of his mien, was firm and dry. He wore one of the rare jackets in the room, a camel's hair, with one of the even rarer ties. His attitude was belied by the quick intelligence in his clear brown eyes.

"Hi, Todd."

"He's taking a semester off from U F to spend some time with his Grandma. Actually, he's running my campaign!"

"I'm a Political Science major," he offered. "I thought, what a chance for field experience, my grandmother is running for public office. My department head arranged for me to receive extra credit. I couldn't pass it up."

"Wow, that's great." I turned toward Dottie. "You must be very proud."

"I am." She patted Todd on the cheek. "He's such a good boy to want to help his old grandmother."

She beamed at Todd and then at me. Then she beamed at Ernie and then Elaine. Ernie smiled at me and then at Todd. I smiled at Todd, Ernie and Elaine. Elaine looked at the floor, seeming to be slightly embarrassed. Finally, a young lady broke into our beaming.

"Would you like to buy some raffle tickets?" she inquired.

"Oh, yes dear, I thought no one would ever ask." Dottie dug into her purse and came up with a wad of bills. "How much are they?"

"A dollar each, 6 for five, 15 for ten and 50 for 25! How many do you want, I mean, would you like? They told us to say would you like," she quickly explained. Dottie plucked a ten from her wad.

"15 should do it," she said. She offered the ten to the woman who was unreeling tickets from a roll she cradled under her arm. When she had unrolled 15 of the double tickets, she tore them off and gave them to Dottie.

"Put one side in the basket of your choice and keep the stub," she intoned. "How about you?" She was looking at me. I took a ten from my pocket.

"Fifteen here, too." She counted them off. Ernie bought some for he and Elaine to share and Todd found a crumpled five pressed into his hand by his grandmother.

"6," he said, somewhat sheepishly. I felt for him. Who could expect a student to be flush with cash? A voice behind me said:

"I'll take 200." We turned to look. It was Toby Chastain, decked out in a white linen jacket, white linen shirt unbuttoned at the collar and white duck slacks with Sperry Topsiders, sans socks, completing his outfit. The linen, as was its nature, was a bit rumpled. He looked like a refugee from that great American cultural icon of the eighties, *Miami Vice*. He held out a hundred dollar bill to the Chamber volunteer. She couldn't hide her surprise. A smile broke out on her face.

"Yes sir," she said. It took her a minute or two to count out the tickets and I used the time to study the man whose deal was about to give me a summer cushion. His nose was straight and sharp, and his longish sun-bleached hair was a bit mussed, I expect on purpose. As he waited for the tickets he seemed perfectly at ease, his cool green eyes taking in our little group and then sweeping the room. It was obvious he'd just arrived. At his side was a remarkable creature, tall, fashionably thin, with tousled blonde hair and tanning bed glow, designer draped in a white sheath so contour-clinging that her braless nipples stood out prominently. She stood close to Toby, her expression vacuous and bored. They looked like an idle rich playboy out on the town with his fashionable and high-priced consort. Something you might expect to see at Cannes, I imagine, but not very often in good old Mangrove Springs.

The volunteer finished counting out the tickets and gave the not inconsiderable wad to Toby in exchange for the C-note.

"Gee," she said, admiration clearly inflected in her voice, "I thought I was going to run out of tickets." She smiled up at Toby and he grinned, somewhat condescendingly I thought, back at her.

"But you didn't, lucky for us. We all know that the money is for a good cause."

If you haven't caught it yet, I was feeling a bit put off by the tone of the whole thing. First, I couldn't understand the volunteer girl's obvious infatuation with a fashion throwback to an era some twenty years in the past. Even though, as I freely admitted, retro was currently cool. Second, the fashion, the girl-on-the-arm, and the flashing of big bucks created an impression of assumed superiority that rankled. I'd met Toby on previous occasions but always in the company of his Grandmother, or, at least, in her shadow. Other than the funeral, this was the first time I'd seen Toby Chastain in a social situation, or any situation, since Alma's death. I thought about that for a few seconds and realized that a young man suddenly without family could react in a wide variety of ways. In fact, he would probably react in a number of different ways until he found one that comfortably fit him.

As he coolly looked out over the gathered assemblage I changed my view of him and the somewhat grandiose impression he was evidently trying to create. I decided that he was probably a sensitive soul suddenly thrust into a cold and uncaring world without the one person who loved him, and he was trying to put on a brave front, stiff upper lip and all that. The blonde waif I viewed as just an expensive prop. Toby was, I convinced myself, under the veneer of urbane, though dated, toughness, just a frightened and vulnerable victim of having to enter the adult world at too young an age. He was only twenty-one or so.

Dottie, Todd and the rest of their group were by this time wandering toward the row of prizes and the baskets that held ticket stubs. Toby had begun separating the tickets wadded in his left fist as the blonde carefully scrutinized a small mole on her thin and fragile looking left forearm.

"Hi. My name's Roy. Dixon. I knew your grandmother." Toby looked up from the tickets and peered at my face in the subdued lighting. I stuck out my hand and he took it and shook it once before dropping it.

"Yes, I saw you at Grandmother's funeral." He continued to look at me and he seemed to be waiting for me to say something further. Or maybe he was waiting for me to leave.

"You're grandmother was a lovely woman and a pioneer in the community. We miss her." I gave him my most sympathetic smile, trying to convey my sincerity, but it seemed to hit the chill air surrounding him and slipped, dying, to the floor. He managed a small 'thank you'. He'd evidently built a wall around his grief and bewilderment, I reasoned. I decided not to let this deter me in my effort to be civil.

"Tell me," I said, trying to make conversation. "Is that old guy, the Indian gentleman, still living on your gran..., on your property?" He looked up at me sharply. I'd have to be more careful to remember that it was his now. "There was an Indian family, right? They worked around the place," I hurriedly said to hide my discomfort. Toby's eyes narrowed a bit as if he was trying to recall.

"You must mean old Dent. He and his wife lived in servant's quarters on the back of the estate." I snapped my fingers.

"Yeah, that's him. Dent, uh, Billie. That's his name. Dent Billie. Is he still there?" He peered at me again.

"Do you know him?" I shook my head.

"No, I don't know him, but I know something about him." He was looking more and more confused. "I mean, I dabbled a bit in graphology one time, you know, handwriting analysis, and I deduced certain character traits from his signature." The blonde was beginning to tug on his arm, pointing vaguely toward the bar area, but he shook her off, not allowing his eyes to leave my face.

"I don't understand," he said. "Why were you looking at his signature?" Suddenly I realized that he wasn't aware of the work I was doing on his behalf. I explained it to him.

"And so I ran across his signature as a witness to your grand-mother's will and I noticed some very distinct characteristics, some things that he and I share, as a matter of fact. You know, leadership, that kind of thing. It's all right there for anyone to see, if you know what you're looking for." He relaxed and grinned for the first time. The change was remarkable.

"The servant had leadership qualities, huh?" He chuckled a bit and I didn't know whether to be offended or not. "Dent and his wife took care of things. Dent washed cars, did mechanical repairs and stuff. Sometimes he drove Grandmother or me around. Lontine, his wife, tended the vegetable garden in season, did the laundry and housework and helped Grandmother with the canning. After Gran died I didn't really need them anymore, so they left. Grandmother left them a little something so I wrote a check against the estate and they moved. His family runs an airboat service in Everglades City. Alligator farm, Indian artifacts, that kind of thing. They went there to help out with the family business, I think, but I don't really know." As I digested this he seemed to recall what I'd told him about what I was doing. All expression left his face and the tension was suddenly returned to his wiry frame.

"Muncie's having you do this work for the estate?" I had no reason to believe that Jack would discuss the day-to-day workings of his law firm with Toby so I wasn't surprised that he didn't know that I was involved. I would just be a line item on the detail of Jacks billing summary, yet I felt a sense of alarm at having revealed myself to him. I chalked that up to a fear that somehow I'd endangered my fee. I figured I would be honest with him but not offer anything further and hope that it made no difference. The blonde was simpering and shifting her weight impatiently from foot to foot. Toby's quick, cold glance caused her to freeze in mid simper.

"Well, it's nothing, really. Just a bit of drudgery that Jack farmed out. Happens all the time. You know, Jack's the contractor, I'm the sub-contractor."

"But I thought he would be doing the work. Confidentiality and all that." He was peering intently. The blonde was still frozen, watching him, all traces of vacuity gone, feet still.

"Hey," I explained, hands spread in supplication. "I'm part of that whole confidentiality thing, you know, by law. Jack will review my work so you can be assured that everything is as it should be." Where had I heard that phrase before? I was a bit dismayed by the wheedling tone of my voice and the general flavor of what I was saying, but it seemed to be having the desired effect. He relaxed once more and the blonde let out with a soft giggle.

"Yeah, I guess." Suddenly, he was all business. "Well, it's nice to see you again, uh, Roy. I know you'll do a good job for the estate. If Jack has faith in you, so do I. Now Tara and I need to place our bets, so to speak." He smiled again and grabbed the blonde by the arm. She looked startled, though she'd been angling for just such an outcome. He pointed to the tickets, forgotten, in my own hand. "You, too." His look was piercing. Even, in my anxiety over my fee, a bit menacing. "Good luck, and I hope to see you again." For a grieving and bewildered youngster he sure was smooth. Breeding will tell, I thought, as he and the blonde turned in lock step and walked away.

I was startled by Dottie's voice at my elbow.

"He gives me the creeps."

"What do you mean?"

"Toby was a student at Rivers High for three years." Rivers was the school Dottie'd been principal of. "Let's just say he wasn't like the other kids." She was watching as, in the distance, Toby and his girl ambled along the tables holding the prizes.

"How was he different?" Dottie snorted.

"He was very bright but only an average student, except in biology."

"Hey, lots of kids are like that, huh?" She turned to look at me.

"He was a loner, seemed as if he felt superior to the others. He was quiet, could sneak up on you it seemed. Listened in without taking part, you know?" I nodded, though I wasn't sure I did know.

"Man, the dude was weird," offered Todd.

"Todd went all through high school in the same classes as Toby," Dottie said. "Tell Roy about him," she urged.

"Well, like you said, he was a loner, in school and out. Never played sports though he sure liked to use the exercise equipment in the gym. And, there were the stories." Todd paused so that he could be urged to tell more. He'd done this before.

"All right," I said. "What stories?" He shrugged.

"Several. Like the time that a dead cat, you know, one of the ones in formaldehyde that we used for dissection in biology lab?" I nodded. "Well, one showed up in Melissa Lambert's locker, its fur skinned and muscles peeled back from the bones and arranged on a satin pillow. It had its eyelids sutured open and Melissa's name was printed on a card hung around its neck. Someone said they saw Toby hanging around her locker that morning." I frowned.

"That doesn't mean anything." Todd shrugged again.

"There were other things that happened that made people, students and faculty, view him as strange," Dottie offered, but before I could ask her to tell me more, Ernie LaPointe and his wife appeared and, after parting words, the four of them went off together.

I stood for a minute, mulling over my conversations with Toby, and then Dottie and Todd.

"Having fun yet?" I looked down at the pert face suddenly hovering about chin level.

"Hi. Having a ball, as usual. What's up with you?" Jenna grabbed suddenly at my tightly held tickets.

"Hey! We have to get those tickets in baskets. They're about ready to start drawing winners." I looked at the distant figures of Toby and his paramour, moving along the prize tables, and had an urge to flee. I pressed the tickets into Jenna's soft, yet firm, hand.

"You go place our bets. I want to get another drink. Want anything?" She counted the tickets.

"Another white wine, please. I'll meet you by the basket we donated." She looked up at me and I thought maybe there was hope for us. I squeezed her arm and wandered off toward the bar area.

I procured drinks, shifting, despite my recent aversion to alcohol, to a vodka martini, which is what I continued to drink for the rest of the evening, and met Jenna by the prize tables. We mingled, I mean marketed, until the prizes were awarded. Jenna excused herself. She was a runner, holding up the prizes and, when the winner was determined (you had to be present to win, occasioning several re-drawings), delivering the prize to the winner. She obviously relished her role, holding up the prize for all to see, and, when the winner was announced, scanning the crowd until she spotted the lucky person, or a re-draw was declared. If a winner was spotted, she let out a war whoop and pranced her way across the room, prize held high and warbling a victory sound until the sheer infectiousness of it got everyone involved in the joy of the moment. Someone was actually lucky enough to win a dried flower arrangement in the shape of Elvis!

I paid fairly strict attention, but Toby, for all his tickets, didn't win anything. In fact, I didn't see him or his blonde again that evening. Todd, Dottie Springbridge's grandson, won a hundred dollar savings bond. Good for him. There was some confusion when Jenna won a prize; they didn't seem to realize that the prize runner was also the winner. Now we would have something to donate for a Naples fundraiser.

Awards were handed out and Jenna was honored for her community involvement. I knew how seriously she took her commitment to the under-privileged and I felt good for her. She'd always been a warm and caring person, but after Patrick disappeared and the problems that caused for Bobby Jane, her level of commitment to the community ratcheted up a couple of notches.

After grabbing a bite from the buffet, I was able to convince Jenna that we ought to head for home. I followed the taillights of her Taurus and we made it without incident. It was only ten-thirty but we were ready for bed. The kids were up and watching a rented DVD, observed by my mother. Jenna and I headed upstairs. At her room, she didn't hesitate at all, went through the door as quick as you please. I slunk into my room and lay still until I drifted off.

Chapter Thirteen

Saturday morning. The sun was streaming in past the open shade at my window. I stretched luxuriously and considered turning over and going back to sleep but my brain was awake and chewing on some things that were bothering me. About Toby Chastain. About the DEAL. I gave up the idea of more rest and struggled from the bed.

A glance at the battered clock on the dresser told me nothing. I'd forgotten to wind it again. I picked up my watch from the nightstand and saw that it was after nine. The house had that quiet, lonely feeling that told me I was probably alone inside the big, wooden structure. I tottered to the bathroom down the hall, cranked the shower wide open, and let the needles of steaming water bring me to full wakefulness. I urinated while in the shower. I shaved and brushed my teeth at the sink. A look at the mirror confirmed that I was, indeed, getting older. The hair was a little thinner and the crow's feet around my eyes gave me a slight perpetual squint. Scrubbed, brushed, shaved, scented and a little melancholy, I went back to my bedroom and dressed.

To help dispel the slight case of the me-grims I chose my most faded jeans, no underwear, no belt, no socks, aged deck shoes and a time and elements softened short sleeved denim shirt, which I left outside the jeans, with the top two buttons undone. Except for thinning hair and crinkled eyes, and maybe a couple extra pounds, another peek in the mirror revealed much the same look I'd sought to achieve some twenty years before. Excellent. Toby Chastain wasn't the only throwback.

Downstairs, I confirmed my hunch that I was alone. It didn't take much searching, as Jenna'd left me a note. A thoughtful woman, instinctively doing the proper wifely, motherly thing, even in our strange estranged situation. She and Bobby Jane were at a swim meet in Cape Coral. Rae was spending the day boating with a friend and her family and Cleve was hanging with his buds, whatever that meant. The note revealed they would all be home by early evening and urged me to have a nice time and enjoy the quiet, as it couldn't last.

I made a pot of coffee and some toast before loping to the big caddy. I put the top down and gunned it toward the interstate. As I passed the motel I'd stayed at on Wednesday night, I averted my eyes. The air was smoky and fire trucks with flashing lights and blaring sirens were hurtling eastward.

I considered what I was about to do, why I thought it was necessary and what I might accomplish. At the root of it all was that I was supremely uncomfortable with the Chastain deal. What I wanted was to reassure myself that all was kosher because I really wanted that fee. But I'd been burned twice by claims and above all else I didn't want to go through that again. I'd rather lose the fee than ultimately lose my underwriter, and then be unable to continue to work in the title insurance business. What would I do then? There were only three other ways I was even vaguely acquainted with to earn a living (four, if you counted pool, but I was awful rusty) and the tomato business and the fishing business, neither of which I liked, were both almost gone from Southwest Florida. I wasn't particularly suited to the traveling carnival business anymore, being, ahem, almost middle aged and rooted in a community, with family and responsibilities and such.

A lot of people I'd talked to agreed that Alma Chastain hadn't wanted her property to be developed and some contended that she'd have taken steps to make that eventuality a non-starter. And yet, the will I'd been presented with hadn't made any provisions that would impede development. And, it was several years old, opening speculation that there might have been wills that did indeed offer such impediments. If a more current will was being suppressed, then there was probably a conspiracy involving at least Toby Chastain and Jack Muncie, possibly others. But, maybe I was all wet, maybe everything was on the up and up. I hoped so.

In any event, I hoped that a visit with Dent Billie might shed some light on the matter. He'd witnessed the will I had and logic would dictate that, in his capacity as a Chastain employee, and since he'd been asked on at least one occasion, he might have been asked to witness other documents, perhaps another, more current will. The problem, as I saw it, was that I didn't really know where, exactly, to find him. Toby had said that he was working with his family at an airboat tour/alligator farm somewhere around Everglades City. There were at least umpteen dozen such places.

And that was assuming that Toby had been forthcoming about Dent's whereabouts.

What I had going for me, or so I thought, was his name. Dent Billie was an unusual name and I thought it would be relatively easy to locate him with just a few well-placed questions. If Dent told me that he'd indeed witnessed the latest edition of Alma Chastain's will, and the copy that I had was indeed that edition, I'd feel much better about the deal and accept that providence had delivered financial salvation to us.

My plan was to head south to Immokalee Road and then exit the interstate, heading east on State Road 846 to where it intersected State Road 858. This would allow me to bypass Immokalee, a sprawling community where fishing, farming and the Seminole Casino were the main sources of livelihood. Located in Collier County and made up of equal parts of Crackers, migrant farm labor and Indians, it was the nearest major settlement to Lake Trafford and the ever-popular fishing camps along that lakes perimeter. I'd also miss paying a toll when the Interstate turned east.

Over the years Naples had spread north and east but after Immokalee Road the route I chose traveled along a flat, two-lane black top with only an occasional grouping of mobile homes, sheds for grading and packing produce, equipment repair barns and, sporadically, a general store or a farm equipment supply. This far inland, farming was still a major industry, though one that was dwindling. Interspersed among the sparse indications of human habitation were signs declaring the names of the various farms and ranches owned by large corporations. There was the Double Diamond Farm, the Carrey Enterprises Farm, the Harger Brothers, and the Three B's, to name a few. There was no traffic to speak of, just the occasional four-wheel drive pick-up passing by or entering the road from a sandy, two-track path. Fires burned to the north and the east, orange and black images reflected in my rear view mirror. Here and there was a burned out parcel, still smoking. Small whirlwinds of ash kicked up as the Caddy rocketed past, like flurries of dandruff from the scalp of the earth. I turned south on route 29.

I traveled through SunniLand, and then Miles City, where 29 crossed the Alligator Alley, fabled east-west corridor between

Naples and Ft Lauderdale that was now part of the interstate system. I passed the communities of Rock Island and Deep Lake, and crossed the Fakahatchee Strand.

I passed through Copeland and Carnestown before crossing U.S.41. If I'd turned east on 41, toward Miami, I'd have come to Ochopee within a few miles. I'd been there several times during my youth, my mother or uncle or whatever stopping on a vacation trip to Miami because the Ochopee Post Office was the smallest in the United States. It was only a little larger than an outhouse. Its postmark was widely coveted and it had the dubious distinction of being the most photographed Post Office in the country. I always wondered how, exactly, they knew that.

I passed several airboat and/or alligator emporiums but none seemed overtly Indian, with names like Trader Jack's, Tropical Tours, Jungle Sid's, Alligator Acres and Gator Gertie's. Just before I entered Everglades City proper I noticed a small weathered sign at the end of a dirt lane that disappeared into palmettos and Australian Pines. Indian Joe's, it said, Airboat Tours, Humongous Alligators and Venomous Snakes. I turned around in the parking lot of a general store a bit further along 29 and drove back to the dirt lane where it left the black top and headed in the direction the sign had indicated. The track twisted and turned through the semi-tropical vegetation that brushed the sleek flanks of the Caddy from time to time while the big car bounced and swayed over the ruts.

After about a quarter mile I emerged into a large clearing surrounding a small lagoon. One side of the horseshoe around the water sported a motley collection of weather beaten structures and a rickety dock where an astonishing collection of airboats, canoes, motorboats and one half-sunken sailboat were on display. Directly in front of me was a parking lot and a rotting boardwalk leading off to the other side of the horseshoe where it wound in and around some fenced-in pits and two Chickee huts. In the pits were mud, water and what appeared to be a number of bumpy logs. I parked and got out of the car. There were two other cars and an old pickup in the lot. I heard the unmistakable sound of a screen door slamming closed and looked toward the buildings near the dock. I saw a tall, thin, longhaired figure wearing jeans and a ball cap, with no shirt, heading toward me. I began walking his way.

When I was close enough I could make out a toothy grin in a ruddy face with high cheekbones, long shining black hair and expressive brown eyes. He wiped his hand on a denim clad right leg before offering it to me.

"Hey, there," he said in a raspy voice. I shook his hand, which was strong and dry. Then he swept it in an expansive arc seeming to indicate all that the eye could see.

"Welcome to Indian Joe's and all its wonders." He dropped his hand to his side and looked me up and down, still grinning. He appeared to be in his forties.

"Well, let's see. You want an airboat ride?" He gestured in the direction of the docks. "Whizzin' along at break-neck speed over the Everglades, which is Indian for 'river of grass'. Wind in your face, bugs in your teeth, earphones protecting you from the roar of the powerful aircraft engine." He grinned even wider as he pointed to the fenced in pits. "Or I could wrassle one of them mighty gators, risking life and limb for your enjoyment." He glanced at the inert logs. "If I could wake 'em up," he concluded. He looked at me expectantly.

"What about the venomous snakes?" I inquired, amused at his spiel. He frowned and looked real sorrowful.

"Ain't got no snakes right now," he lamented. "Had two. One run off and the other got so sad he done bit hisself and swelled up and died." His smile told me he was enjoying this as much as I was. I hoped he wouldn't sour on me when he realized I didn't really want his services, just some information. I thought I might as well break it to him.

"Well, really, I just want some information."

"No airboat ride?"

"No."

"No alligator wrasslin?"

"No. Sorry."

"Well, you got off Route 41 before you were supposed to. You go back out the dirt road to 29, the hard top, and turn right. When you get to 41, it's marked real plain, you turn right if you were heading for Miami or Fort Lauderdale, or left if you were headed for Naples, Ft. Myers, Sarasota or Tampa." He grinned, though not as widely as before, turned and headed back the way he'd come. I hurried after him.

"I'm trying to find someone. An Indian." He looked at me but didn't slow his pace.

"You found one. Now what?"

"I mean, I'm looking for an older fellow, last name is Billie." He stopped and I did too. He leaned toward me as if he were going to share an important confidence with me.

"Half the Seminole Tribe is named Billie." I guess he saw my consternation. "Half ain't." He shrugged and began walking again and I moved to keep up.

"This one's first name is Dent. I stopped because I think he works at an airboat ride place around here and the name of this place, you know..." I gestured about helplessly.

"You thought, hey, an Indian is an Indian and you might as well ask old Indian Joe if he knew this Dent guy." He stopped again and looked at me.

"You're Indian Joe? Hi, I'm Roy." I smiled with what I hoped was humility to hide my embarrassment.

"Jr. Indian Joe, Jr. Indian Joe was my dad and he built this God awful place and then had the nerve to leave it to me." He surveyed his domain ruefully. "Why couldn't I have brothers and sisters? Who ever heard of an Indian with one kid?" He pointed to one of the structures by the dock. "My mother lives there. She's 71. She wouldn't understand any life but this one. As long as she lives, I'll be here. When she's gone, I'll take my family and move on. The swamp can have this place back if I can't sell it. MY children are going to have better." He paused and seemed to come to some decision. "Dent? Is that his name? Dent Billie?"

"Yeah, Dent. It's important that I locate him."

"Hmm. Let me send some smoke signals, see what the drums say." He must have seen the puzzlement on my face.

"I've got to make some phone calls," he said.

"Oh. Okay."

I followed him to the nearest building, which turned out to be a sort of bait shop, with aerated tanks holding live bait, and, piled everywhere, rods, reels and any other fishing gear you could think of. He saw me looking around.

"Fishing's big in the Ten Thousand Islands. Anything to make a buck. Excuse me." He picked up a cordless phone from a nearby counter and wandered away as he punched in a number. I looked out over the dock again and noticed something I'd missed before: a gas pump. Fishermen must stop here to gas up and get bait and supplies, I realized. Turning back to the bait shop I noticed a well-stocked beer cooler.

Indian Joe, Jr. made four or five calls while I killed time wandering around the bait shop. I marveled at the variety of implements for catching fish. There were lures, nets, gigs, hooks, rods, reels, baits, electronic gadgets and clubs to knock fish senseless. Then there was a selection of items to keep fish alive, and, or, captured, once they'd been caught: aerators, oxygen releasing tablets, stringers and creels. And there was a shelf devoted to the needs of the fishermen; lip balm, sun block, Slim Jims, crackers and cheese, pastries, nuts and candies. And the beer. And wine. Indian Joe, Jr. stocked everything for the comfort and efficacy of the modern fisherman. I was unwrapping a Slim Jim when Joe returned.

"Dent Billie is Claude Billie's uncle and he recently retired from his job working for a white family. Dent, not Claude." I chewed a two-inch segment of the spicy sausage.

"Claude got him a job with his niece, helping out with maintenance of the boats and feeding the gators at her place. The name is Josie's Airboats and Alligator Emporium." I thought about that for a minute.

"But I didn't pass a place with that name coming in. Is it in Everglades City proper?"

"It's not really in Everglades City. It's back on 41, east of here, toward Ochopee, but before that. Now, anything else I can help you with?" He looked at me, eyebrows raised slightly.

"Look, ah, I really appreciate this. Maybe I can pay for an airboat ride, you know, like I really took one. You know, for your trouble." I could see distaste beginning to cloud his features. I hurried on. "Maybe I could take a real ride, you know, I think I'd like that, 'whizzin' along at break neck speed', with the 'wind in my face, bugs in my teeth', and listening to 'the powerful, throbbing engine.'" He made shooing motions with his hands and walked toward me, forcing me to retreat from the bait shop.

"Just pay for the Slim Jim."

"How much is that?" I continued to back-peddle.

"A buck'll do." I dug out a single. "What business are you in?" That threw me. I fumbled for an answer.

"Uh, title insurance, uh, we insure real estate…" he cut me off with a wave of his hands.

"Don't, I repeat, DO NOT try to force your children to take up the same business." He grabbed the dollar from my hand and abruptly turned and headed back toward the bait shop. I looked after him.

"Thanks," I called. And I meant it. "Thanks a lot." He raised his hand to acknowledge me but didn't turn. As I backed out of the parking lot I noticed a bass boat, a 15 or 20 footer, gliding into Joe's dock.

Chapter Fourteen

I followed the dirt track back to Route 29 and took a right. When the two lane black top intersected with the Tamiami Trail, I turned right again. I stayed below the legal speed limit, searching for Josie's Airboats and Alligator Emporium. Soon, on the right, brightly colored blankets suspended from clotheslines began appearing every two hundred yards or so. They had hand-painted lettering announcing the nearness of Josie's, home of airboat rides, alligators, tribal crafts, tribal foods and a genuine Indian museum. A final blanket, bright red with yellow letters, screamed 'HERE IT IS!'

Just beyond, on the same side of the road, a long, narrow strip of land covered with crushed shell and rock served as Josie's parking lot. It was at least two hundred feet long and held more than three-dozen candy colored cars baking in the early afternoon sun. As I pulled in and parked I marveled at the level of activity as compared to Indian Joe's. As any real estate agent could tell you, only three things mattered in real estate: 'location, location and location.'

I could see people in twos and threes wandering along a pathway that meandered in and out of the vegetation. Several buildings were partially visible. Signs identified these as a Gift Shop, Cafeteria, Museum, and Restrooms. They were of a modified Chickee hut design, closed in with tinted glass, and obviously air-conditioned. The logs and thatched roofs appeared to be of some synthetic material. The signs along the walkway pointed toward Alligators, Airboat Rides and a Nature Trail, which were out of sight beyond the wall of greenery. There were trashcans strategically placed about and a teen-aged Indian boy was patrolling with a short broom and a dustpan. I headed toward him and he didn't look up until I stopped a foot in front of him. He looked at me without curiosity and without saying anything.

"Hi," I said. He nodded.

"I'm here to see Dent Billie. Do you know where I can find him?" I smiled and if I'd been wearing a hat I'd have taken it off and twiddled it in my hands. He nodded again. I waited but he didn't say anything. I began wondering if he might be dumb, not the stupid kind, but mute, and I started to feel a bit of embarrassment.

"Uh, where is he?" He shifted the broom to the hand that held the dustpan and pointed without looking. I looked to where he was pointing.

"Alligators? He's down by the alligators?" He was still looking at me and he nodded. I thanked him and he turned and resumed his search for candy wrappers and cigarette butts.

I followed the path into the vegetation and about ten yards later I emerged in an open area where the land disappeared into dark, still water. Five feet before the waters edge was a ten-foot tall cyclone fence. Wooden stairs led to a sturdy looking wooden bridge that extended to a platform built above the water about forty feet from the near shore. I couldn't determine where exactly the far shore was. The expanse of water was dotted by mangrove trees and small, sandy islands. To the left I could see gleaming airboats at two long docks. There were small ones which could carry two to four people in addition to the pilot and a couple of larger ones that appeared to seat ten or fifteen.

Several people stood on the bridge and the platform with what appeared to be cane poles, the kind you use for fishing. As I watched, an elderly man, an Indian I thought, carried a large white bucket to a man on the platform and attached a hunk of something to the line on his pole. Nearer to shore, there was a violent splash and a couple on the bridge jumped back, startled, the woman emitting a yelp of surprised fear. I made out the shape of a large alligator, maybe ten or eleven feet long, sliding under the water. The elderly fellow was attaching something to another person's line. There was a splash and another alligator slid into the murky water clutching his treat.

I climbed the stairs and walked out on the bridge as the man with the bucket was headed my way. When he was close I stopped and smiled at him.

"Chicken?" I asked, nodding at the bucket.

"You bet." He set the bucket down and dragged one denim-clad forearm across his brow. "Want a pole?" His long-sleeved shirt was buttoned at the wrists and throat and he sported a bolo tie. His jeans were tucked into well-worn boots with improbably pointed toes. He wore a wide leather belt with a large silver buckle. A design that I was unfamiliar with was etched onto it. His dark, broad face was crinkled with laugh lines and slick with sweat. There were dark stains under his arms.

"No thanks. Are you Dent Billie?" His eyes narrowed.

"You bet. Why?" A woman on the bridge near shore called 'yoo-hoo' and waved one arm at us. He picked up the bucket and began to walk slowly toward the woman. I walked along with him.

"My name is Roy Dixon. I'm from Mangrove Springs and I'd like to talk to you for a few minutes." He switched the half-full bucket to his other hand.

"You the guy Jerome called about?"

"Jerome?"

"Indian Joe."

"Oh. Yeah, I am." He nodded as if strangers inquired about him every day. He stopped just before reaching the woman who had called to him and was now looking at us a bit impatiently. He pointed toward a park-type bench on the grass.

"I can talk to ya when the bucket's empty." He didn't wait for an answer but reached into the bucket and pulled out a piece of the cut-up chicken and began to attach it to the woman's line.

I headed for shore, the snapping and splashing of alligators following behind. When I reached the bench I sat and watched as one of the big airboats, fully loaded with tourists, backed away from the docks and began to glide forward, faster and faster, skimming the top of the water and emitting a huge roar. I could feel the backwash from the prop blow across me, cooling the beads of sweat that had appeared on my forehead. If I still smoked this would be a perfect time for one, I thought.

As I waited I thought about what I was doing and how futile it might ultimately prove to be. But damn it, I had to be sure. I watched Dent Billie as he moved from tourist to tourist, attaching piece after piece of chicken to their lines, alternately berating myself for running this fool's errand and congratulating myself for my dedication and tenacity in the pursuit of truth. Finally, the bucket was empty and Dent came down from the bridge and went to a small concrete pad where he rinsed out the bucket with a hose coiled on a post set in the concrete, before setting it upside down to drain. Then he unbuttoned his sleeves, rolled them up and washed his hands, using a piece of soap he took from the top of the post. He dried off with a large, colorful kerchief he pulled from his back pocket. He used the cloth to wipe his sweating face dry before rolling his sleeves back down, tucking the kerchief back into his pocket and heading my way. He sat down on the bench next to me.

"Tie the chicken with lightweight thread," he said. "Snaps easy. Don't want no tourists pulled over the rail and swallered by no gator." He pulled a pouch of Tops tobacco and cigarette papers from a shirt pocket and proceeded to roll a near perfect tube. He offered the fixin's to me and I shook my head. Then he returned the items to his shirt pocket, buttoned it up, and reached into his hip pocket and retrieved a battered Zippo lighter that was emblazoned with the insignia of the 101st Airborne. He returned it to his pocket and took a deep drag on the homemade cigarette. He closed his eyes and a look of utter satisfaction came across his face and his body visibly relaxed.

"Learned to roll these as a kid, when I couldn't afford store-bought." His eyes remained closed. "Now I just prefer 'em." He took another drag before opening his eyes and focusing on me. "Now, how can I help ya?"

"Were you in the 101st?" His eyes narrowed a bit at that.

"Yeah. You bet. Is that what ya wanted to know?" His expression for the first time was a bit puzzled.

"No, no. I just admired your lighter. My uncle was in the 82nd. He told me a lot of stories about the rivalry between the two units." It sounded lame, even to my ears, but it was true. He just looked at me.

"Were you in the service?" I felt a slight flush creep up my neck.

"Ah, no." He grunted and smoked.

"Actually, I wanted to talk to you about Alma Chastain."

"What about her?" His weathered face was totally expressionless.

"Well, you worked for her, right?" I fidgeted some on the bench. He wasn't making this easy. He leaned forward, forearms on his knees, and stared out across the water. The tourists were moving on now that the fun was over, casting curious glances our way as they left the bridge and crossed the open ground to the pathway that led through the vegetation to the highway.

"Hey," I said. "Do you have to go back to work, give them more chicken or something?" He dropped the short remains of his cigarette and ground it out with a boot heel.

"Naw, we won't put no more chicken out 'til two o'clock. Damned tourists would feed 'em all day if ya let 'em. I started in workin' for Clive. Alma's husband. Me and the wife worked for him and then for Alma for forty-five years altogether. Well, Lontine, my wife, worked four years more than that. I was in the army for four years. Married her when I got out." He dragged the Tops back out and made another near perfect cigarette.

"I'm interested in the last few years when you were working for Alma." He took another drag on his cigarette and blew smoke at the swamp.

"Why."

"Well, I'm doing a property search, a title search, actually, on a piece of Chastain land and I have some questions about the propriety of the sale." He looked me in the eye.

"What?"

"I mean, I saw your name, your signature on one of the documents concerning this piece of property, well, concerning all Chastain property…" He shifted his weight on the bench and seemed a bit annoyed.

"Look," he said. "Slow down. Pretend I don't know a thing about what you're saying. I don't, ya know." I took a deep breath and started over.

"Alma Chastain made no effort to hide her feelings concerning the development, er, over-development, of Mangrove Springs, and she swore she wouldn't let developers get at her land, even after she was gone." He nodded as if he was now following me.

"In fact, she told several people that she'd taken steps, via her last will and testament, to protect against just such an eventuality." I glanced over to see if he was still with me. I couldn't tell.

"CIT-GIM was a group of..." He abruptly stood up and ground out his cigarette.

"I'm gonna get some lunch," he said as he headed for the pathway. I hurried to catch up.

"Wait! Don't you want to talk to me?"

"I don't mind talking' to ya if you'd make sense. So far everything ya said just confuses me. Besides, it's lunchtime. If I don't get somethin' to eat now I won't get nothin' 'til suppertime. Come on, you should eat too. I've lived a long time and one of the most important things I've learned is to eat reg'lar."

I followed him along the pathway to the building identified by a sign as the Cafeteria. We entered through a smoked glass door into a dim, cool interior, with a serving line to one side and the rest of the space taken up by small plastic tables with uncomfortable looking plastic chairs. It really was set up cafeteria style and Dent grabbed a plastic tray, plastic utensils, and paper napkin and pushed them down the stainless steel tubes toward the food. I followed behind with my own tray. Dent chose a green salad, dinner rolls, and a fish stew type thing over rice at the steam table, served by a wide Indian woman with an infectious smile and a huge apron stained all colors of the food spectrum. I took a plate of beans and franks I was sure I'd regret later. Dent took a huge bowl of lime gelatin filled with canned fruit, coffee, iced tea and iced water. I selected a diet cola. The cashier waved Dent through but insisted that I pay seven-fifty for the privilege of eating genuine Indian food. I followed Dent to a table by the smoked glass window overlooking the parking lot. A glance about the dining room told me that only a few tables were in use and looking at the parking lot I could tell that there were fewer cars than when I'd arrived.

Dent spread out a paper napkin and tucked it into the collar of his shirt at his throat. He sprinkled generous amounts of salt and pepper on every thing but the bread, the gelatin and the drinks. He began eating with deliberate and mechanical motions.

Over the course of the meal I managed to fill him in on the current situation vis-à-vis the Chastain property, including my flattering assessment of his personality traits as gleaned from his handwriting. He grunted at that and otherwise only interrupted my story about two-dozen times. Whenever, it seemed, he was between mouthfuls. As we lingered over my diet cola, his coffee and Tops, I asked if he remembered witnessing Alma's will.

"You bet. Several times. I think." He dragged deep on the wonderfully noxious smelling weed.

"What do you mean," I asked, my interest piqued.

"Well, I witnessed things all the time for Clive and Miss Alma. So did Lontine. They was always havin' important papers done that needed witnesses to be 'ficial. Wills. Deeds. Trusts and Corporations and who knows what all. I never really read any of 'em. Didn't need to. None of my bidness, anyway. I was witnessin' their signatures, swearin' that it was them who was signin', that's all. Leastways, that's the what the lawyer fella told me." He slurped some black coffee. I digested this information for a minute.

"The will they entered in Probate," I began.

"What? Speak plain, man. So's an old Indian can understand ya." I started over.

"The will the court is using to dispose of the land is one she had Ralph Rennegar draw up for her several years ago. Does that sound right to you?"

"You bet. Until he died Ralph did all the Chastain legal stuff. I was always drivin' 'em over to his office while they, and later just her, would meet with Ralph, sometimes an hour or more. I always waited in the waitin' room, lookin' at those magazines and enjoyin' the air-conditionin'." I thought some more, trying to figure it out. The old man interrupted my thoughts.

"'Course, when that new one took over her legal stuff, I kept witnessin' things."

"Jack Muncie?"

"You bet. Never really warmed up to the man but I didn't have to. He wasn't taking care of my legal things and Miss Alma seemed happy enough with him. Mostly."

"What do you mean?" He shrugged and dropped his butt into the melting ice that was all that was left of his tea.

"Well, couple of times she seemed a bit put out when she came out of a meetin' with him. I think some other people were in the meetin' with them on those times. Anyways, she was agitated and there was no papers to sign."

"What else can you think of?" He squinted his eyes and studied me for a moment.

"Ya know, you're askin' lots of questions bout someone else's private bidness. I'm not sure I should be talkin' to ya like this." I dug out a business card and gave it to him. He studied it carefully.

"Look, Alma Chastain is dead and the estate, er, the heir, Toby, is trying to sell some of what was once her property. Muncie hired me to make sure that all the paperwork is in order." I gestured toward the card in his hand. "That's what I do. I can give you Muncie's office number if you like. Or you could call Toby." He looked me over then looked at the card again. After a few seconds he seemed to make up his mind and he put the card in his shirt pocket.

"No need to talk to him."

"Who, Toby?" He began rolling another cigarette.

"You bet. Never did talk to him much. Tried to when he first come, figured he needed a man's hand. Thought I could learn him a little, ya know, to fish and the like. They said he was trammatized a bit, ya know, hurting over what happened to his folks." He snorted. "Nothin' ever hurt that boy. Least, he didn't show it. But he liked to hurt things plenty." I shifted a bit on the plastic seat.

"How so?"

"Bugs, insects and such. He'd catch 'em and then pull 'em apart, set fire to 'em, that sort of thing. Later, I think he messed with a few bigger animals. Gave me the willies. Didn't hang around much with the other kids, not that there was many in the area, but he didn't have any friends at school, neither. Creepy."

"Did Alma know, you know, about the animals?" He shrugged.

"Tried to tell her once, she 'bout bit my head off, she got so mad. And she was the most even-tempered soul, least to Lontine and me. She'd bark and carry on with others when she felt cranky or put upon, but she was never like that with us. Only that once, with me. I never brought it up again." We were quiet a moment, both lost in our thoughts.

"Anyways," he said as he sat up straight. "I guess I can't really help ya much. I mean, they might 'a been a will after the one you're talkin' 'bout, I just don't know for sure. If Lawyer Muncie had done one for her, that would be the one he'd give ya 'stead of the old one." He glanced at the clock on the wall, which was fashioned out of a slice of a cypress tree that had been covered with a clear-cast resin.

"Two o'clock. I got to get back to work." He grinned at me. "Them gators might get tired of waitin' and start eatin' the tourists." I stood and stuck out my hand.

"I appreciate you speaking with me. You've been most helpful." I smiled as he shook his head and headed for the rear door. He stopped abruptly and came back.

"Ya know, we kind a got side-tracked and I nearly forgot what I was going' to tell ya."

"What's that?"

"That CIT-GIM ya was talkin' bout. I used to drive Miss Alma to those meetin's. And she'd talk at those meetin's, say things about developers and how she wasn't gonna let them get a hold of her land. Not over her dead body."

"You were there?" He grinned a sly old man's grin.

"Why, those women in CIT-GIM would fuss over me and make sure I was asked in and given a soft seat and a glass of ice tea. No waitin' in the car for ole Dent, I'll tell ya. Hope that helps." He turned and once more headed for the exit.

A young Indian girl came over with a plastic tub and began to clear away our mess. I fumbled two dollars onto the table and she gave me a huge smile, radiant with gleaming white teeth. I felt bad because Dent had left nothing. I had no more singles so I retrieved the two ones and laid a five on the table. Her smile got even bigger. I headed for the parking lot.

As I pointed the Caddy back toward Mangrove Springs I replayed the conversation in my head. Some interesting tidbits but nothing that really could help me. No, I realized, that wasn't quite true. I'd eliminated one possible source of contradiction, or problem, concerning the will. Like the man had said, if Lawyer Muncie had prepared a later will for Alma Chastain that would be the one he'd have given me. You bet. Evidently all the talk at the CIT-GIM meetings and elsewhere was just that. Talk.

After thinking it over I decided the best that I could do was give Ralph Rennegar's longtime Assistant, Linda Wong, a call. She could tell me if there was a later will prepared by Ralph. About halfway home the beans and franks began working on me. I was glad the top was down.

Chapter Fifteen

Moonlight illuminated the small clearing where the older trailer sat, shadows cast by the encircling cypress trees whipping about as the wind kicked up. On the breeze was the acrid scent of the wildfires burning to the north. The air was filled with the night sounds of chirping insects and the furtive rustling of nocturnal creatures in the underbrush surrounding the clearing. A ten-year-old station wagon rested in the ruts carved into the sand in front of the trailer amid the litter of children's toys.

His own pickup was down the lane a bit, out of sight, as he watched from behind a gnarled tree more than six times his age. He felt the thrill of an adrenaline rush as an armadillo scurried past him into the clearing and disappeared into the brush on the other side. All senses keenly focused, he peered intently at the vicinity of the electrical junction box near one end of the trailer, where he had made some adjustments to the wiring within. The public library had provided him a wealth of useful information over the years, and it had not disappointed this time. Of course, the Internet was much more convenient, and maybe more comprehensive, but it left traces, clues, for anyone who cared to look for them.

As he watched, a small flame sprouted and grew quickly, spreading rapidly, engulfing the sides of the trailer and quickly reaching the tarred roof. He had spread a little gasoline about, not much, hopefully not enough to be identified as an accelerant. Just enough to help the fire on its way. The fire and the moonlight allowed him to see from a glance at his watch that it was after three a.m. Hopefully everyone in the trailer was deep asleep, even dreaming pleasant fantasies. He couldn't suppress a grin at the thought.

Suddenly, a door halfway down the length of the trailer burst open and a tousle-haired child stumbled onto the wooden steps, coughing and rubbing its eyes. Flames were roaring along the entire length of the trailer now and he could feel the heat licking at him. He felt a moment of panic before the icy calm that accompanied his escapades, as he thought of them, returned.

Moving quickly, he darted forward and caught the child as it was descending the stairs, just beginning to scream, and grabbed it up. He crooked his elbow about the tiny neck and squeezed just hard enough to choke off the screams and the breath of the child, but not hard enough to do any damage to the soft tissue of the throat.

When he felt the child go limp after a brief struggle, he went as far up the steps as the heat allowed him and, swinging the dead weight of the child two-handed, like it was a sack of flour, he tossed it back through the doorway and into the raging inferno. He quickly went down the steps and retreated a safe distance into the trees, where he watched until he was satisfied that no living thing would emerge from the burned out hulk of the trailer. It was still burning furiously, rivets popping from the heat, sheet metal and rubber melting, thick smoke roiling skyward, as he calmly walked to his truck.

Chapter Sixteen

The next day, Sunday, was my Aunt Chili's birthday. It was her 70th and the clan had decided to celebrate with a Dixon Family Cook-Out. By ten o'clock I was helping to build the chicken pit.

We built it on a cleared, sandy piece of ground away from the houses and other structures. Because the fire index was so high we were extra careful. My cousin Aubrey and I worked quietly, familiar with each other and the work at hand. First, we raked a plot approximately four feet by twelve, smoothing the sand and removing sparse vegetation and the charred remains of the wood used for a previous cookout. Next, we laid the split wood, cut a couple of weeks before by some of the others and stacked nearby, in the pit, filling the raked area. Then we outlined the perimeter of the pit with cinder blocks, two high. Aubrey took a gallon can of charcoal lighter and splashed the contents more or less evenly over the wood. While that was soaking in, we placed sections of cast iron grating side by side until the entire pit was covered. I stretched a 75-foot hose from where it was connected at an outbuilding to a spot near the pit. I opened the spigot and depressed the nozzle to make sure there was water. Aubrey had a box of strike anywhere matches and we each took a handful and worked our way around the perimeter, throwing lit matches in toward the center and applying others to the wood at the edges. The fire would burn for 1-2 hours until white-hot coals were left and it was time to put the chicken pieces on the grate. I left Aubrey to tend the fire and went to help with other preparations.

Dixon family members scurried here and there for the next couple of hours like worker ants, performing familiar tasks like some ancient ritual until the sights and sounds began to coalesce into the shape of a large family cookout. From a storage shed we drug out two dozen old fashioned wash tubs and filled them with canned beer, sodas and ice from the fish house. The same shed yielded half a dozen wheeled grills made from 55gal drums split lengthwise. Four large smokehouses, made from gutted and vented refrigerators, had been in operation since before dawn, the tantalizing scent of wood smoke tickling our nostrils. An eclectic array of folding tables, picnic tables, assorted lawn and kitchen furniture and canvas shelters supported by aluminum poles swiftly appeared. The number of people milling about slowly increased as more family and guests began arriving. At some point preparation transitioned into party and voices were raised in merriment while music from at least four boom boxes around the camp serenaded the growing crowd.

The food was incredible in its volume and variety. We grilled chicken quarters at the pit. We used a commercial floor mop, new of course, to baste the quarters with vinegar as they cooked, thus ensuring crispy brown skin. When the chicken was done and the skin nice and crispy, the meat receded from the joints, we mopped on a barbecue sauce Uncle Buster made with honey, blackstrap molasses, catsup, onion and spices and cooked until it was as thick and dark as used motor oil. We removed the pieces to waiting commercial kitchen sized pans and threw on another batch.

The smokers were disgorging ribs, turkey breasts, pork loins and a variety of smoked fish. The grills were used for hamburgers, hot dogs and mullet. The fish was split and grilled with a stuffing of rice, tomatoes, and jalapenos. Large propane powered deep fryers were used to cook battered fish and hush puppies. Some of the fish being cooked were snook, that most prized of game fish and the most delicious fish caught in Southwest Florida. Its flesh was firm and white and not fishy at all. Snook fishing was regulated fiercely by the state. My mother's grandfather, Rufus Dixon, gone to his reward, had told me that when he was young snook were thought to be trash fish, like ladyfish, fun to catch because they fought so gamely, but impossible to eat. They were nicknamed soap fish because of their taste. It was a while before anyone caught on to the fact that after death something in their skin, some chemical, seeped into the flesh rendering it inedible. It was discovered that if the snook were skinned or filleted within a reasonable time after death they were delicious.

Two of the deep fryers were filled with water instead of oil and these served up corn on the cob and boiled shrimp. Tables groaned under the weight of an amazing assortment of casseroles, potato dishes, pastas, vegetables and breads. A new child's plastic wading pool in the shape of a frog had been set on a table and filled with tossed salad and at least seven different dressings sat before it. And the desserts!

I worked, sweated and talked with guests until the last of the chicken was done and the coals were burning down. Aubrey and I reached under the grates with long handled rakes and moved the coals around and covered them with sand. Then we watered down the whole pit until the sand and embers were a muddy mass and white steam had stopped hissing up from the coals. Aubrey said he'd keep an eye on them for a while longer. I went home and took a quick shower and changed clothes. Much better. I rejoined the party and relaxed and visited with others, only occasionally having to return to work to refill wash tubs with drinks and ice. I had a can of beer in my favorite Koolie Kup and wandered the grounds listening to the various conversations, joining in sometimes. I ran across Jenna at one of the dessert tables, serving cakes and pies and puddings to the children who had stopped running around long enough to get another sugar fix.

"Hi," she said when I caught her eye. "Chicken done?" I reached for one of aunt Chili's double chocolate chip cookies. I knew they were aunt Chili's by the index card propped against the plate that read 'Chili's Blue Ribbon Chocolate Chip Cookies.' Her cookies had won a blue ribbon at the Lee County Fair in 1973 and she was proud of the achievement.

"Yeah. We cooked three grates." I looked around at the crowd of humanity. "I hope it's enough."

"Are you kidding? There's enough food here for TWO armies." She placed a gooey looking brownie type of thing on a paper plate and handed it to a chubby kid with glasses and balls of dirt in the creases of his neck. The lenses of his glasses were streaked with sweat and his tongue protruded from his lips in anticipation.

"Yeah, well, there's a lot of people here. Aunt Chili sure has lots of friends and family."

"She and Lemuel are the leaders of the clan now."

"You think the turnout is due to family politics?"

"Well, the land here is worth a lot of money and opinions run hot in and out of the family."

"Uncle Lem and Aunt Chili have never made any secret of their stance concerning the Dixon family policy." I waved my arms about. "The land is for the family, not high rises." Jenna shrugged and scooped some pudding into a bowl.

"I agree. But listen closely to the talk here today and you might be surprised at the range of opinion on the matter."

"All right, I'll listen. But Lem and Chili have my support."

"I don't want to see it go, either." She dipped her eyes and lowered her voice. "But I'm afraid times are changing." I didn't want the conversation to travel any farther in the current direction.

"You and Bob Dylan. Don't worry, they're not going to kick us out of our house anytime soon." She handed the bowl of pudding to a freckled young girl and we were suddenly alone. She came from behind the table and took my elbow in her warm grip.

"It's all changing," she said, her pert face peering intently at me, eyes squinting at the early afternoon sun. In the back of my mind I found myself wondering if one could peer and squint at the same time. "But let's not worry about it too much today." I looked at her earnest face, the face that I knew so well and which had changed so much and so little over the years, the face that was as dear to me in it's maturity as it had been years before in it's youthful vibrancy, and my chest felt hollow. I felt the mucous thickening in my throat but was spared the need to answer when a voice, lilting with alcoholic musicality, interrupted us.

"My boy Elroy!" Jenna's hand slipped from my elbow and we turned toward the voice.

"Lonzo," I said. "Good to see you. How you doing, my friend." I'd seen Lonzo just days, or rather nights, before at The Grouper Hole. I wasn't sure, though, that he remembered the meeting. Jenna smiled and mouthed a hello.

"I'm doin' good, boy. This is a red letter day, the second sightin' of the elusive Elroy in a matter of days." He did remember. Lonzo raised a Koolie Kup to his lips and swallowed deeply from the beer encased there. Another loaded Koolie was clutched in his other hand and the tops of unopened sweating beer cans protruded from both hip pockets of his ragged cutoff jeans. He wore an unbuttoned button up shirt, un-tucked, his scrawny chest marked with the deep red vee common to all fishermen.

"Have you sampled some of the fine food that's available?" Jenna was trying to be diplomatic but Lonzo would have none of it.

"Jenna, is that Jenna?" He leaned his unshaven face in close to hers, but she didn't flinch, God love her. "I don't want none a that lumpy stuff. Hell, I can eat any time. This here is an honest to God OCCASION and I plan to act accordin'ly." He belched and spilled a few drops of beer in his haste to do the polite thing and cover his mouth.

We all stood there, looking expectantly at one another, quizzical expressions turning uneasy as the silence spread out and engulfed us. Lonzo suddenly seemed much more sober.

"Well," he said, "it's really good to see you two. We ought to get together again real soon. When it comes down to it, family's all ya got in this world." He began to back away and his body language gave the odd impression that he was bowing as he retreated.

"Good to see ya, we'll have to get together sometime, like the old days. Like back when I was fishin' and we'd go out for fun some times. We really should, ya know." He was smiling a wide idiot's grin and looking like he wanted to turn and run.

"We'd love that, Lonzo. Call us, or we'll call you. Say hello to Betty and the kids for us." He turned and headed toward a group of men twenty yards away who were engaged in an animated discussion, arms flailing, obviously accentuating points made, but the words were indistinct at this distance.

We watched as Lonzo hurried on past the group and continued toward the fish house where a large number of the clan that was still engaged in the fishing or boating business in one way or another were congregated. He waved a Koolie Kup at them and they returned the salute.

Jenna and I talked for a few minutes more and the awkwardness that had developed when Lonzo was there melted away into the glorious day. The temperature was about 85 degrees but kept from being uncomfortable by the breeze blowing in off the bay. A few more children wandered up and requested their allotment of sugar.

"How long you been on dessert detail?" Most of the food tables were unattended except by a patrol charged with re-supply, but the dessert table was always manned, or woman-ed, so the children wouldn't indulge themselves to the point of stupor.

"Oh, about half an hour. I'll be free in another half hour or so."

"How about the kids?" I hadn't seen any of them for a couple of hours. Jenna shaded her eyes with a hand and looked about.

"Cleve and Larry and a couple of the others are out on the jet skis. Rae and Bobbie Jane are around here somewhere. They were watching Markie and Colette for Diane while she and Bruce went into town to pick up ice cream to have later with the birthday cake." She dropped her hand and looked expectantly at her newest customer.

"I'd like some of my Aunt Denise's homemade apple pie, please."

"Why, Frankie, how nice and polite you are." Jenna cut a large wedge of the deep-dish pie 12 year-old Frankie had pointed to, and placed in on a paper plate, handing that, a paper napkin and a plastic fork to the boy.

"Thank you, Ma'am." Frankie grinned hugely at Jenna before turning and walking away.

"That boy is going to go far with manners like that. Women will just melt and give him whatever he asks for."

"Yeah," I admitted, "but the guys are going to hate him." Jenna scowled at me briefly before smiling.

"You should be so polite." I shrugged a 'what you see is what you get' look at her and picked up another cookie. The cookies weren't especially good with beer but they *were* award winning.

"Look, I'm going to wander around a bit, see who I can talk to. Some of these people I only see a couple of times a year anymore."

I headed off in search of someone to talk to, some way to interact with the clotted humanity swirling across the fish camp landscape. I drained the beer and discarded the empty in a large barrel lined with a white plastic bag. I was able to recharge my Koolie within twenty-five feet, dragging a cold, dripping can from a conveniently located wash tub. People were gathered in knots of anywhere from 2 to 20, eating, talking, and drinking, with participants breaking off and others joining in with some frequency. I hooked up with my first group and spent twenty minutes listening to a debate over the relative merits of the different regional methods of preparing seafood. I moved on.

I moved from group to group, joining and leaving conversations about everything from health care to reality TV to politics, local state and national. I knew most everyone, at least in a nodding fashion, family or not. I came to a group of people arrayed about the veranda of Uncle Lemuel and Aunt Chili's house. I moved in a bit closer, eager to hear what the birthday girl had to say.

"I don't care what they offer, this land ain't for sale." That was Aunt Chili.

"My God, Chili, that development group offered millions, for Chris' sakes!" The speaker was Thomas Dixon, son of Elliot and Clarice, who were of my generation. Thomas couldn't have been more than twenty years old. I could have been his father!

"No need to use profanity, young man! I can hear ya without that." Chili looked about, surveying the group congregated about her ancestral home.

"Alright," she said, pointing a knotted finger of her gnarled right hand and sweeping the gathering. "If the family sells and divides the money fairly among the clan, after all notes and obligations are paid, and there are a bunch since the net ban, each qualifyin' member of the family, and there are over a hunnert, would receive 'bout $250,000! Now, I realize some families would get two or three times that, but for most of us that's all we would get. Now, let me ask ya..." there was a general murmur from the members of the group who evidently supported the idea of selling the property. "Let me ask ya," Chili continued with increased volume, "how ya gonna replace this property for that money?" She looked defiantly out at the congregation. "Where can ya buy gulf access waterfront property, house included, for that kind of money. The average price in Mangrove is a bit over $350,000 and that includes all the crappy land east of the interstate, excuse my French!"

"Besides," she continued, " these are our HOMES! Where we grew up, where our roots are. Do ya really want some retirees from up north, willin' to live in dinky 'partments stacked up thirty high, to take over the land ya grew up on? Is that really what ya want?" Chili stared defiantly at the assembled crew and awaited an answer. There were murmurs of 'that's right,' and 'don't you know that's true,' before Thomas found his voice and answered.

"Aunt Chili, I love and respect you and your opinions, but I've got to tell you that you don't speak for us all." There was a mumbling of assent. "Not all of us want to live on the water, not all of us need to keep connected to these roots you say we have. For us, the past is gone and the net ban has changed everything. Now, lots of us have regular jobs and we'd be happy to give our families the American Dream, a 3/2 with a double garage and a barbecue in the back yard. Hell, some of us might actually want to move to other states, someplace with hills and mountains, deserts and plains, somewhere where hurricanes, red tide, fires and water shortages don't reach."

"Yeah," a voice chimed in. "We can't fish no more cause a the net ban, can't boat nor drive no more cause a the crowds. The water's bad, the air's bad, an there's drugs everywhere corrupting our kids!" Some in the gathering muttered an angry assent. Aunt Chili leaned forward in her rocker and cast a withering glance at Thomas and his supporters.

"I swear child, as long as Lemuel and I are members of this family, there will be no sale of Dixon's Fish Camp!" She set the rocker in motion, rocking to and fro' with some force. Lemuel peered around the gathering with a set jaw in support of Chili's statements, but it was apparent who spoke for them. Thomas shook his head, nodded gracefully toward Aunt Chili, and wandered off. About half the crowd went with him. I stepped up onto the veranda and leaned against the porch railing. Lem and Chili rocked with jaws set and eyes on the planking at their feet. Gradually, the rest of the crowd left, some offering encouraging comments to the elderly leaders of the family. I stayed where I was until I was alone with Lem and Chili. They seemed unaware of my presence and were startled when I spoke to them.

"Quite a mess, isn't it?"

"How's that?" Chili asked. I shrugged and sipped from my Koolie Kup.

"Some want to sell and some don't. As long as that's the case nothing will get done. How'd that happen?" She squinted at me across the eight feet of porch that separated us.

"You're Elroy, right?" I raised my beer to her. Lemuel seemed interested in what was going on a couple of houses away where a crowd had congregated about some people playing guitars, banjos and other instruments and singing. "You're Callie's boy. My eyesight ain't what it used to be."

"Yes'm. I was just wondering how this problem came to pass. You know, half the Dixon clan wanting to hold on to the homestead and the other half wanting to sell?" She looked at me a moment, thinking, weighing possibilities.

"Calvin Dixon was a salvager of naval wrecks. He worked out a Key West 'til the number of salvagers made makin' a livin' in the Keys a bother." She looked to Lem for support and, though I could detect no movement on his part, she seemed satisfied with his response.

"In the Eighteen Twenties he came here. Not many wrecks to be found and Calvin and his family took up fishin', stakin' claim to this piece of ground. Right from the start he had the idea of a family compound. Every time there was a birth, a new deed was issued giving the new Dixon a piece of the land." Of course I'd heard all of this before. Every Dixon grew up hearing the story of Calvin The Founder and the share in the family compound that was a Dixon's birthright. It was an undivided share however, and no Dixon could sell their interest without all agreeing to sell.

Even so, "Wow," was what I said. I still loved hearing it. Aunt Chili looked at me somberly.

"Ya know what that means?" I shook my head at her even though I had a fair idea what that meant.

"It was his way to protect the family. Keep it together. Keep it strong. But now it seems like its gonna tear us apart. I guess old Calvin didn't foresee the temptation that a large piece a money could be." Her voice faded to a whisper and she clasped her hands in her lap. Lem slowly rocked and nodded.

"Maybe he saw just that, Aunt Chili." She looked up at me, her sun weathered face with its laugh-crinkled eyes reflecting all her years.

"What ya mean, son?" I'd moved closer to her during our talk and now I kneeled by her rocker and covered her knobby hands with mine.

"I mean maybe he saw just such a thing happening. Rather than let the family land disappear little by little, lot by lot, as might have happened if the land had been sub-divided among the family members, he wanted to be sure that all would have to agree before the land was sold. Make sure that there was ample discussion and that no decision could be made in haste or the property lost incrementally." I patted her hands reassuringly.

"You're a good boy Elroy." I heard the Jetson's tune in my head as she said that. "And what ya say is prob'ly true. But do ya know the headaches involved, even if everyone does agree to sell? Oh," she flushed a bit and blinked a few times. "I guess ya do, being in your line a work and all." I thought about what would be needed to legally convey title and mentally winced.

Then her expression hardened into a grim mask.

"But that won't be necessary in my lifetime." Her voice rose in pitch and picked up volume. "As long as I'm alive, I swear, this property won't be sold! The damn developers and money grubbers won't get their hands on Dixon land!" The vehemence with which she spoke, not to mention the profanity, surprised me a bit, but not the meaning of the words. I already knew that Aunt Chili would never agree to sell. Uncle Lemuel rocked and nodded. I leaned over again and planted a kiss on her wrinkled forehead.

"Don't worry," I told her. "You're not the only one who feels that way." She smiled at me again and leaned back in the chair, closing her eyes. I held her hands a few seconds longer and, when I was sure that she was calming down, I wished her happy birthday, assured her that I loved her and left the porch, waving to Lem as I went.

I set off in search of the nearest washtub. The parking areas were full to overflowing and all the boat slips were taken, many guests having come via the water. Not surprising, given the location and the family. People wandered everywhere over the grounds. It seemed the cookout was at its peak. People sat, stood, walked and ran, clasping beers, sodas and plates of food. The sun was still fairly high in the western sky, about four-thirty by my watch. I found a washtub and grabbed a beer. I stopped at a table laden with food and filled a plate with fried fish, hush puppies, coleslaw and smoked turkey breast and ate leaning against a twenty foot pontoon boat on a trailer parked in front of the bait house. Ten or twelve men were assembled about the boat, drinking beer and lamenting the loss of the good old days. I ate and listened, not joining in the conversation, not asked to.

Finished, I dumped my trash into a barrel and resumed my wandering. I passed Rae and Bobbie Jane, who were eating watermelon with several other young people, seeing who could propel the seeds the farthest using only their mouth. I said hi to them but they ignored me, as youthful etiquette required. I didn't make an issue of it, having been there myself.

The afternoon and early evening passed as people ate, drank, played softball and horseshoes, and ate and drank some more. I roamed from group to group, from activity to activity, more an observer than a participant.

Eventually, I came upon a group that included Jenna, my mom, and others of both of their generations, about fifteen people in all.

My mother was singing and accompanying herself on the Martin acoustic guitar that was her physical link to the sixties, the age that had shaped and defined her. The song was "Where Have All The Flowers Gone," that seminal folk song made famous by Peter, Paul and Mary or some other Beatnik to Hippie transition group. It had been my mother's misfortune to be on the cusp, age wise, between two culturally significant, but essentially different, subcultures. She'd been the latest Beatnik, fully familiar with Maynard G. Krebs, and the earliest Hippie, in tune, spiritually, with Ken Kesey and the Merry Pranksters. Now, as she sang in her clear, sweet contralto and strummed the chords on her mellow-voiced guitar, I wondered how many beers she'd consumed. Generally, she didn't become emboldened enough to perform publicly until she had half a snoot-full.

I slipped into the group gathered in a semi-circle in front of my mother and settled to the ground on a blanket occupied by my former wife. She scooted over a bit to make room for me without looking up. I wondered briefly if she had any idea to whom the warm body pressing into place next to her belonged or even if she cared. Watch out, I told myself; those kinds of thoughts won't get you where you want to be.

Callie had her eyes closed. She swayed gently from side to side as she played and sang. She looked transported to another time, a time that seemed more relevant, more real to her. She sat in a green plastic lawn chair and an opened beer stood on the grass beside her. I recalled the words from my youth, when my mother would entertain me for hours with music as she drank beer. I was an only child, my mother never meeting anyone after my father with whom she wished to cohabit. True love or a supreme lack of self-esteem, I could never be sure. At any rate, I had no siblings to divide my love between, and my mother had no other children to dilute her maternal affections. Thus, we spent a lot of time together. The result? I knew the words to all of her songs. And knew the order in which she tended to perform them when loosened by alcohol. And knew where her performance usually ended. I figured she had about six songs to go. With in between song time, beer sipping time, and adding a couple of minutes for good measure, I figured there was about forty minutes left.

I snuggled closer to Jenna and she finally turned her head in annoyance until she recognized me, whereupon she snuggled back.

Chapter Seventeen

After the singing, I sat and talked with my mother awhile and then helped her to the cottage she shared with two other unmarried female clan members, where I saw her to bed. She was sleepy and bleary eyed, still humming "Tom Dooley," though she paused long enough to wish me good night. Then I roamed the grounds some more, listening in on conversations and sometimes offering an opinion of my own. There was more talk about the Dixon family land and what should be done with it. Other subjects included: fishing for a living, farming, sports, the last presidential election, sex, the upcoming special election, and the fires to the east. A wide variety of issues and candidates were discussed but one consensus was reached: Evan Muster, in attendance and brimming with confidence, was a shoo-in for District 3 Council member.

The cookout had begun breaking up about eight and the hard-core partiers probably lasted until midnight or later. Jenna, the kids and I spent about an hour on cleanup and got home about ten-thirty. Everyone was tuckered out and we were all in bed by eleven. I was at my desk on Monday at 10:00 sharp.

I reached for the Lee County telephone book and looked in the white pages for Linda Wong's number. There were only a few Wong's and Linda was the fourth entry. After the third ring a frail voice answered and I hesitated a moment before identifying it as a thinner, weaker version of the voice I remembered answering Ralph Rennegar's phone.

"Hello, is this Linda Wong? Used to work with Ralph Rennegar?" There was a moment's hesitation as if she needed to rest a bit before answering.

"Yes. Yes, this is she. How can I help you?"

"My name is Roy Dixon. With Mason Dixon Title?" Silence. "I used to do business with Ralph. I spoke with you and met with you on a number of occasions." I waited through five uncomfortable seconds.

"Yes, Mr. Dixon, I remember you." Her voice had the power of a reed instrument blown by a first year band student.

"Well, it's been some years since we've spoken but it's good to hear your voice. You're well, I hope?" My southern upbringing took over and the platitudes gained a life of their own though it was obvious to me, by her voice, at least, that she was not well.

"Well, Mr. Dixon..."

"Roy, please."

"Thank you. You can call me Linda." I murmured an assent. "I must admit I have enjoyed better health. A recent scare required hospitalization and I haven't fully recovered." Her voice trailed off into a breathy whisper.

"I'm sorry to hear that, Mrs., er, Miss Wong," I was unsure of her marital status but I remembered the rumors of her romantic involvement with Ralph.

"Miss will do fine if you insist upon formal name usage. I have given you permission to call me Linda." Her breath ran out and she audibly gulped for air.

"I'm sorry, Linda, but I'm a southern boy, born and raised. Give me a moment to adjust to your kindness."

"What are you calling about, Mr., er, Roy." She was susceptible to autonomic manners as well.

"I'm calling in regard to the Last Will and Testament of Miss Alma Chastain. As you may know, we lost Miss Alma this past summer, and now the probate court has ordered the sale of a portion of her estate. Our firm is handling the title insurance for the transaction and the will entered into probate is one that was prepared by the law offices of Ralph Rennegar." God that sounded official.

"We, I mean, Ralph, handled all of Alma Chastain's legal affairs. Right up until Ralph passed away."

"That's why I called. There is some question as to whether the will that has been entered is, in fact, Alma Chastain's final will and testament."

"I'd like to help you, Roy" her voice gained a husky quality and I silently rooted for her to clear the phlegm. "But Ralph prepared several wills for Miss Alma, each making changes, some small, some rather large, to the basic disposition of her assets."

"Do you remember the last will he prepared? The major points? I'm most interested in her desires as they concern real property." I just wanted to know if she'd blocked developers from access to Chastain lands, as CIT-GIM members seemed to believe.

"No, I don't remember the particulars. But then, I don't remember the particulars of many, MOST of the documents Ralph prepared for his clients. There were so many!" Her voice trailed off into a huffing sound.

"Linda, this is very important to me. Can you help at all?"

"Yes. All of Ralph's files are in storage, in a U-Store-It, right here in Mangrove Springs. They're in cardboard file storage boxes. I have the key. The court appointed me executor. I get requests for documents, well, copies of documents all the time. That is, I used to. There haven't been too many calls lately. In fact, none in the last year or so."

"Could you look in Alma Chastain's file and see what her last will said should be done with her real property? I could come and give you a hand."

"That's nice of you to offer but I can manage. All I'll need is the court order or executor's request for the document search and I'll check it out."

I thought that over. Jack was out of town and I didn't want to ask Toby. I could call Beverly, Jack's receptionist. He'd told me to just inform her of what I needed. But I didn't want to do that, either. If there was a problem, some sort of chicanery, Jack Muncie was probably involved up to his eyeballs. And if everything was as it should be (that phrase again!) I'd rather not have everyone think me a paranoid fool.

"Well…" I began. Linda snorted politely.

"Not exactly an official enquiry, huh? I remember you, Roy Dixon. Ralph always had good things to say about you. I'll tell you what I'll do." Her voice lowered to a conspirator's whisper. "If you'll bring me a copy of the will you now have, the one that's being probated, I'll check it against the file and let you know if there's a later one there. If there is you can get an OFFICIAL request." I could almost hear her wink.

"Linda, you've made my day. I'll owe you a nice dinner at The Grouper Hole in payment for your kindness." She giggled a bit until interrupted by a wheezing cough.

When the paroxysm subsided, she gave me her address and informed me that she'd be home all day and that she'd be on the lookout for me. I told her I'd be there in an hour or so, thanked her and hung up. I wrote down the address on Tangerine Terrace.

I finished a file that Jenna needed for a closing. Everyone wanted their file to be treated as a rush job so Jenna and I had developed a rating system, communicated on a yellow sticky attached to each file: rush was a regular, no particular hurry file. An extra-rush was needed a bit sooner than that. Ultra-rush meant that the closing was expected to occur within two or three weeks. A Turbo-rush was the most urgent classification, meaning that Jenna needed the file back from me as soon as possible. This file was a Turbo-rush.

When I finished with it I took it to Sigrid and asked her to tell Jenna, who was conducting a closing, that I'd return after lunch. Then I made a copy of the Chastain will and headed for the parking lot.

It was another beautiful day and I'd left the top down. The leather seat was hot but not unbearable and I headed upwind into the stink of petroleum fumes mingled with the sweet smell of citrus and the dark odor of wood smoke. Traffic was horrendous, of course, and it took me fifteen minutes to travel the four miles to the old section of town just east of Old 41. New 41, completed in the mid seventies, was four-lane and three miles west of Old 41. Our office was a mile farther west and perfectly situated as to be convenient to modern mercantile needs. Old Mangrove, however, was a bit to the east, up-river, and a separate community in the old days from Mangrove Beach. Tangerine Terrace was in a section that had been sub-divided into Mangrove Farms, back when it was believed that potential investors would look for ranches upon which to grow grove crops, like oranges and grapefruit. The forty-acre plots, though, had eventually been further sub-divided into residential developments consisting of building lots measuring 75' across the front and 100' deep. That is, most of them. Some had been divided into lots 50' by 75' and zoned multi-family, meaning for duplexes. This alone could explain why, in the old section of town, streets didn't line up, one sub-division to another, and trailers and duplexes shared neighborhoods with single-family dwellings, some with double lots sporting miniature citrus groves. The river and several creeks crisscrossed the area.

Tangerine Terrace crossed an intersection of four different streets radiating outward like the spokes of a wagon wheel. I turned onto it from Loquat Lane and followed it as it meandered in a southerly direction, following Linda Wong's directions. Her house stood at a point where the street curved to the east, giving her a fifteen-foot frontage and a hundred foot rear, a pie shaped lot. There was just enough width at the street for a concrete driveway that led to a stucco house with a terra cotta tile roof. A double attached garage was at the end of the driveway, with a recessed and covered entry framed by twin royal palms.

I parked in front of the garage and opened the screen door of the entry. Two more steps and I was at the front door. I pressed the bell and heard the muted sound of brass chimes. After a few moments I pressed the bell again. No sooner had I done so than the inner door opened and Linda Wong stood there squinting into the mid-day sun.

The sight of her jolted me. I remembered Linda Wong as a squat, substantial, meaning stocky, Oriental woman with porcelain skin, black hair and vivacious ways. The Linda Wong that greeted me was a shriveled, dried, yellowed shadow of her former self. It was obvious that something was eating her, stealing her vitality. It wasn't just a matter of a middle-aged woman losing weight, shrinking in height. She was definitely in trouble. She sported a thin matte of stringy gray hair over her age-spotted cranium, but even that looked as if it might be gone tomorrow. Her skin was a yellowed, dry parchment covering her bony frame.

"Hello, Roy. Come on in." I just stood there dumbly. She looked at me, a quizzical expression on her lined face. "You are Roy Dixon, aren't you? Or should I be apprehensive at the appearance of a stranger at my door?" A few more seconds passed and still I couldn't bring myself to close my mouth, let alone respond. A tired, resigned look came over her face. "It's all right. I know the way I look is shocking to someone who hasn't seen me lately." She turned and walked into the cool, dim interior of the house. Finally able to move, I closed the door behind me and followed her.

"No, Linda, I just have trouble with my eyes adjusting to ..."

"Don't." That one word made me stop in mid sentence. There was such anguish and despair in her voice that I realized anything I could say would sound extraordinarily lame. I followed her in silence through a living room, past kitchen and dining room to the left and hallway to the right, into a Florida room that would have been gloriously bright and sunny, a celebration of the sunshiny wonders of southwest Florida, except for the heavy ceiling to floor drapes that were shut tightly against the outside. In the dim room we found our way to facing loveseats, covered in a bright and flowery fabric, and settled in. I had a great number of questions I wanted to ask her, many of them about her health, but I held my tongue.

"I imagine you're wondering about my appearance?" I toyed briefly with the idea of politely denying the obvious.

"Yes, Linda, I am. You can tell me that it's none of my business but, if you like, you can tell me the truth. You'll find that I'm a good listener and sometimes it can be a help to have someone to talk to." I remembered more of the stories that had circulated about her, about her relationship with Ralph Rennegar.

She'd gone to work for Ralph right out of Edison Community College. She'd graduated with a two-year degree in secretarial science. She was conscientious, industrious and willing to work late. Ralph often worked late, trying to build his practice. They spent long hours together, many evenings away from his family home and her lonely bachelor-ette apartment. They eventually fell into one another's arms out of sheer loneliness and opportunity.

The affair, as the story goes, lasted even after Ralph's wife and ultimately his children knew about it, until Ralph's death. According to the gossip of the time, Ralph not only provided for his legitimate family but he made sure that Linda had a home and a secure retirement, purchasing several annuities, and certificates of deposit to provide her with an income stream. Ralph's family overlooked the situation, happy to accept the balance of his estate, which had swelled to impressive proportions.

"I have a cancer." She looked at her fingers, which were intertwined in her lap. I didn't say anything right away. Finally she raised her eyes to mine.

"I'm sorry, Linda. Is there anything I can do?" What a lame response. Here, I showed up in her life, having not seen her in years, and I was trying to come off as an intimate. I was feeling mildly disgusted with myself but I still had feelings of empathy and was casting about for ways to express them. Linda, bless her, attempted to put me at ease.

"There's a good chance that it will go into remission. Between the chemo and the radiation, the doctors seem to agree that I have an excellent chance of surviving." She smiled wanly. "All I have to do is think positive thoughts and it'll be all right." She smiled again in recognition of the banality of that.

"They're doing wonderful things in the field today." I was just as guilty as she.

"It's in my left lung. Nowhere else up to this point, not that they can detect. Of course, by the time they find any metastases, that's what they call it when it spreads to other organs, it would probably be too late."

"Is surgery not an option?"

"No," she said with finality, changing subjects. "So, how have you and yours been?" She folded her hands in her lap and waited for me to reply. She was at least thirty pounds lighter than I remembered and the weight loss was accentuated by the way her housedress sagged about her body. Her eyes were smudged, with dark patches of skin surrounding them, looking like an inexperienced hand had liberally applied mascara and shadow. This, along with the too large clothing, brought to mind a young girl playing dress-up. The bone deep fatigue and despair evidenced by her expression and by her body language quickly dismissed that image.

"Same old same old," I assured her. "The kids are bigger, the bills are larger, and I'm older. Still doing fascinating title searches for good old Mason Dixon." I placed my hands on the knees of my polished khaki pants and leaned my shoulders back until I couldn't see the tassels on my cordovan loafers.

"Ollie Mason!" Her voice was a veritable chirp compared to her previous sepulchral tones. Ollie still has that power with women, I guess. "How is he? I haven't seen him since I ran into him in the supermarket a couple of years ago."

"Ollie? He's doing fine. Got his finger squarely on the pulse of Mangrove Springs, as usual." I thought of his network of spies and informants and how he'd known all about my escapade with Rita Muncie.

"Yes, he always did have that. I remember Ralph used to take him to dinner whenever he needed the most current information available." Knowing Ollie, I bet he got more than a dinner out of it. "How's your family?"

"Jenna and I are divorced now."

"No! That's a shame."

"Well, we still live together," I hastened to add. Linda's worn face showed a glimmer of surprise. I spent the next few minutes explaining, briefly, our present situation.

"How interesting," she murmured politely. A cat wandered out from under the loveseat Linda was seated upon, stretched luxuriously, and then leapt into her lap where it stood on hind paws, front paws on Linda's chest, and began nuzzling her chin. Linda gathered the cat in, one hand cupped about its furry bottom and the other ruffling the scruff of its neck.

"Mrs. Benz! Where have you been all day?" The cat was audibly purring as it energetically rubbed its nose on Linda's chin and pawed the front of her housedress. Linda looked at me while continuing to nuzzle the longhaired white Persian. "Mercedes Benz is her name. A joke, get it? Ralph gave her to me shortly before he passed away. He named her." I smiled politely and thought briefly about several articles I'd read concerning the palliative effect a pet, or animal companion as the p.c. crowd would say, could have on a seriously ill person. My grin widened a bit.

"Beautiful." Linda lifted the cat and placed it into a purring pile in her lap. It seemed content to settle into a humming, furry ball.

"Well, do you have the copy of the will you'd like me to check out?" Linda had turned serious, the crisp, business-like manner of old presenting itself. I handed her the manila envelope I'd dropped into the loveseat next to me. She didn't open the envelope to look at the document. "I can go to the storage room in the morning. It's air conditioned so it won't be too bad. I have a radiation treatment in the early afternoon. If I feel up to it afterward, I'll call you late afternoon. Otherwise, it'll be Wednesday."

"Thanks, Linda." I stood to go, my knees protesting the move. "I really appreciate it. Like I said on the phone, there's probably nothing to it but I'll rest easier if I know for sure." She started to lift the cat from its place in her lap. "Don't bother to get up. It's a straight shot to the front door, I see it from here." She eased the cat back into place and smiled weakly.

"Thanks, Roy. I am a little tired. I'll call you."

I crossed the floor to the entryway, where I turned and waved at Linda and Mrs. Benz. Linda lifted a hand in farewell. Mrs. Benz snubbed me. I let myself out and on the way to The Grouper Hole for lunch I considered what joke might be hidden in the cats name. The only thing I could come up with was that Ralph Rennegar could say that he gave his mistress a Mercedes Benz.

Ha, ha.

Chapter Eighteen

He had parked two streets away, finding his way through the moonless, smoke-filled night by following a drainage ditch that ran between the rear boundaries of quiet residential properties. He looked and listened carefully for signs of a pet on the loose or a resident taking a bit of air before catching the news on the tube. Nothing.

The screen door to the lanai was unlocked and with his Leatherman multi-tool, it was easy to jimmy the slider from the lanai into the house. If there was an alarm, it wasn't set or it was silent. Either way, he would be long gone before anyone could respond.

The room just inside the sliding glass doors was darkened but a light shone weakly up ahead and he duck-walked toward it as silently as he could, pausing occasionally to listen for any sound.

He had reached a junction with a hallway that ran at right angles to the room he was in when a kimonoed figure emerged into the hallway from a doorway to his left and came toward him. He pulled back and waited until the figure came into view again, striding purposefully past him, blissfully unaware of his presence. When it had passed he moved quickly and took it from behind, grabbing it in what the pro wrestlers called a Japanese headlock, jerking mightily with his scissor-ed forearms until he heard a bone snap, and the form went limp in his arms. He breathed deeply for a moment before casting about for a way to make the death he had just caused appear to be an accident.

Chapter Nineteen

Linda didn't call me on Tuesday so I assumed she got home late, was too tired, or something. The lady was obviously at less than her best. I felt somewhat guilty about asking her to check the files for me but I reasoned that she'd probably feel better with something meaningful to do. That sounded lame, even in my inner-head voice, but I needed the rationalization. I really felt bad for, and about, Linda Wong. I hoped her doctors weren't just blowing smoke about the chances of remission.

Early Wednesday morning, well, about eleven o'clock, I looked up her number and placed the call. A machine answered and I hung up, not wanting to put any pressure on her. She WAS doing me a favor, after all. I hoped she didn't have caller I.D.

I left the office a little before twelve, checking out with Sigrid before I went. Wednesday was MNMC+2 lunch day and I headed for Luchese's Italian Grill on new 41, just south of the Collier County line. From the county line to well past the restaurant, 41 was under construction, being widened from a four-lane thoroughfare to six lanes. The work was half done and had already taken about two years. There were large earth moving and road paving machines lined up along the road on both the north and the southbound sides. Traffic sped along at a crawl, except when it stopped outright, and I could see but three men, two of them leaning on shovels, and the other pointing at something lying in the sand. No one else was in sight, not on foot nor astride any of the yellow behemoths parked on the side. I estimated that those three men could finish the work in another fourteen months, give or take a month or two. They may have been the same three men who had taken 36 months to complete the widening of a stretch of 41 in south Collier County, near the government complex where I went once a week to record deeds and other Collier County documents. But I'm not complaining.

When I got near the restaurant a blue sign the size of a matchbook cover, erected on a piece of steel driven into the sand, alerted me to a temporary entrance, over the biggest hill in southwest Florida, to the restaurant. If I hadn't known what to look for it would have been almost impossible to spot. As it was I had to creep the Caddy over the pothole riddled mountain, wondering if the cars beefed up suspension would be turned to hamburger. No wonder that, during these fits of construction, businesses complained of a drastic drop-off in trade, with about a third of independently owned operations forced to close their doors.

Inside the restaurant I could see that the place was more than three quarters full in spite of the traffic problems. A tribute, no doubt, to the excellence of the restaurant which, in turn, was a tribute to the discriminating taste of the nominating member of MNMC+2 responsible for the selection of Luchese's as a luncheon destination: me. Harry Oatman, the Pete in Pete and Repeat, waved both arms at me from a big, round table in the middle of the large dining area. Don Stone was seated at the table, along with Marcus Hopmann and Jim Bruzzi. The only MNMC+2 member not present was Barry Oatman, Harry's twin brother. The two were usually inseparable.

Marcus was a real estate agent, a local, who worked in a C-21 agency. He was known far and wide, at least in the voluminous advertising he purchased in the local print media, as Mangrove Marcus. Bruzzi was a transplanted Ohioan, a retiree who had been invited into our exclusive group after he'd caught a 27-inch snook off the Mangrove Pass Bridge and Don and Marcus had been present to witness the feat. They'd been fishing, also, and his catch had drawn them into a conversation during which they'd found out that, snowbird or not, he was an okay fellow. Hence, the invitation to join our luncheon club. I walked past the questioning look of a Maitre'D type and pulled out a chair at their table.

"Hey, guys. What's up?" I glanced around the table and asked the obvious question: "Where's Repeat?" Pete answered me.

"He'll be here in a minute." He held up a cell phone. "He just called. Tied up in traffic."

"I thought you twins didn't need cell phones," said Marcus as he lifted a sweating glass of iced tea to his lips.

"We don't, really," said Pete. "Just didn't want to spook all you normals." Most of us chuckled but Pete seemed serious.

When Repeat joined us a few minutes later, he sat down and picked up his menu just as a waitress appeared, pencil and pad poised to take our orders. I ordered my favorite Luchese's dish, the spaghetti and meatballs. The menu was full of exotic choices representing the culinary specialties of different regions in Italy and Sicily but I preferred the simple, universal appeal of the basic Italian combination. The meatballs at Luchese's were still prepared the old country way. I'd met Mama Luchese when they'd closed upon the property that housed their business and she'd assured me that she and her husband, though officially retired, still made it into the kitchen each a.m. to make the meatballs and the sausages and to bake the wonderfully crusty, absolutely delicious breads served in the restaurant.

"How'd that Chastain deal come out?" Repeat asked, looking directly at me.

"I'm not sure yet. I checked with Dent Billie, the old Indian who witnessed the will, but he wasn't much help. I've asked Linda Wong to look into Ralph Rennegar's dead files for wild wills, but I haven't heard back from her yet."

"When'd you ask her?" Don wanted to know.

"Monday. But she's pretty sick. Cancer. Might take her a little time to get the information for me."

"I remember her," Pete said. "She did the closin' on our first house. Ralph was the lawyer but we never saw him. We just dealt with her. She did a fine job."

"Yeah," I agreed. "She knows her stuff."

"She has cancer?"

"Yeah. Didn't look so good. She seemed kind of weak, at low ebb. The treatment, I guess."

"I've known Linda for twenty years," Marcus said. "Though I haven't seen her more than once or twice since Ralph's death." He began to butter a freshly baked roll. There was a shallow dish of olive oil and spices on the table for dipping. "She's always been a pleasant woman, competent, knew her stuff when it came to real estate." Marcus paused, buttered bread poised to enter his mouth, and smiled. "She's a sweet lady."

"This is Wednesday," Don said. I looked at him.

"What do you mean?"

"Well, you talked to her Monday. This is Wednesday. You should call her. I know she's sick and all but maybe she forgot or lost your number." He sipped at his iced tea.

"I did."

"Did what?"

"Call her."

"And?"

"Got her answering machine." Marcus was buttering another roll. That boy could sure eat.

"Leave a message?" Pete asked.

"No. I didn't want to seem like I was pestering her."

"I think you should go see her again," Don told me. I thought about that and slowly shook my head.

"Naw. She'll let me know when she checks it out."

The waitress appeared, carrying plates balanced from her wrist to the crook of her elbow. We dug right in, not the least bit concerned with what Emily Post might think of our table manners. I'm a twirler, and when I eat spaghetti the sauce tends to fly. The waitress appeared a couple more times to refill drinks and all conversation was on hiatus.

When the plates were cleared away and we were politely and quietly belching and sucking morsels from between our teeth the waitress asked if we would like dessert. A collective groan arose from our group but we all feebly placed orders for coffee and cannolis.

We paid the tab and collected tooth picks at the cashiers station before heading for the parking lot. Someone suggested Claws for the following weeks get-together and the rest agreed. Claws served Maryland style steamed crabs and crab cakes and was one of our favorite places.

I dawdled the afternoon away with a couple of files and the daily crossword. An hour spent at The Grouper Hole after work left me much relaxed and after dinner and a couple of hours of the boob tube with Jenna and the kids I was more than ready to snuggle under the covers in my cozy little room. Jenna had hurried to her room without a backward glance.

Thursday morning was spent in a hectic atmosphere of panic. Two closings that Jenna had originally scheduled for the end of the next week had been moved up at the lender's request. One problem. No one had informed us and the necessary searches and paperwork hadn't been completed. By one o'clock all had been straightened out and Sigrid agreed to sacrifice and let Jenna and I escape to a well-deserved lunch. We took the Caddy, top down, hair blowing in the breeze; well, Jenna's hair was blowing in the breeze. My short cut and thinning mop kind of ruffled a bit but I don't think you could accurately say it blowed, er, blew. We went to Juanita's, an authentic little Mexican joint that the in crowd avoided because of its location in a heavily migrant area of town. We loved the place. The owners served up genuine Mexican cooking from an unpronounceable region of that country. No Taco Bell versions of Tex-Mex here. After we had ordered we relaxed with two cold Dos Equis. No Coronas for us.

I sipped the beer and looked carefully at Jenna's beautiful face. I noted the faint lines beginning to appear around her eyes and mouth and marveled at how I felt even more affection for her because of them. In her youth she'd been a stunner, with creamy, unlined skin, toned muscles and a vibrant youthfulness. That's what I'd fallen in love with, originally. But as her face slowly changed over the years, becoming more care-worn, as her body showed the changes caused by years and use, childbearing included, I found my regard shifting from the superficial to the bone-deep qualities of the woman. That's not to say that Jenna was disintegrating before my very eyes; she took pride in her appearance, worked hard at retaining as much of her youth as she could. But time will have its way with you, its effects postponed but not denied. Jenna was maturing with extreme grace, but she was maturing. And I felt only increased affection for her in spite of the years. And in spite of, maybe because of, the divorce. I wanted her more than ever, needed her, and the need was growing, coming to a head. But every time I tried to talk to her about the situation, tried to let her know what I was thinking, how I felt, I seized up like a schoolboy.

This lunch was no different. No matter how I tried, I just couldn't tell her what was really on my mind, in my heart. So, we talked about work, the weather, Sigrid's eccentricities (of which there were a few) and any inanity we could think of. I tried to get a read on her, tried to determine if she was roiling under the surface, as I was, with a need to talk about our situation, but failed to reach a conclusion. Maybe there just wasn't anything there but I refused to admit it to myself. There just had to be. Something. After all the years together, the kids, there had to be something. That's what I told myself, anyway.

After lunch, when I was back at my desk, I checked my message slips and realized there had still been no call from Linda Wong. I dialed her number, only to get the answering machine once again. A quick survey of my littered desk revealed that I had nothing extremely pressing, so I headed for the parking lot, waving my cell phone at Jenna, who was covering the front desk as Sigrid finally took her lunch break.

"Call me if you need me for anything. I'll be back soon." Jenna looked up from the computer screen and nodded. I drove the Caddy over the familiar streets of old Mangrove Springs toward Linda's house. As I went I reflected on how much Mangrove Springs had changed since my childhood. There were four and six lane highways where once there had been narrow two lane paved roads and sand and shell streets. There were sprawling shopping centers where there were once groves and pastureland. Million dollar plus homes behind security berms and gated entrances were replacing the modest cracker homes that had once been at the heart of the community. The population of the United States had nearly doubled in my lifetime, that of the world had nearly tripled and in Mangrove Springs the year round population had more than octupled. Is that a word? Anyway, eight times as many people were here year round. It amazed and saddened me. Yes, we now had the convenience of multi-plex cinemas as well as a vibrant and varied nightlife scene thanks to the proliferation of restaurants and bars. We had groceries, doctors, a hospital, even. We had big chain stores, department and home improvement among them, and we had enough gas stations with convenience stores to service the entire state. But, what about what we had lost? The slower paced life? The sense of community? Knowing your neighbors? The enjoyment of the regions natural wonders? You could still take a boat out on the river or the bay, or the Gulf, for that matter, but it wasn't the same. There was no sense of nature, no awe at the natural beauty. Now, it was more like an amusement park, a poorly run one at that. There were lines everywhere. In the stores, at the restaurants, at the boat ramps, even at the hospital! If you tried to serenely float down the river or calmly fish the bay or Gulf, everywhere you looked were scads of other people trying to do the same. And obviously insane people piloting all forms of watercraft from pontoon boats to deck boats, from bass boats to skiffs, from cabin cruisers to personal watercraft. If you attempted a leisurely drive on an off day to take in the sub-tropical scenery you were honked at, cursed, and given one finger salutes. That's if you were lucky! Your very life was in danger from the madly streaking lanes of traffic. Not to mention road rage. Lee County traffic fatalities had skyrocketed to all time highs in recent years. And just try to find a U-Pick or a working grove or farm.

Here, in the older section of town where Linda lived, you could remember a more serene time though rot had started to creep in. Where once these homes had provided the standard in housing for the community, today they were aging and had become mostly rental properties, housing the workers necessary to operate all the restaurants, bars, stores, construction and service companies now needed for the higher classes. The small section around Linda's house still exuded dignity and was well kept, but the blight, as the Mayoral candidates called it, was creeping nearer. At one time Mangrove Springs had been a nearly classless society, without most of the frills necessary to the well to do and without most of the ills associated with poverty. Much of the year round population had been working homeowners and the winter residents had been modest retirees and snowbirds, not the wealthy that the Miami area attracted. That world was gone forever and we had to adjust to the new reality. Bummer. I chased the depressing line of thought out of my head before pulling into Linda's drive.

I rang the front doorbell and heard the chimes distantly echo. After about thirty seconds I rang the bell again. Still nothing. Two more rings with appropriate intervals between and I conceded that perhaps Linda wasn't home. On the way back to the car I eyed the house for any sign of occupation. The garage door was window-less, and tightly closed. A walkway consisting of round concrete pavers set in a field of crushed white rock led along the side of the house. I hesitated a moment, looking around carefully, then followed the path toward the rear of the property, past a whirring A.C. unit to the screened lanai in the back. Drapes were drawn across the sliders and nothing was visible inside. From the corner of my eye I spotted a movement inside the lanai. I slowly scanned the porch for the source of the movement. There, behind a white wicker chair, was the cat, Mrs. Benz. She seemed nervous and a bit unkempt. My eyes focused on the sliding glass door at the edge of the wicker chair and I could see that it was open half an inch, an opening too small to allow the cat entry. I thought it a bit strange that Linda would leave her home with a door unlocked, let alone so obviously open. It was even stranger that Mrs. Benz was stuck on the outside.

A screen door connected the large, by today's standards, back yard with the screened porch and I walked to it and tried the latch. Unlocked. I opened the door and stepped inside feeling a ten-degree drop in the temperature once I was out of the sun. Two fans graced the ceiling of the lanai but they were still, unmoving. I peered about carefully, especially on the lookout for a curious neighbor looking at me. I walked carefully to the sliding door and slowly pulled it open far enough to admit my large frame. Mrs. Benz had initially retreated at my approach, fearful, wide eyed. When she realized I'd opened the door she made a decision and dashed past me, under the drawn curtains on the other side, and disappeared from view. I stepped closer to the drapes and called out softly.

"Linda?" I found myself holding my breath for some reason. I added volume to my voice. "Linda? Miss Wong?" Silence. I looked warily around again, not exactly sure what I should do. Linda Wong might have been out, going about her legitimate business. She might have been at her doctor's or at treatment or even in the hospital for some reason or other. She might have been inside the house, perhaps napping. But she could also have been in some sort of trouble. She was seriously ill. Maybe she'd collapsed, unable to reach a phone, unable to summon help. I hesitated a moment longer, considering all scenarios, weighing all options. Finally, I swept the drapes aside and stepped into the Florida room. I was very aware that I might be shot dead in a moment, or mortally embarrassed, or anything in between.

The Florida room was very still, dust motes released from the drapes spinning in the sunbeams now entering the room through the two-foot opening in the glass doors. Movement drew my eye to the tail of Mrs. Benz where it was disappearing into the kitchen off to my right. I decided to begin my search on the trail of the cat.

The kitchen was dark, no lights on, blinds on the windows that looked onto the back yard closed. I moved carefully, unwilling to turn on a light, following my instincts and the cat. Somewhere ahead a light was on, illumination leaking into the kitchen entryway. A breakfast bar gave way to a dining nook with a small table overhung by a faux chandelier looking thing that housed multiple light bulbs disguised as candles. All bulbs were burning except one. A chair was pulled out from the table and overturned, and on the tile floor was what appeared to be a shattered light bulb. So was the pale, housedress-clad form of Linda Wong. Her legs were twisted grotesquely beneath her. Her eyes were open and sightless. The housedress had risen above her knees, revealing pale, lumpy thighs. Her thinning hair, pale features, and artificially reddened lips gave her the waxy appearance of a discarded and forgotten doll, the property of an indulged and bored adolescent. I stood motionless for a few moments before it occurred to me that I needed to be more than an observer of the situation. I slowly moved forward and reluctantly pressed my fingers to her cool neck. No pulse. I moved my fingers to the crook of her twisted right arm. Still nothing. I knelt and put my ear to her left breast, recoiling a bit at the stiffness of her body. Silence. Mrs. Benz sidled up to Linda's body, mewling and rubbing against her. I sat back on my haunches and admitted it: she was dead!

Chapter Twenty

"So, this is just the way you found her, right? You didn't move her or anything?"

"Well, I checked for a pulse."

"How?"

"I felt her throat, the inside of her wrist, and put my ear lightly to her chest. But she didn't move at all. I had to check, you know, make sure that she wasn't alive, that I couldn't help her."

"Sure, I understand. Just need to be exact." The Sheriff's Deputy waggled his notebook at me. "Paperwork, you know?"

After I'd determined that Linda Wong was indeed dead I called 911 on my cell phone and told someone with an attitude of exaggerated calm what I'd found. I gave the address and my name and the soothing voice instructed me to remain at the scene but not to touch or disturb anything. The EMTs and a Deputy would be arriving shortly.

I backed up until my backside encountered the breakfast bar at the kitchens end. I gratefully leaned against it, noticing for the first time the trembling in my legs and the bile churning in my stomach. I'd seen many dead people but most had been within the ordered and expected confines of a funeral home, being presented for a last, cathartic viewing for the benefit of the grieving. Other than the occasional possibly dead body briefly glimpsed at a roadside accident scene before police officers waved me impatiently forward, I'd never seen a dead person in the wild, so to speak. And never anyone that I'd known. That I'd been speaking to just a few days before. I stood there, head bowed, trembling and thinking dark and morbid thoughts. After a few minutes I realized that the emergency personnel and the deputy probably weren't in much of a hurry and that I could be waiting for a while. I didn't want to spend the time alone so I took out my cell phone again and called the office. Sigrid surprised me by answering.

"Sigrid?"

"Ya?"

"That was quick."

"Roy? Is that you?" She sounded a bit apprehensive.

"Of course, Sigrid, I…"

"You sound weird!" she blurted out. "Is something wrong?" I realized that my voice was a bit higher pitched and more brittle sounding than usual. I made an effort to speak more normally.

"No, no, I just didn't expect you to be back from lunch yet, that's all." I could almost hear her shoulders squaring.

"It has been forty-eight minutes. I am allowed forty-five minutes. I have been back at my post for five minutes, just slightly sooner than I was required."

"All right, Sigrid, I know you are a punctual person. I just meant that the time had passed more quickly than I'd thought. That's all." I squeezed my forehead with my left hand and hoped that would do it. To my relief it seemed to.

"You should pay more attention to your watch, then time would not seem to confuse you so." Whatever, Sigrid. I didn't need to deal with this right now.

"Is Jenna there?"

"Yes." She said it crisply; glad to be back on familiar ground. "I'll ring her."

"Thank you," I said, and meant it. Jenna picked up almost immediately.

"Hey. What's up?"

"Linda Wong is dead."

"What?" I remembered that I hadn't kept Jenna current on my doubts about Alma Chastain's will or my efforts to dispel those doubts.

"You remember Ralph Rennegar," I began.

"Oh, yeah. Linda was his secretary. What happened?" I proceeded to tell her all that had occurred during the previous week and about the doubts that had dogged me. Finally, I told her about finding Linda Wong's body.

"You're there right now?"

"Yeah, I'm waiting for the EMTs and the cops. I just needed to talk to someone, this is a little spooky."

"Whoa, I can imagine! Just relax, Roy, they'll be there soon. Then it won't seem so bad, you know?" She prattled on a bit and I was indeed reassured by the soothing sound of her voice but I found my mind wandering as she spoke. As I considered the sad state of affairs it occurred to me that Linda's death did not mean that she hadn't been able to check out the old Rennegar files, just that if she had she'd not been able to communicate the results of her search to me.

I straightened my spine and began to take more notice of my surroundings. It wasn't entirely dark in the house. There was the glow of the chandelier in the dining room and the sunlight that made its way around the drapes and blinds, especially where I'd partially opened the sliding glass doors of the Florida room. Plus, my eyes had adjusted to the dimness. As Jenna extolled the virtues of remaining calm and focusing on positive things I found myself wondering if Linda had found anything and, if she had, where she'd have put it. I began to recall the house as I'd seen it on my way in. I'd come through the Florida room first and I strained to remember all that I could about it. Nothing stood out.

"Uh, look, I think I hear them coming." I didn't but I wanted a graceful way to get off the phone.

"Are you going to be all right? Do you want me to come over there?"

"No, I'll be okay. It was just a shock, finding her like that. I'll come back to the office as soon as they're through with me here. Might take a while, though."

"Call me on your way. I'll be wondering what's going on. Call me first, okay?"

"I will. It'll be all right. I've got to go now." After I disconnected I found a wall switch that turned on the overhead light in the kitchen. A purse was sitting on an old-timey butcher's block thing standing at the end of the kitchen counter. It was a large bag made from a dark green, heavy fabric and had a flap that was folded over the rest of the bag in a closed position. I flipped it over and saw that the purse was divided into two main sections, or pockets. I used a fingertip to spread open first one compartment and then the other, peering intently into the interior. Keys, wallet, the usual feminine litter was evident, but nothing that seemed connected to Alma Chastain. I listened closely for any sound of arriving vehicles but heard nothing.

I went into the living room but saw nothing of interest. I entered the hallway, turning on another light, and looked into a starkly clean bathroom obviously reserved for guests. It looked like it hadn't seen any in some time, as did the small bedroom just beyond.

At the other end of the hallway was the master bedroom. I flicked the light switch and entered. I felt creepy, like some sort of peeping Tom. No, it was more ghoulish than that. The woman who had slept in this room, who had laced it with her scent and her preference in bedding and reading material and furnishings lay dead just a couple of rooms away. I felt positively uninvited. But I still gave the room a once over before deciding that there was nothing there, either.

I turned off the light and went to the living room where I sat in the dimness on a sectional. I got right up again and went to the front door. I tried the knob and found that it was locked. I unlocked it for the expected emergency workers. I looked at my watch and realized that twenty-seven minutes had elapsed since I'd called 911. Ought to be here soon, I thought, as I headed back to the living room where I once again sat. Then stood up again. Her car! The garage was through a door in the kitchen and the light switch was just inside.

It was a double garage with her silver Camry parked in the middle. Along the wall in front of the car were a washer and dryer and a laundry tub. A water heater stood a little farther on. The side walls were lined with an assortment of cleaning tools, brooms, mops, etc., mostly hung on hooks. The other wall was mostly taken up with the garage door. The light was part of the overhead garage door opener.

I went to the car and tried the passenger door. It was unlocked. I stuck my head inside and gave the interior the once over and saw nothing but a cable-knit sweater draped over the back of the passenger seat. I reached down and opened the glove compartment. It contained the registration, owner's manual, lube receipts and a map of Mangrove Springs printed by the Chamber of Commerce. I closed it and flipped the sun visors over. The only item I found was a garage door opener on the driver's side. No paperwork anywhere. With a sigh I closed the car door and retreated to the living room, turning off the light and closing the door on my way. Seated once again, I looked at my watch and saw that thirty-six minutes had elapsed since my call to 911.

All of which I related to the Deputy who was questioning me. All but the fact that I was looking for evidence that Linda had found something in Ralph's files concerning Alma Chastain's will. I thought that would only complicate matters. I told him that I was looking around for any other people and/or pets who/which might need help.

"So why were you here?" The question startled me a bit.

"Uh, I'd asked her, Linda, I mean, to check a file of her old boss's for a document I needed. He's dead and she was administering the records. I stopped by to see if she'd had any luck." He glanced toward the dining area.

"Seems she didn't have much luck." He wrote something else and then thought for a moment. The EMTs had loaded Linda's body on a gurney and were preparing to wheel her from the house.

"Do you know if she had any relatives close by?" I thought back to the conversations we'd had over the years, passing time while waiting for some bit of business to be completed in Ralph's office.

"I'm not really sure. I know she never married and she lived alone. Except for the cat." I pointed to Mrs. Benz sitting on the back of an overstuffed recliner. The Deputy wrote some more.

"What do you think happened?" I asked.

"Looks like she was trying to change a light bulb and fell. The back of her head was stove in. That will happen when a head hits ceramic tile with force. Shouldn't have been on that chair. Older, with health problems. We see similar things all the time. Will you come in to the sub-station to make a formal statement? Anytime in the next few days. But call first to make an appointment. I don't know which investigator will be assigned to the file, but just ask." He looked sternly at me. "If you don't come in they'll come to you. Then they won't be happy."

"I'll come by. And I'll call first." He stood up and prepared to follow the EMTs from the house. I stood also.

"What about the cat?" I asked, nodding toward Mrs. Benz. He shrugged.

"Got any kids?"

"Yeah, three. Why?" He shrugged again.

"Maybe they'd like a cat. Looks like a nice one. Otherwise I'll have to call animal control. Chances are they'd end up destroying it." He retrieved his hat from the arm of the sofa and looked at me expectantly.

"Do you have any children?" I asked. He raised his brows a bit.

"Two. And they have three cats, two dogs, a turtle, a hamster, two guinea pigs, five gold fish and three parakeets." He smiled tiredly.

"I'll take her," I said. He nodded and motioned for me to get the cat. I approached Mrs. Benz, who eyed me warily, but let me pick her up and tuck her to my chest. I went out the front door ahead of the Deputy.

I held Mrs. Benz firmly in my lap as I put the top and then the windows up on the Caddy. Then I released her and she didn't bolt as I'd expected, but settled more deeply into my lap where she closed her eyes and began purring. I started the car but before I put it into gear I reached for my cell phone and called the office. When Sigrid put me through to Jenna, with no nonsense this time, I told her that I was on my way.

"Was it very bad?" she wanted to know.

"I'll tell you about it when I get there." I didn't mention the cat.

Chapter Twenty-One

"How awful!" I'd told Jenna about my search of Linda's house and my conclusion that she hadn't found anything concerning Alma's will. I couldn't even be sure she'd checked the records. I told her about feeling bad about conducting that search while Linda lay dead in her dining area, a victim of an apparent light bulb changing accident.

"Could you tell how long she'd been dead?" I looked at her sharply.

"How would I know? I don't really have much experience with this sort of thing."

"I know, I know, I'm sorry. It must have been awful. So, tell me about the cat." We both looked at Mrs. Benz.

"Well, the Deputy said they'd probably put her to sleep if he called Animal Control. I didn't want to contemplate that at the moment. We can always go that route." Jenna looked up from the cat and right at me.

"You know we've always had horrible luck with pets." I thought about the tropical fish that had been lost down the sink during a water change, and the chameleon that had succumbed to a rare virus.

"But look at her," I said, fondling the furry form in my lap. "She is a loveable, nearly self sufficient creature. If we don't take her she will surely be put to an early death." I lifted Mrs. Benz and cradled her furry face in my spread fingers. "How can you NOT love that face?"

"I DO think she's adorable, I think the kids will find her adorable, but who's going to take care of her? Everybody will want to love and pet her but who'll feed her and groom her on a regular basis?" I didn't respond to Jenna's questions because they weren't really questions at all, just her way of convincing herself to do something that logic said she shouldn't. I gently removed Mrs. Benz from my lap and deposited her in Jenna's. My thighs were suddenly cool where the cat had been. Mrs. Benz didn't protest, as I'd feared she might. Nor did Jenna.

"So," I said. "I guess there really isn't anything else I need to check on the Chastain deal, nothing I can think of, anyway." I leaned back, fingers linked behind my head, and looked to Jenna for her response. Mrs. Benz had snuggled into her lap and had resumed purring. Jenna wrinkled her brow and thought for a moment.

"I'd say if you're comfortable with it then we should go ahead with the commitment and send everything to Muncie so that it can close. Judge ordered the sale, right?" I nodded. "Well, if the chain of title is good," more nodding on my part, "and the will checks out," this time I sort of shrugged, "then I guess it's as clean as it needs to be. Right?"

"Right." I agreed with her but wished I felt better about it. Jenna was stroking the cat in her lap with loving care. I knew she was hooked.

"Well," I said as I stood up. "I'll gather up everything Muncie needs and fax it to his office." Jenna looked at me with a twinkle in her eye.

"I'm finished for the day. Guess I'll head on home." She looked at the cat. "I'll take her with me. Introduce her to the kids."

"Fine. Oh, just a second and I'll print out the commitment for Muncie and you can sign it before you leave." As the license holder she was required to sign all insurance policies and commitments.

"Okay. Be quick, though. We want to get home."

Right." I hurried to my office and brought up the commitment on my computer and began the print job. While it printed, I organized the other paperwork that Muncie would need. When I had the printout I rushed it back to Jenna's office. She signed it and gathered up her purse, the cat securely tucked into the crook of her left arm like an infant.

"I'm going to be stopping by The Grouper Hole for a bit on the way home," I told her. "Make sure your windows are up so she doesn't jump out." I pointed at Mrs. Benz.

"Don't worry, we'll take good care of each other, won't we Mercedes? I can call you Mercedes, can't I?" Jenna was cooing baby talk as the cat closed her eyes and purred even louder.

"Look, I know you don't like her, and all, but..." Jenna looked at me and slowly grinned and then laughed out loud. I was chuckling too. My eyes locked on hers and my knees were suddenly weak. We stopped laughing and, when she spoke, Jenna's voice seemed a bit husky.

"I like her just fine and you know it." And to my surprise and delight she brushed her lips across my cheek as she stepped around me and out of the office. "See you at home," she called over her shoulder. I heard her saying goodnight to Sigrid, who'd made a fuss over the cat when I'd brought her in, and then the door opened and closed with a pneumatic sigh. I stood a few moments as I enjoyed the glow Jenna's kiss had left me with. Eventually, I roused myself enough to head back to my office where I began gathering the rest of the material necessary for the Chastain closing.

When I had it all together I composed a cover letter, printed it and signed it, and took the whole mess to Sigrid. She felt my presence and looked up from a file she was working on.

"Yes?" she said in her crisp manner. Before I could answer, she began chattering about Mrs. Benz.

"That lovely little cat won Miss Jenna's heart right away, just like I knew ahead of time. What a lovely present to be bringing home to the family. The kinder will love her too, the children, I mean." The embarrassment at her slight lapse in language slowed her down enough for me to tell her what I wanted.

"Fax this package over to Jack Muncie's office before you leave, will you, Sigrid? Then put it in the file. I'm going to be leaving a bit early."

"The big deal, it is ready? Sure I will fax it, you can believe it." She took the sheaf of papers and headed for the fax machine.

"Have a good evening," I called after her as I opened the door to the outside.

"Ya, you too," followed me out.

As I stepped off the veranda and headed for the parking lot a chill wind sent shivers racing up my spine. The sunlight had turned pale and windswept clouds, leaden and dull and gray, were brushed across the cold, light blue that was the sky. I hurried toward the Caddy and opened the trunk. I took out a jacket that I kept there for just such occasions and hastily put it on, straightening the collar that had turned under and pulling the cuffs to their rightful place.

The newspaper had reported that we were going to experience some cooler weather, that which passed for winter in southwest Florida. It was forecast that it would drop to sixty by nightfall and to a low in the forties over the next couple of nights, with the day time high reaching only seventy or so. The weekend and halfway into the next week was supposed to be cold, with temperatures returning to normal by Wednesday. It felt like it had dropped fifteen degrees just since I'd returned to the office an hour or so before. Still no rain in the forecast.

The jacket helped a bit and as soon as I got into the car and out of the wind I began to warm up. I cranked the engine and headed for The Grouper Hole. Halfway there the engine had warmed enough for me to turn on the heater and by the time I arrived at my destination I was downright toasty.

"The usual?" Dan said after I'd taken a seat.

"Don't you ever take a day off?"

"Sure. But only on days when you don't stop by." We both grinned and chuckled as only men can at a bon mot shared between a guy and his bartender.

"Yeah, the usual. And do you have any popcorn or pretzels or something." He nodded and moved off to prepare my drink. In a moment he was back with a vodka martini and a basket of goldfish.

I nibbled some as I looked about. Just exiting the men's rest room was my soon-to-be city councilor, Evan Muster. He headed for a stool at the other end of the bar and when I caught his eye I waved my drink at him. His eyes lit up and he said something to Dan before scooping up his drink and heading my way.

"Roy, how the hell ya doin'?" I took his outstretched hand and withstood his newly acquired politician's grip. Evan grabbed a stool next to me. Before long we were talking about the election.

"You're going to win, aren't you? That's what they all say." He grinned.

"Well, that's a matter of opinion, Roy, but I hope so. The race is sure hard on the nerves and on the family." I thought I saw a hint of sadness in his eyes that belied the hundred-watt grin he was projecting.

"You really want this? I mean, you're running for a reason, right?" His grin faded and his face became serious. He began speaking in a low voice and I leaned closer.

"Roy, I'm 'fraid they're gonna steal this place clean away from us, that's why I'm doin' it. They've already taken our jobs and they're tryin' to take our land." He leaned closer and wrapped his free hand about my left arm. I could smell alcohol and realized he was probably tipsy.

"I know our time is past, Roy. Ain't never gonna be like it was before. I just hope to slow it down enough so that we can adjust. Can't all of us be like you and adapt to the new ways so easy." He grinned sadly at me. "Course, we're all proud of ya, Roy. Proud of the fact that ya can beat them at their own game." He shook his head. "Fittin' that ya should make your way servicin' the real estate crowd, the very thing that's forcin' the rest of us out." I was stunned.

"Evan, I just scrambled around for a way to make a living. I never meant to betray my family!"

"I don't think you're betrayin' us, Roy. I don't think that at all. You're leadin' the way, settin' an example for the rest of us 'bout how to survive. If ya can't beat 'em, join 'em, that's what I say. I'm just tryin' to buy enough time for the slower ones amongst us to see the light and make the shift before bein' chewed up and spit out by this here progress. THAT'S why I'm runnin' for the council. To slow things a bit and give our kind a fightin' chance, a chance to adapt the way you and Jenna have." He stopped and took a sip of his drink.

We sat without talking for a few moments. He seemed lost in his own thoughts and I had no reply to what he'd said. Evan had always seemed to be a steady, decent man with good common sense, but I'd never suspected that he was prone to such analytical thinking. I'd never concluded that we locals needed to adapt to the growth and changing demographics of the area. I disliked much of the change going on around me at such a frenetic pace but had never formulated a plan to deal with it, to adapt to it, regardless of what Evan read into my lifestyle. I, we, Jenna and I, had just gone with the flow, followed the path of least resistance. We'd taken advantage of openings and relationships, such as our friendship with Ollie Mason, to finance our lives. Mostly we, I, had tried to avoid being trapped in an occupation that I couldn't stand, such as fishing or farming. I knew I didn't want to pursue either, family history notwithstanding, long before I realized those occupations were dying. Serendipity? Desperation? Adaptation? I just didn't know.

Dan came down the bar and pointed toward the door.

"Cab's here, Evan." Evan followed Dan's pointing finger, as did I, and saw the man standing just inside the door and looking about the room. Evan waved to him and drained his glass before standing a bit unsteadily.

"I'll catch the tab next time I'm in," he said to Dan, who smiled, nodded, and walked away. Evan then looked at me.

"Keep on adaptin', Roy. The next big change will come when they take the family land. Be prepared. Cause they will. And don't forget to vote for me." He made his way through the crowd, chatting with some and glad-handing others, working the room as any politician would. I watched his progress until he'd followed the cab driver out into the parking lot.

I had two drinks more, polished off the goldfish and occasionally made the rounds of the room chatting up people I knew. Slowly, I worked my way out of the funk that my visit with Evan Muster had left me in. At seven o'clock I paid my bar bill and bid my farewells. The Caddy's engine had cooled so I shivered a bit until I could turn the heater on. The temperature had dropped another ten degrees.

At home we decided to order pizza and as we waited for the delivery person Jenna regaled me with an account of her brief but productive (expensive) stop at the pet store. She showed me her purchases and gave a detailed recounting of the tortuous logic involved with each buy.

"And you didn't say, you probably didn't know, what kind of food she ate, not the brand nor even whether she likes wet or dry..." Jenna rattled on, an animation infusing her that I hadn't seen in a while. She showed me the food she'd decided on, buying some canned and some dry so that "... Mrs. Benz can communicate her preference to us."

There was a little catnip mouse and a ball and something that resembled a baby's rattle for her to play with. There was a nifty litter pan with a patented disposal system that, the label claimed, was superior to anything on the market and guaranteed to be the least stinky available, or words to that effect. And a bag of the newest aid to neatness, clump-able cat litter. Supposedly, when the cat used the litter pan, this litter would carefully envelop the offending substance, locking it away inside an aromatic little ball of sweet smelling wonder crystals ready to be scooped out of the pan with the handy plastic, slotted, shovel thingy. Watching Jenna's joyful animation as she talked about and displayed the cat wares for me, I wished I had gotten her a cat months before. I tried not to think of how this one had come to us.

Meanwhile, Mrs. Benz was on the living room floor closely attended by three adoring young people to whom it had not yet occurred that the cat was something to be fought over.

Chapter Twenty-Two

About ten on Saturday morning, I wandered downstairs and found my way to the kitchen, where Jenna was drinking coffee with the newspaper spread before her. She was wearing a shapeless nightgown under a velour robe, and fuzzy blue slippers. One leg was tucked under her on the chair. I heard conversation in the living room. Jenna saw me cock my head at the sound.

"Good morning. That's the girls, all three of them. Rae, Bobbie Jane and Mrs. Benz. They're getting along splendidly, thank you." I plopped into a chair across from her and eyed her coffee mug enviously. The heat kicked on and warm air flowed over me from a vent in the ceiling.

"How old's the coffee," I croaked.

"It's empty. But if you say pretty please I'll put a fresh one to brew." I smiled and nodded my gratitude and she un-tucked her leg and got up. As she prepared the coffee for brewing I snagged the local section of the paper and began looking it over.

"Where's Cleve?"

"He's helping Sonny pull the transmission from his swamp buggy. It needs inserts, or something, I forget what he said. The races are coming up and Sonny's running in the modified 2-wheel class. He's asked Cleve to work in the pits." Sonny was Sissy's son, Sissy being the daughter of Aunt Chili. He was about nineteen, a good boy by all accounts, respectful of his elders and recently graduated from high school. He seemed intent on making a life that included boats or fishing or mechanics of some sort. The conversation with Evan Muster came to mind.

"I wish Cleve would spend more time fooling with computers or something. That's where the future is, not in swamp buggies." Even I could hear the sour grapes in my voice. Jenna stopped what she was doing to turn her head and look thoughtfully at me.

"Sonny's a good kid and I'd rather have Cleve hanging out with him and learning about work than with some of the other young people you read about. Cleve's a good kid, too. Give him some credit. He enjoys working on Sonny's swamp buggy, but you know his heart is set on being an architect." I knew that, and that certainly seemed to be adapting to the new southwest Florida world order according to Evan, but the swamp buggy thing reeked of un-adapted locals.

"I know, I just worry about the kids, that's all. We won't be around for ever and they'll need to be self sufficient at some point." I buried my nose in the paper. "You know what I mean."

"Yes, I know," she said in a low voice. She came back to the table and sat down. I could hear the coffee start dripping and the aroma came to me, rich and heady.

Sometime during the scanning of the local section the coffee finished brewing and Jenna got up and prepared a cup for me. Black with one artificial sweetener, just the way I'd learned to like it.

"Thank you," I said as she set the mug before me. We sat and drank coffee while reading the parts of the paper that interested us, occasionally reading bits out loud to one another. I turned the page and looked at the obituaries, something I wouldn't have done just a couple of years earlier.

"Well..." Jenna stood and tugged at her nightgown. "I'm going to shower and get dressed. I promised the girls we'd go to Edison Mall this afternoon. Want to go?" I most certainly did not want to tag along on a female window-shopping tour. My feet hurt at the mere thought. They'd handle every article of female apparel in the place and some of the men's, most notably the boxer shorts. For some reason, all of my women loved the things. They'd spend four to six hours in bliss and then leave, buying little or nothing. Ice cream sundaes at DQ would cap their dream adventure.

"I'd love to, but I have to stay home and change the fat in the deep fryer." I grimaced with a great show of regret and sighed as loudly as I could. "Sorry."

"Right." Jenna knew when she asked what my response would be.

"Actually, I have some errands I need to run. I'll be done by late afternoon. You planning on dinner here?" I asked, trying to keep my tone light. For all I knew she could have had plans for the evening, maybe with Vern. To think, I used to like that guy.

"Yeah. What would you like?" I thought briefly about telling her what I'd really like but I knew she meant for dinner.

"I don't know. You pick."

"Well, it's cold and something really filling and warming sounds nice. Maybe some of your stew or spaghetti would be good. That is, if you feel like cooking." I admired her maneuvering.

"Sure. How about spaghetti?" She headed for the hall staircase.

"Perfect," she called over her shoulder. I finished with the paper then rinsed the coffee cups and placed them in the sink. I went up to my room and laid out the clothes I'd wear that day. I heard Jenna leave the bathroom and I headed in for my shower. Our house was an older one and the master bedroom didn't have its own bathroom. One off the hall serviced the whole upstairs. Downstairs was a half-bath. But we did have a huge water heater. I'd made sure of that when the old one died. We had always been running out of hot water. No more.

When I was showered, shaved, and dressed I headed back downstairs. In the kitchen was a note from Jenna.

"See you later. Don't let Mrs. Benz get out as you're leaving, she doesn't know where she lives yet. Jen." There was another note for Cleve explaining things to him and instructing him to be home and cleaned up for dinner. As usual, she had all the practical needs of those for whom she cared covered. I called Ollie at home and he answered on the third ring.

"Got any plans for lunch?" I asked him.

"Nothing special, why? Do I smell an invitation in the offing?"

"Yeah, I thought maybe we could get together, you know, have a nice lunch somewhere. It's been a while"

"What are you in need of, Elroy?" His voice was soft, not accusatory. I thought about how to answer him.

"Just some conversation, Ollie. That's all. Well, maybe some advice. But mostly conversation. I need to put some things in perspective. You can always help me do that. You're so, what's that California word, centered? Grounded?"

"Boston Charlie's in half an hour." Boston Charlie's was a seafood joint at the north end of Mangrove Beach frequented by bikers and hell raisers, though it did serve some fine New England style seafood, including outrageous fried clams. The increasingly upscale residents of Mangrove Springs had been trying for several years to close the place down.

"Boston Charlie's? Why there?"

"I have a private table there, we can talk in confidence."

"Why would you have a private table there?"

"I, ah, have a small ownership interest in the establishment." I should have known.

"Okay, thirty minutes." I grabbed my list, cell phone and a jacket and was very careful to let myself out without the loss of cat that Jenna had warned against.

It was about fifty-five degrees out, colder even than forecast for midday. I let the engine warm for several minutes before putting it into gear. My backside noticed how well the leather seat reflected the coolness of the day through the rather thin material of my Levi Action Slacks. The sky was lead gray and streaked by wisps of smoke drifting out of the east. Cooler weather didn't seem to diminish the fires.

Twenty minutes later I was pulling into the shell parking lot of Boston Charlie's where I didn't have much trouble finding a parking spot. It was a little cold for bikers, I thought. And maybe a little early. It was just after noon.

Inside the restaurant it became apparent that food was only part of the attraction. The cavernous building was divided roughly into thirds with a bar residing in one section and the actual restaurant occupying another section. The final third was taken up with pool tables arrayed in the center, eight of them, and arcade type game machines, as well as several old-fashioned pinball machines, lining the perimeter. The areas were separated by waist high barriers that provided a place upon which to set drinks while allowing the patrons in each section a relatively unimpeded view of the other sections. The pool tables were not the traditional regulation size of four and a half feet by nine feet, or even the new regulation size of four feet by eight feet, but were rather smallish three by six foot models. I couldn't imagine ever missing a shot on such toy-sized tables. They were coin operated, a dollar (four quarters) a game, and, even though the parking lot had been relatively empty, five of the eight tables hue in use.

The tables in the restaurant were another matter. No more than a third were occupied and the uniform of the day seemed to be boots and jeans. The male patrons were mostly longhaired (graying and thinning), potbellied, with unkempt facial hair, wearing sweatshirts emblazoned with various rude sayings and graphic insults. Females mostly wore halter-tops, from which excess flesh spilled, and big hair. Almost all, male and female, had draped greasy denim jackets over the backs of their chairs. A folding Chinese screen was spread about the table farthest from the entrance and I could see Ollie's profile around one corner of the stretched silk. I made my way to the screen and stepped around it. When Ollie saw me he half stood and motioned me toward a seat.

"Roy, Roy, sit down, please. It's good to see you. Sit down." I seated myself in the chair he'd indicated and looked at the table. It was set with snowy white linen and gleaming silver and was adorned with a tropical flower and fruit centerpiece. And candles. Tall tapirs of a pearly, swirling wax design, in baroque silver candleholders.

"Ollie, how are you?"

"I'm fine, just fine. I hope you don't mind, but I've taken the liberty of ordering for the both of us. I'm a bit strapped for time and I knew that you were a fan of the fried clams that are served here." I nodded at him and said that the clams would be just fine.

"Oh, here they are." A waitress had appeared around the screen, two plastic baskets balanced upon her crooked left arm and two long neck bottles of beer grasped in her right hand. Quite a contrast to the linen and silver, but no one seemed to notice.

"Here you go," she said. "Need anything else?" I looked at the basket in front of me and saw that it contained a generous portion of clams, fried to a pleasing golden hue, a heaping mound of

French fries, and two small plastic containers, one filled with creamy looking Cole slaw and the other with tartar sauce.

"Cocktail sauce and malt vinegar," Ollie informed her without hesitation. "Anything that you require, Roy?" I looked at the waitress and smiled.

"No, I think this will do it." When the waitress returned with the items requested by Ollie, he sprinkled vinegar on his fries then forked a clam and dredged it in the cocktail sauce.

"Is there something wrong with the food, Roy? Why aren't you eating?"

"No, nothing is wrong." I speared a french-fry with my fork and popped it into my mouth. I immediately opened my mouth as wide as I could and began huffing like the prize pupil at a Le Maz class. The fry was hot! He nodded as if my answer was sufficient and returned his attention to the food.

I filled him in on what I'd been doing and what I'd learned since last speaking with him concerning the Chastain file. I informed him in some detail about the circumstances surrounding the finding of Linda Wong's body and my search for any documents related to the Chastain will. He listened attentively as he ate, occasionally wiping his lips with the linen napery and swigging from the beer bottle that the waitress kept replacing. When I'd told him everything he pursed his lips and belched.

"You didn't find anything that would lead you to think she found something that applied to your file? No paperwork of any kind?"

"Nothing." He cupped his right hand beneath his chin and thought a moment.

"Hmm," he said. I finished my second beer as I waited for him to provide me with some insight into a mystery that I'd not been able to make any sense of, that I'd just about decided was nothing more than what it appeared to be on the surface: an embittered old woman who had threatened, but failed, to provide protection from development for her property.

"That's funny," he said, hands clasped under his chin.

"What?"

"You found nothing. Nothing at all."

"What do you mean?" Ollie looked right at me.

"You didn't find anything? Not even the copy of the will in question that you'd given her?"

"She could have thrown it away. Or maybe she left it wherever Ralph's files are stored."

"Perhaps."

Chapter Twenty-Three

Monday morning I called the Lee County Sheriff's sub-station and spoke to the Detective assigned to investigate Linda's death, one Cleon Service, spelled 'S-e-r-v-a-i-s, ' he informed me. I told him I could come right over to give a statement and he said that would be fine, he was going to be in all morning.

The sub-station was housed in a five thousand square foot retail space in a strip mall on new 41 near the county line. I had to wait in a lobby for about ten minutes before a uniformed Deputy led me back into a warren of cubicles. The Deputy motioned me into one and then turned and headed back. I did as I was motioned. A black man in shirtsleeves stood and pointed to a chair before sticking out his hand for shaking.

"Mr. Dixon. I'm Detective Servais. Please sit down." I shook his hand, which presented a dry, firm grip, and looked over the top of the wall dividers before sitting on the steel and gray fabric side chair that looked as if it might have come from the local Sam's Club. He sat also.

"I've never been in this new space," I offered. "Lots bigger than the old Community Hall down by the park." He looked at me a moment before speaking.

"Did you have occasion to visit there often?" Either his upper lip had a nervous twitch or he was suppressing a smile.

"I was there a couple of times. Back when all those kids went missing a few years ago." He placed his elbows on the desk and tented his hands. His lip had stopped twitching.

"Ah, yes. The Kelly case." It was and forever would be known as the Kelly case though he had not been the first child to disappear.

"You know about it?" Silly question. People in town still talked about it occasionally. He gathered up a sheaf of papers that lay spread on the desk before him and placed them in a manila folder, which he then placed in a neat pile of folders on a corner of his desk. He then straightened the pile of folders, squaring them with the edges of the desk.

"That was before I came here but I'm familiar with the basic facts." He reached into a drawer of the desk and located the file he wanted. "Everyone here is. What was your involvement with the case?" He stopped fooling with the file and once more gave me his complete attention.

"My daughter was Patrick's best friend. She was playing with him on the playground when he went for a drink of water. She required counseling and I think it still bothers her some." I knew it still bothered her; I just wasn't sure how much.

"Yes, yes, Dixon. I remember. Your daughter would be Bobby Jane." I nodded. "I've talked with her about it at her school." He must have seen my eyes narrow. "Did she mention that to you?" I shook my head.

"I would think you'd have to get permission from her parents to interrogate her again." He raised his hands in a defensive motion.

"Whoa, it wasn't like that at all. She wasn't interrogated by any stretch of the imagination. I gave a talk in the auditorium about strangers and the need to be careful in dealing with them. After, Bobby Jane and several other students, as well as a couple of teachers, approached me with questions and comments. She brought it up, told me, told the group about her experience. Once she started talking I knew what case she was referring to but I did not interrogate her. Didn't even ask her any questions, though the others had a few for her."

"I'm sorry, I didn't …" He laid his hands on the file before him.

"That's all right. I should have presented the information in a different fashion." He got that right.

"So, I guess nobody works on that case anymore, huh. Probably closed."

"No, it's still open but classified as a cold case. When a Detective has a light caseload it's required that they spend spare time on cold files. Lord knows we have plenty of those. But that one doesn't get looked at too much these days. When a Detective is working a cold case he needs to read the entire jacket first, to re-familiarize himself with the case." He allowed a small grin to appear briefly. "The jacket on that case occupies two large file cabinets."

"I imagine." It was all I could bring myself to say. He began leafing through the file in front of him.

"Who knows? We may get lucky and close it out one of these days." I waited quietly as he read the details of the open file.

As I waited, I had a chance to observe him and to form some first impressions. When he'd stood and directed me to the chair I'd noticed that he was tall, not just a little, but basketball tall, 6'5" to 6'6" maybe, and slim. Not in an emaciated way but in a lean and well-muscled fashion. I got the feeling that this man was on top of his game. In the zone, as the sportscasters, the younger ones at least, were fond of saying.

"Now, Mr. Dixon..."

"Roy." He didn't seem offended that I'd interrupted him.

"Okay." He flashed a genuine smile at me. "Roy. And you can call me Cleon." He looked back at the file before him.

"Okay, Linda Wong." He peered at a form from the file. "You were the one to discover the decedent?" I'd expected him to say body. Decedent was so much more dignified.

"Yes."

"I have the Deputy's report here," he waved the form about, but his cool, though not unfriendly, brown eyes were on me. "But, why don't you tell me about it and I'll pretend I'm hearing it for the first time. Sometimes it helps to do it that way." He relaxed in his swivel chair and assumed a listening attitude.

"Sure. I'd asked Linda to check on a file of her previous employer's, a lawyer, now deceased, and for whom she was administering the files. It concerned a piece of property on which my firm, Mason Dixon Title Associates, is responsible for the title insurance. I was trying to determine the marketability of the property in question and had some legal questions as to its pedigree. She, Linda, agreed to look into the law firms files, held in a storage facility, to see what she could tell me about certain

151

legal documents, previously executed, that pertained to the property in question." His look had morphed into one of amusement.

"You're a lawyer." He said it as if that would explain everything.

"No, not exactly. I'm just a title examiner, though we often deal with the same criteria as lawyers concerning real property." I bristled a bit at his unfair and degrading assumption until I realized that I'd been trying to sound exactly like a lawyer, trying to impress him. I smiled sheepishly.

"I'm sorry about the legalese," I said. "I'll try to keep it informal." He shrugged. "At any rate, Linda had promised to check the files and get back to me. I didn't hear from her, so I called her several times. But all I got was the answering machine. Eventually, I decided to stop by her house and see what was up." I paused but he waited patiently for me to continue. I thought about the best way to relate the sequence of events that followed. I gave him a verbal picture of my movements on Friday, from my final call to Linda's residence to the actual discovery of the body, er, decedent. I told him of my search of the premises though not the real reason for it. I told my tale with a straightforward sincerity that would impress anyone. Anyone but me, that is. I was definitely beginning to feel a bit queasy about hiding my less than noble motivation from the authorities. If I had any proof that Linda's death had been anything but an accident I would change my tune, but it seemed to be a clear-cut case of death by misadventure. I'd picked that term up sometime during my years of perusal of the public records. Or, maybe during the hours I'd spent watching crime dramas on TV. When I'd finished relating the chronology of events to him, Cleon just sat, eyes closed, hands clasped under his chin. He sat that way for so long that I began to suspect that he'd fallen asleep. Not so. Eventually his eyes opened and he seemed to drag himself back to the here and now.

"Well, that matches with what we now know. Of course, the ME's report, which we'll have in a couple of days, will put a lid on it. Probably death by misadventure." I felt a thrill as I heard that phrase.

"You don't suspect foul play?" Another term I'd heard many times over the years in TV dramas.

"No, I guess it was just an accident. An elderly lady with a life-ending disease, undergoing debilitating treatments, treatments that made her weak and susceptible to accidents. She tried to change a light bulb, attempting to stand on a kitchen chair, on a tile floor, no less, and the chair slid out from under her. She smashed her head on the tile floor and the accident resulted in her death. No surprises there."

"But," he continued. I tensed up, knowing what I usually mean when I utter that word. "But, there is the anomaly concerning the light bulb."

"What anomaly?" I wanted to know.

"Well, it's probably nothing." He seemed genuinely reluctant to bring it up.

"What is it?" He worked his hands in a scrubbing motion and thought a moment longer before apparently coming to a decision.

"I went to the scene and looked around a bit, you know, after the report landed on my desk. The place was taped off and hadn't been disturbed since the first responders had left. The EMTs had been pretty careful not to disturb the physical scene. Evidently there hadn't been a need for emergency resuscitation efforts." He looked soberly at me. "The decedent had obviously been dead for some time." I remembered the cool, marble-like touch of Linda's skin when I'd felt for a pulse. I nodded my agreement.

"Did you find something?" He shrugged.

"Not really. Just an anomaly, as I said. There was a curiosity concerning the light bulb she'd been attempting to change."

"Oh? What was that?"

"The bulb that was burned out was a forty watt bulb. All of the bulbs in the light, you know, were forty watters. The bulb on the floor was a sixty-watter." I thought about that a bit.

"How do you know? It was busted all to hell, excuse my French."

"I examined several of the larger pieces and noticed that one had been printed with the wattage."

"Why would she have two different wattages in those candle-flame shaped bulbs?" I wondered aloud.

"There are two wall sconces on the lanai that had the sixty watt candle flame bulbs in them."

"Then, maybe that's all she had," I ventured. He nodded.

"Just what I thought. To confirm that conclusion I looked around, searching for the place where she kept spare bulbs." He tented his hands again, resting his chin upon them.

"Well?" I prompted.

"Eventually I found spare bulbs kept in the linen closet in the hallway between the bedrooms. On the top shelf, behind some sheets. Hard to reach for someone of the decedent's size, but not impossible."

"And?" I urged. He placed his hands flat on the desk and looked me steadily in the eyes.

"There were several cartons, you know, those corrugated tubes that light bulbs come packaged in, stacked neatly behind the sheets. The neatness struck a chord with me, made me feel closer to the woman. That's what we detectives do, you know, try to place ourselves in the shoes of the victim or the perpetrator, try to make a connection. Think as they do." I had the feeling that he wasn't talking to me at all.

"So, she was neat. I have no trouble believing that about Linda Wong." He shook his head almost imperceptibly.

"The front cartons in the stack contained sixty watters. The next row contained forty watters. Behind them, there were several cartons of hundred watters and seventy-five watters. Regular bulbs, I mean." I chewed on that a moment.

"She was tired. It was maybe dark in the hallway. She was going through chemotherapy, she had cancer, for God's sake!" He nodded through my comments.

"I know, I know. Like I said, an anomaly. But there was only one light bulb burned out, there were several still burning in that fixture. If she was tired, if she didn't feel up to changing the bulb, what was the rush?" He spread his hands out in a gesture of sheer futility.

"I don't know," I told him, and I didn't. He collapsed his arms and they landed on the desk top in an ungainly heap. He gave me a tired smile.

"Well, it's probably one of those things, you know, we'll never know the exact details of what happened, but I don't think we need to read anything sinister into this."

"Will you be needing anything else from me?" I had a sudden need to escape the cubicle. Cleon Servais smiled at me as he placed the Wong folder back in the drawer.

"No, no, I think we have all we need, at least until the ME's report is issued."

"When will that be, again?" I rose from the uncomfortable side chair. He stood also, towering over me by a good three or four inches. He stuck out his hand once more.

"They're pretty backed up right now, what with it being tourist and snowbird season and all. Increased rate of death this time of year, you know, traffic, and elderly visitors. We should have the report in the next several days, week at the outside. Don't leave town." He molded his right hand, which I'd just shaken, into a pistol that pointed at me.

"I'm not goin' anywhere, Sheriff," I said in my best western drawl. His visage sobered once again.

"If I have any more questions, or if I find out anything new, I'll be in touch." I stepped out of his cubicle and headed for the lobby, passing a uniformed Deputy on the way. I crossed the lobby and exited the sub-station, squinting in the noonday southwest Florida sunlight. On the way to the Caddy I reflected on my impression of Detective Servais. Here was a man, I thought, who was dedicated to order. When a grain of sand caused an irritation to his detective's machinery, he took notice.

It was still cool, though not as cold as over the weekend, so I left the top up on the Caddy, though I did crack the window just a bit for the fresh air. On the way back to the office I drove through the, well, drive through of the local Checkers franchise. Though Checkers was mainly known for its Champ Burger, I was a big fan of their hot dogs. I ordered up a couple, of the chili-cheese variety, with onions and mustard, along with a large order of seasoned fries. I called the office to see if Jenna or Sigrid wanted anything but was informed that they had other plans for lunch.

At the office, after a cursory hello to Sigrid in passing, I grabbed a drink from the kitchen and spread one of the napkins from the sack on my desk, pushing assorted papers and a few pens to the side. I arranged my food items on the napkin and discarded the wrappers. I was an old hand at cafeteria style dining. Before I could take a bite of the aromatically enticing tube-steak, Jenna stuck her head into the office.

"Hey," she said. I paused, a chilidog inches from my mouth.

"Hey." I lowered the dog to the desktop.

"I'm going out for lunch. Might be a little longer than normal. Just wanted to let you know." I thought that I'd never seen her glossy hair hang so attractively, her short "do" framing her face and creating a pixyish sort of look.

"Oh? Where are you going?" Her left hand grasped the doorframe and the scarlet nail of her forefinger scraped at the green paint.

"I'm having lunch with Vern at IHOP." I felt myself shrink to no more than half my usual size.

"Oh," was all I could manage. She squinched her eyes and pursed her lips together. Vern Otto's head came into view behind and above hers. I closed my eyes to rid them of the hateful hallucination, but when I opened them it was still there. It was a big head. A big, ugly head, with thinning, sun bleached hair, ridiculously deep tan and obviously artificially whitened teeth.

"Hi, Roy," he said, waggling his fingers and giving me a sheepish smile. Jenna looked over her shoulder at him.

"I asked you to meet me outside." Her voice barely escaped the straining muscles of her neck and her tightly pursed lips. Vern nodded, still grinning stupidly.

"I just wanted to say hi to Roy. Haven't seen him in a while." Yeah, hadn't rubbed it in for a while.

"Hi Vern. Bye Vern." The words seemed to burn my lips and I could feel my blood pressure rising. Vern and I had once been friends. Evidently he harbored the illusion that we still were. Jenna dug into his ribs with her elbow. I knew what that could feel like. Vern recoiled and made a face.

I stood and went around the desk, the dog forgotten. I could feel the blood pounding at my temples and I wanted nothing more than to grind my fist into Vern's grinning, idiot face. Jenna was between us, and Vern started to dance and hop behind her. I feinted left and moved right but she anticipated me and blocked my move.

"Roy! Stop that."

"Yeah, Roy. I just wanted to say Hi. We're still friends, aren't we?" Vern was still moving side to side to elude my pawing efforts to reach him. Jenna kept shifting in the doorway to block me and I didn't want to hurt her, so I was stymied.

"Wait for me outside!"

"Okay, okay. See ya, Roy." He disappeared. For good, I hoped. Jenna looked at me and her eyes seemed to soften. Blood was roaring in my ears, like a seashell when you listen to the sea, and my stomach contracted in pain. Vern was gone and I was suddenly deflated, in the aftermath of a severe adrenalin rush. I felt drained and my head hurt.

"Sorry," she said. I swallowed a sharp retort and just shrugged with my face.

"Don't be." She started to say something more but stopped and looked toward the window. She leaned heavily against the doorjamb. Her big brown eyes glistened. When she looked back my way, she said: "I don't have anything important on my calendar. I should be back before I'm missed. Sigrid can reach me on my cell phone if there's any problem." Her eyes seemed to be pleading for understanding. I wasn't sure I understood the messages her body language was sending me.

"Okay," I said in a flat tone. She looked at me a moment before catching her breath in a sort of hiccup. She pushed herself off of the doorframe into an upright position.

"I guess I'll see you later. I guess," she said as she turned away and disappeared down the hall. I didn't know what had happened between us but after that exchange the chili-cheese dogs tasted like cardboard.

When I finished the corrugated lunch I reluctantly turned my attention to the files on my desk and worked industriously until I heard Jenna return sometime later. Curious, I glanced at my watch and was somewhat surprised to see that it was after three-thirty. It had seemed like an eternity since Jenna had left for lunch. I continued to work until nearly five, well, if you can count a few hard fought games of Spider as work. The office was quiet, with only Sigrid's voice occasionally carrying to me as she answered the phone. None of the calls required me to speak to anyone, though I couldn't be sure how many people Jenna had needed to talk to.

Just before five Jenna stopped by my office again and informed me that she had a meeting of one of her real estate oriented clubs to attend and that she'd made arrangements with my mother to be with the kids. She seemed breezy and relaxed. I told her that I planned to stop by The Grouper Hole for a bit and then I would be home to relieve my mother.

"So, if you have plans, don't worry about us. We'll make out all right."

"No, no, I have no plans. Just the meeting."

"Okay, then. I'll see you later at home." She smiled, a small, wicked smile.

"Yeah. At home." She was beginning to scare me. My face must have revealed some of my concern because her face cleared.

"No, really, I'll see you at home." I tried to keep my face as neutral as possible. Evidently I succeeded because she suddenly broke into a large grin and pointed her left forefinger at me.

"You da man," she said, in her best impersonation of Bobbie Jane. I was reminded of a large, maternal animal playfully consorting with her cubs. Thank you, Discovery Channel.

Chapter Twenty-Four

The Grouper Hole was waking from its afternoon lull and the bar area was starting to fill up for Happy Hour. The early birds were arriving also for the dinner specials. Those who came to eat at five or six o'clock must be the ones who were on the many area golf courses by seven a.m. More power to them. I hurried to the bar to claim a seat while there was still one available.

"Hey, Roy," Dan said. "The usual?"

"Please."

"Will you be eating tonight?"

"I'm not sure. Probably." Dan smiled at me and moved off down the bar.

After I got my drink, I swiveled on my stool and surveyed the room. I saw Barry Oatman and his wife coming in from the parking lot. They paused just inside to orient themselves before heading for one of the small tables around the perimeter of the room. I tried to catch their eye but they didn't see me as they seated themselves. I made a sign to Dan and he stopped by when he had the chance.

"Bring me another of these," I said. "I'll be right back. Don't let anyone take my seat." He gave me a thumbs up. I made my way across the barroom floor to where Repeat and Donna sat, just giving their drink order to their waitress. I said hello. Repeat seemed a bit surprised to see me.

"Hey," he said. He motioned to his wife. "Donna and I came by for dinner."

"I couldn't believe my eyes when I saw you two coming through the door. I didn't know you frequented this dive."

"Oh, yeah. We eat here sometimes. We don't usually get here early enough to have a drink before dinner so we just head right on into the dinin' room." The waitress arrived about this time and put their drinks before them. Repeat placed a twenty on the waitress's tray and she made change.

"They have really good seafood," I said, apropos of nothing.

"We love the sautéed grouper, that's why we come," Donna offered.

"Sit down," Repeat said before nibbling at the fresh fruit on a toothpick that adorned his drink. Donna was drinking white wine. "Hey, I heard about Linda Wong." I pulled out a chair and sat.

"Yeah, I'm the one who found her."

"No! I didn't hear that."

"Yep,"

"You were talkin' about her last lunch day!"

"Yeah. I went to see her in connection with the Chastain deal." Donna kind of picked up her ears at that.

"I told you about that, right?" Repeat asked his wife.

"No, I don't think so."

"About sellin' some of the Chastain land to a developer." Donna looked surprised.

"She swore it was all fixed, no one could get hold of her property for any kind of development."

"I've checked the will three ways from Sunday and nothing is mentioned about development, pro or con. She left a big hunk of her estate and executive control to her grandson, Toby," I said. "That's why I was checking with Linda, asking her to search Ralph Rennegar's old files to see if there was another, later will." Donna looked back to me.

"Ralph's been dead for years. Jack Muncie was her attorney after that." I shrugged.

"Well, Jack provided me with the will that's being probated, said it's the most recent. I even tracked down one of the witnesses, Dent Billie, her Indian caretaker and chauffer. He remembered attending some CIT-GIM meetings with her and the way she spoke against development but he didn't recall a later will."

"Hell," Donna said, "Dent don't know anything. The times he drove Alma to meetings he only came in to enjoy the air conditioning and pig out on finger food." She squinted in my direction. "Did you talk to Lontine? His wife?"

"No. Should I?"

"Of course! Lontine was more than a maid or someone who drove Alma 'round when Dent was busy. She was a member of CIT-GIM. She cared as much about it as Alma did."

"So, why do you think Linda committed suicide?" Repeat said. "The cancer?" I swiveled my head in his direction.

"Suicide?" Where'd you hear that?"

"Harry." Most everyone referred to them as Pete and Repeat but they called each other by their given names. "He said the woman who clips his dog told him, said her sister's husband's brother or somethin' was an EMT. He got it from one of the squad that took the call. Said it was awful, blood everywhere. Why?"

"It was an accident." I told him about it and he seemed disappointed that it wasn't a suicide. We sat there for a few moments more and eventually finished our drinks. Repeat started to fidget a bit and finally asked Donna if she was ready to go to the dining room. She nodded and Repeat asked if I'd like to join them.

I politely declined. We said our goodbyes and I worked my way back to my stool. I was afraid that I might have lost it to someone else but Dan had come through for me, placing a tented RESERVED sign on the bar in front of the stool along with a fresh drink. I slid into my seat and on his next pass, when he scooped up the sign, I mouthed my thanks and asked for a menu. I ordered the Rueben and fries, with extra Russian dressing on the side and extra pickles. After I finished my meal I had one more drink and mingled with the crowd for a bit, seeking out those in real estate.

It was a little before ten when I entered the house. My mother and the kids were lounging on the living room furniture, engrossed in a network crime drama. The only illumination was from the TV. I grabbed a beer from the kitchen and joined them, my recliner being empty, as no one with any sense would dare occupy it. Actually, when I entered I thought that the recliner contained a shadowy shape, but when I got back from getting the beer I saw that I'd been wrong.

When the show ended my mother gathered her medications (she didn't go anywhere without them), glasses, reading material (she liked tabloids and crossword puzzle books, she never went anywhere without them, either) into a plastic supermarket bag. The kids often teased her about being a 'bag lady.' I thanked her for her assistance and thought that we couldn't really get along without her. I packed a little extra sugar into my goodnight peck on the cheek.

The kids, all three of them, didn't move during all of this. They remained splayed across the furniture. My mother looked at them and then at me. I just shrugged. What could you do?

"They're gonna miss me when I'm gone." I stepped onto the front porch and followed her progress as she walked to her small cottage. I re-entered the house. Another, very popular, crime drama was beginning. The children's attention was glued to the tube and I settled into my recliner to watch the hour-long show with them. When it was over I began urging them toward bed, this being a school night.

After the kids were packed away to their bedrooms, I sat again in my recliner and sipped beer with the sound of the eleven o'clock local news turned low. The fires to the east had flared up again and were threatening to move closer to developed areas. Wildfires had become a problem state wide, with large areas burned or burning from Ocala on down. So far over fifteen thousand acres total and nearly two thousand acres locally had been consumed. The Governor had declared a state of emergency and water restrictions were elevated to the next level.

I only half listened to it, preferring, instead, to spend my time fantasizing about the possible antics of Jenna and Vern Otto, whom I visualized in various intimate scenarios. I didn't even consider that whatever meeting Jenna had attended, if any, had lasted this late. I was pretty sure that she'd met Vern but I couldn't conjure a reason to be as angry as I felt. After all, we were divorced, and had been for two years. She'd been seeing him for over a year. It was time to get over it! But all the rationalization in the world couldn't budge the heavy ache that permeated my very being. The beer augmented my melancholy mood and I was feeling pretty low when I heard noises at the door. I froze, listening for the slightest clue that he was accompanying her into the house, mortified that I might have to witness them climbing the stairs together to her room. I shut my eyes and hoped that the dim light and muted sound from the TV wouldn't alert them to my presence. I heard the front door close and footsteps traversed the hall.

"Roy?" I squinched my eyes tighter together. "Roy? Are you asleep?" It finally penetrated my numb brain that there had been the sound of only one person entering the house and I opened my eyes to see Jenna standing in the gloom, peering intently at me.

"Ah, oh, er, um, you're home!"

"Yes. Were you asleep?" I re-arranged myself in the recliner.

"I was dozing, I guess. Meeting run over?" I tried to keep it casual. Jenna moved past the living room and into the kitchen.

"Yeah," she called over her shoulder. "I thought it would never end. And the food was terrible. I'm hungry and thirsty and ready for bed." I rose from the recliner and followed her into the kitchen.

"Well, I don't know what the kids ate, I ate at The Grouper Hole." I opened the fridge. "Let's see what's in here."

"First off, the meeting was an hour late getting started. Then, everybody had something they wanted to talk about. And everything we talked about, there were people who were opposed and the debates went on and on." I began hauling things out of the fridge that I intended to assemble into a western omelet plus, one of my specialties and one of Jenna's favorites. As the number of ingredients grew, she settled into a chair at the table and audibly sighed. She leaned down and removed her shoes. Standing again, she reached up under her calf-length dress and tugged her pantyhose down to her knees. She sat and removed the flimsy garment completely, one leg at a time. Her eyes were closed and a beatific look graced her features. I closed the fridge and retrieved a sauté pan from under the counter. I turned on a front burner and placed the pan on it to pre-heat. I grabbed a small wooden cutting board and began preparing the ingredients.

"Then, after an endless meeting, I was cornered on my way to my car by several members who wanted to discuss, at length, their feelings about several of the issues. These people are all clients, I couldn't blow them off!" I gave her my best 'sincere' glance as I dropped some butter into the heated pan. Jenna had dropped the pantyhose in a ball in the general direction of her shoes, which she'd thrown to one side of her chair. She sat, legs spread, dress hiked up over her knees, and wiggled her toes appreciatively.

I quickly diced some sweet onion and some red bell pepper and some honey-cured ham before cracking three eggs into a bowl. I added a bit of water and beat the mixture into a frothy consistency with a fork. Then I added kosher salt, freshly ground pepper, cayenne, paprika, garlic powder, and herbs before pouring the mixture into the pan. I crumbled some cheese and placed some bread in the toaster oven. Then I ground some coffee beans and set a pot to brew.

While Jenna relaxed, I continued with my cooking. I pried the edges of the egg mixture gently from the pan, working my way around the pan several times. When it was time, I added the remaining ingredients and placed a glass lid on the pan so that the steam could tenderize the vegetables. I removed the bread from the toaster oven and buttered it while it was hot. I readied a plate and, when the eggs were bubbling up around the other ingredients, I removed the lid and folded the mixture over so that it resembled a taco in shape. I cut the toast into triangles and prepared a cup of coffee, just the way Jenna liked it, and placed these before her. Next, I slid the omelet onto the plate and set it in front of her, along with a napkin and utensils. Finally, I poured a glass of orange juice and put it and catsup on the table. Jenna liked catsup with her omelets. She favored me with a tender smile before digging into the food ravenously.

I cleaned up in the kitchen while she ate with manners suitable to a stevedore, devouring the victuals with sheer pleasure. I fixed myself a cup of coffee and sat at the table, transfixed, thoroughly enjoying her pleasure as though it were my own. Not another word was uttered until she finally leaned back, plate empty save for a few crumbs of toast, and said, "Oh, my! Just what I needed!"

I cleared away the dishes, put away the leftover ingredients and moved the pan to the sink where, I hoped, someone would wash it.

Jenna gathered her shoes and pantyhose. Her eyes were trying to close and she was struggling to stay awake. I knew the state very well; if she didn't get to bed soon, she would drop wherever she was. It happened when she was tired and full, all appetites sated.

"You head on up," I said. "I'll finish down here." There wasn't much to finish. I checked the doors and turned off the lights. Mrs. Benz was stretched out on the couch. By the time I made it upstairs, Jenna's door was closed and the house was silent. I went to my room and prepared for bed.

Chapter Twenty-Five

The rest of the week was passed in the numbing humdrum of work. Thank God! We opened more files than we had in any week in recent memory. At the end of the day I took satisfaction in being pleasantly tired. So much so that I forsook my usual evening marketing efforts at The Grouper Hole and gladly went home, where after dinner I'd fall asleep in my chair in front of the TV. I even missed the MNMC+2 luncheon on Wednesday. I made a mental note to call someone for the location of our next lunch. I was able to push the Chastain mess to the rear of my mind.

On Friday evening Jenna and I attended a political forum and listened as each of the candidates for the various new Mangrove Springs public offices told us about themselves and about their ideas for the future of the bustling community. There was a good turnout and the auditorium of the middle school was overflowing. A few of the office seekers were actually heckled by portions of the audience and what had started as a civilized effort rapidly deteriorated into something less seemly. Two of the council seat hopefuls almost came to blows over the allegation by one that the other was, under cover of night, removing the roadside signs of his opponent and replacing them with his own. We slipped out just about then, giggling, and opted for a nightcap at the Hole. We huddled at one of the small tables, heads close together, and engaged in what men and women who are married to one another usually refer to as pillow talk; things the kids did, details from work. You know, pillow talk. It felt very good and right.

Later we headed home to relieve my mother, who was watching the kids. We had a last, small drink, and headed for our separate bedrooms. Progress? I realized I hadn't thought about Vern in several days. I hoped that Jenna hadn't, either.

Just before noon the next day, a gorgeous but smoky Saturday, I sped along 41 after it had turned east, toward Miami. I was mentally kicking myself for the suspicious and stubborn nature that it was my misfortune to possess, but I drove on. Cleve was back at work on the swamp buggy and Jenna and the girls were busy cleaning house, systematically going from room to room, making sure that everything gleamed and smelled of pine.

Between Jenna, the girls and my mother, the house was maintained in passable cleanliness, but two or three times a year Jenna was seized with a compulsion to root out all traces of Demon Dirt. I had politely declined when asked to join in her crusade, citing the need to travel south to check with Dent Billie's wife, Lontine, concerning the existence of another will. I told Jenna about Donna's assertion that Lontine would know more than Dent.

I tried to explain to myself just why I couldn't let it go, why I couldn't accept the obvious fact that the will had been the right one, and get on with my business, my life. Aside from being a major distraction, my unreasonable, and, to date, futile quest was becoming expensive. The Caddy required large quantities of fuel. Not just any fuel, but the platinum plated 93-octane variety. I had to admit that basically, I was just nosy. And those claims still rankled. I knew that I was not sloppy or lackadaisical in my work, despite those liability settlements. And I would not let that happen to me again.

The parking lot of the emporium was almost full and I had to park near the eastern end, the end farthest from the cluster of buildings. Several groups of people were in the parking lot. The newly arrived seemed fresh and eager to explore a genuine Native American establishment while the departing guests seemed wind and/or sun burned, slightly disheveled and tired. The paths around the buildings and exhibits were clotted with people.

I hurried to where I expected Dent to be baiting tourist's poles with chicken pieces. There were only a couple of people on the bridge and the gators in the water below seemed paralyzed, inert masses basking in the sunlight. I quickly scanned the area and then made a more thorough search for Dent Billie's bucket carrying form. He was nowhere in sight. I looked at my watch and saw that it was just before two o'clock. I wondered if he might be taking his lunch break. I made my way to the faux Indian Chickee Hut that housed the cafeteria and cupped my eyes and leaned against the smoked glass that held the air conditioning in. About half the tables were occupied and several people were in line, but no Dent. I straightened up and looked around, trying to decide what to do next. It had never occurred to me that Dent wouldn't be at the emporium.

A figure with a short-handled broom and a dustpan on a stick caught my eye. It was the same teen-aged Indian I'd seen on my last visit, the one who had directed me to the gator feeding area. I headed toward him, feeling as if I'd spotted a long lost friend. He remained focused on the miniscule litter that he was chasing with his apparatus even after I was standing directly in front of him. He attempted to move around me, eyes still on the ground, intent on litter, oblivious to me. I realized that he probably had to ignore lots of people during a typical workday. I moved with him, blocking him once again. We did a two-step for a few seconds until I finally got his attention by saying "hey, hey!" He raised his eyes to mine and stopped trying to get around me. He pointed over my shoulder at one of the buildings.

"It's over there, sir." He lowered his eyes again and made an effort to resume his trash tracking. I didn't move.

"What's over there?"

"The restrooms. Ain't that what you wanted to know? Sir?"

"No. No, that's not what I wanted." He looked baffled, even a little bit fearful.

"Do you remember me?" I asked. He looked at me a moment before shaking his head.

"No, I don't." He began inching backward.

"I was here two weeks ago. You were sweeping, like now." He continued to inch away from me. I followed.

"I'm always sweepin'. It's my job. I see lots of people. I don't remember you."

"I asked you where Dent Billie was, remember?" He stopped his backward motion and squinched his eyes together as he tried to recall.

"Most people ask where the restrooms are. Or where to get on the airboats or get somethin' to eat. I can answer them without thinkin'." He opened his eyes wide and stared at me.

"What?"

"I remember. It was the same day it happened. We didn't hear about it 'til the next day, though." He began moving backward again.

"Hear about what?" I was getting exasperated. All I wanted to do was locate Dent Billie and pose my few pitiful questions to his wife. This guy was acting like he'd just figured out that Mr. Mustard had committed the murder in the library with the candlestick.

"The fire," he said. What was he talking about?

"What are you talking about?"

"There was a fire two weeks ago tonight. Dent's trailer burned up. Killed him and his wife. And two of their grandbabies, Burke and Cremona. Just little 'uns, two and three years old." He stopped backing up and just looked at me as if I'd somehow been responsible. I felt unable to breathe.

"That's awful!" I'd met Dent Billie the one time but felt as if I knew him well, probably because of my expertise in graphology. Now the man was gone, dead by fire, a horrible way to go. Along with his wife. And two grandchildren.

"Was it the wildfire?"

"Naw. Just a fire. Was hard on everybody. Dent was like, you know, everyone's grandfather, and Lontine always had somethin' nice to say when she was around. The little 'uns used to come here with her when she came to pick Dent up after work and they was always laughin'. That's what I remember most about 'em, the way they laughed and ran and seemed so happy, it was like joy, you know?" I was stunned and tried not to envision the small bodies writhing in agony as the flames, smoke and heat stole their lives from them.

"Were they the only grandchildren?" The boy looked down at the concrete walkway and made a half-hearted attempt to sweep up a crushed cigarette butt, probably out of habit.

"Naw," he said. "They had ten, twelve, I'd guess. Just Burke and Cremona was mostly with them on account of the problems that Monique was having. She's their youngest daughter. They'd had her when they was already gettin' old. Then she had those two babies but never married. And she was, you know, involved with the rock, like addicted, you know. She'd do anythin' for a high, a real junkie. They sure worried about her, spent a lot of money puttin' her in treatment places and all. Never seemed to work, though. Spent a lot for lawyers, too. Since they moved back here those babies was mostly with them."

"Where's the mother now?" I asked. He looked uncomprehendingly at me. "Monique. Where is she now?" He nodded his head.

"She's in jail. Over in Miami. Dade County, or somewhere. Doin' time for hookin' and dealing. Got a few years cause a her record."

"And it wasn't a wild fire?" I asked. A creepy thought was beginning to rattle around in my mind.

"The cops, the fire department cops, said it was an electric problem. The trailer was pretty old and the wiring was bad. The main breaker box, I think is what they said."

"The breaker box?" I asked.

"Yep. That's what they said. I remember." He suddenly looked at me with some interest. "You a friend of Dent's?"

"I knew him when he lived in Mangrove Springs," I fibbed, suddenly on the defensive. "If Dent and Lontine moved here recently, how come the trailer was so old?" It was a nonsensical question but I wanted to distract him from whatever thought train he'd boarded. He seemed to seriously consider it.

"I don't know," he said. "It was one that somebody else in the tribe had lived in and it was empty when they moved back here. A tribal thing."

"What do you mean?"

"Well, the Tribe owns the Reservation and the gamblin' rights to a couple casinos. There are only 'bout three thousand or so of us Seminoles left in Florida," he proudly proclaimed.

"The Tribe owns lots of land, lots of trailers and Chickee villages, and the casinos provide every member an income. When Dent and Lontine moved back, the Tribe provided 'em a place. The trailer. It was an old trailer. They got their monthly share plus the housin'. Seminole's take care of their own!"

"Do you get a share?" I asked him.

"When I turn eighteen. That's in only four months." He seemed real pleased to let me know that he was almost an adult.

"What about school?" He looked at me a little suspiciously.

"What about it?"

"Do you go?" He backed up a half a step.

"Naw. Not any more."

"How come?"

"Not necessary," he said. "I'll have my share soon, then it won't matter. Besides, it don't matter how much education a Seminole gets, can't never fit in with the white man." I suspected that he was parroting a sentiment that he'd probably heard repeatedly over his formative years. It occurred to me that he'd laugh at the Dixon family's problems, as Evan Muster put it, adapting to the changes taking place in southwest Florida these days. Native Americans knew a lot about having to adapt. I wasn't sure whether the 'share' was a boon or a hindrance to his people. Likewise, I wasn't sure that 'adapting', and getting our share, would be good for the Dixons. I nodded agreement and he relaxed a bit.

"Do you think that the fire was an accident?" He suddenly got a little wary, casting his gaze about and licking his lips.

"Well, the fire cops said it was, but I know they probably don't want to waste too much time on it. Seminoles bein' involved and all." He suddenly recalled who he was talking to and stammered something about not meaning anything by that, it was just a joke among Indians. I held up my hands and told him it was all right.

"But what do you think?" He shook his head slowly from side to side.

"Don't know. Most likely were an accident, bad wiring and such, but man, to think about them babies dyin' that way. And old Dent and Lontine. They was so nice." He looked so forlorn that I offered my hand to him.

"My name's Roy Dixon," I said. He looked me in the eye for a moment before grabbing my hand with his.

"Ernest," he said as he pumped my hand for all it was worth. "Ernest Osceola. I'm descended from the great chief." When we let go, my hand fell to its natural position by my side but he raised his and, with a mischievous gleam in his glittering brown eyes, said "How." That seemed to tickle him no end and he giggled softly. I chuckled along with him.

"Well, Ernest, it's been good talking with you. It's too bad that it had to be under such sad circumstance." His face resumed its gloomy countenance and the giggles faded away.

"Yeah."

"You really ought to think twice about school, you know? It CAN make a difference in your life." I smiled gently to let him know that I was returning his joke to him. "Even for a Seminole." He studied my face a moment before he beamed a 100-watt smile at me.

"Sure, dude, sure." He lowered the dustpan on a stick and began to once again chase minute bits of litter across the concrete walk. I turned and headed for the parking lot. The Caddy started right up and I turned the air conditioning up full blast.

The tragic and apparently accidental loss of Dent Billie and his wife and their two grandchildren was bad enough in its own right. When added to the apparently accidental death of Linda Wong, the atmosphere of accidental death congealed into a cloud of uncertainty that hovered over the Chastain deal. I was probably being paranoid, but my behind was on the line, monetarily speaking. Though, I was quick to recognize, Linda and the Billie's had suffered far more than I was likely to. But what would happen, I wondered, if I were to mention to Cleon Servais my fear that the deaths were somehow connected? He'd probably, and rightly, assume that I was delirious. There was, after all, nothing to indicate that the tragedies had been anything but a series of unrelated accidents. Nothing but an anomaly. I sped north on Rte. 29, my brain roiling with unlikely thoughts.

Chapter Twenty-Six

Saturday evening Jenna, Cleve, Bobby Jane and I, attended a concert given by Rae's school Orchestra. After, we treated ourselves to ice cream at the 'Shoppe' next to the local multiplex cinema. The concert was good but I was feeling too down to properly enjoy it. I think I successfully hid my mood from the kids but several times during the evening I caught Jenna giving me a puzzled look. Later, after the kids were in bed and we were sharing a small pot of aromatic coffee at the kitchen table, she asked what was wrong. I told her about the fire that had claimed the lives of Dent, Lontine, Burke and Cremona.

"That's awful!" She set her cup down and looked at me with eyes wide open.

"Yeah, it's pretty lousy."

"And two young grandchildren?" I nodded and told her about Monique, the children's mother.

"Jesus!" She reached over and covered my hand with her own. "No wonder you've been acting so strange. How horrible!"

"It's all so senseless. First Linda Wong and now this." She applied a bit of pressure to my hand.

I took my other hand, warm from the coffee cup, and draped it over our entwined hands and returned her pressure. I looked into her eyes and she looked back for what seemed like a full minute but was probably considerably less than that. I was the first to look away, unsure whether I should mention my fear that the deaths could somehow be connected.

Jenna stood and began to clear away the coffee things. I took the hint and made the rounds of the first floor, turning out lights and locking the doors, something I still resented having to do.

Sunday we spent a family day at the crowded Mangrove Springs public beach, playing in the surf and lathering ourselves with SPF 30 sun block. We had a lunch of cold sandwiches and cold drinks from a wheeled cooler that didn't wheel too well in the sand. The depression slowly lifted.

Monday morning I called Ollie. He was in and had time to see me, so I hurried on over. His secretary announced me and then ushered me into his private office. She withdrew and quietly closed the door behind her. Ollie leaned his not inconsiderable bulk back in a huge, padded brown leather chair, hands clasped across his middle.

"Roy! Twice within a matter of days you have sought my advice and counsel. I am always glad to entertain you, my friend, but it is curious, don't you think?" I just loved the way Ollie talked. "Sit down, sit down." He motioned to one of two club chairs arranged before his massive oak desk. I settled into one and glanced at the Remington prints that adorned the oak paneling. The thick rust colored carpet was freshly vacuumed, as indicated by the telltale tracks of the sweeping machine. Barrister type cases, with glass fronts, filled with an eclectic assortment of books, took up most of two walls.

"Ollie, you know I wish I had more time to visit with you. But when I'm busy, when Mason Dixon is busy, it's hard to get away."

"We're in the middle of the busy season," he said, a small grin tugging at the corners of his mouth. "Aside from that, I know what you mean." I decided to get to the point, as I never seemed to fare too well when verbally sparring with Ollie.

"I'm still uneasy about the Chastain deal." I held up my hands as if to ward off attack. "I know, the will was probated and at first blush everything seems in order." I paused, not knowing how to continue.

"But?" Ollie prompted, leaning forward to cross his arms on the desk. The big brown chair creaked slightly.

"But," I repeated. "There are, ah, anomalies."

"Anomalies?" he asked.

"Yeah, anomalies. That's what Detective Servais called them."

"Servais. He's a good man." Did he know everyone? As if to answer my unspoken question, he continued. "He investigated a burglary of one of my businesses a few months ago. Very organized, methodical."

"Found the burglar, huh?" Ollie smiled at me.

"No. But he was able to find out who didn't do it and that was just as important because then the insurance company had no reason not to pay the claim."

I told Ollie all that had happened since I'd met him for lunch at Boston Charlie's. I told him about my meeting with Servais, what Donna Oatman had told me about Lontine Billie, and of my trip to see Dent and Lontine. I told him what I'd learned about their deaths and the deaths of their two grandchildren on the night of the day that I'd first visited Dent. When I was finished I leaned back in the chair and waited for Ollie's reaction.

He remained motionless for a few moments; eyes closed, lips working in a way that reminded me of a baby sucking at a pacifier, though I'd never tell him that. He opened his eyes and reached for the phone on his desk.

"Would you bring a club soda please? And a diet cola?" He looked at me for confirmation. I nodded. "Thank you." He replaced the receiver in its cradle and leaned back again. He closed his eyes and remained motionless until Rhonda, the secretary, knocked and entered bearing a small tray she held head high on her bent wrist like a waitress. She crossed the rust colored carpet and briefly rested the tray on the corner of the desk while she placed coasters, drinks and napkins before us. The coasters were thick cork on teak, the glasses appeared to be lead crystal and the napery was fine linen whose color matched the carpet. She was a trim blonde, about twenty-five or so, wearing a flowery dress cut low enough to exhibit some breathtaking cleavage when she bent over the desk, and cut short enough to reveal nicely dimpled knees and four inches of thigh. She removed the tray and left the room, gently closing the door behind her. Ollie picked up his glass of club soda and regarded the bubbles a moment before draining three quarters of it in one noisy quaff. I took a sip of my cola.

"Anomalies seem to abound in this affair," he said, after patting his lips with the napkin.

"What do you mean?" He reclined once again and thought a moment longer before looking at me intently.

"Anomaly one. Jack Muncie calls to have you do the search and exam and write the policy." I shrugged.

"That's because he had to be out of town and he couldn't meet the deadline imposed by the contract."

"Nonsense. He'd had the contract for some time before he passed it on to you, certainly long enough to complete the necessary work. Muncie is, after all, engaged in the business of selling title insurance, among other things. The policy fee is large enough in this case as to be a compelling reason for him to keep the work in house. I hear he definitely could use the money."

"What are you saying?"

"Anomaly two. You almost immediately are enticed into the bed of Muncie's wife." I sat up straight and made a sound of protest.

"Wait a minute, wait a minute. I was under the influence of an ocean of vodka and can't be held accountable for that. Hell, I couldn't even consummate the affair."

"No matter. There was intent. On both sides. You have to ask yourself why." I started to point out that just maybe I was a highly desirable commodity to women in general and to Rita Muncie in particular, but he hastened on.

"Anomaly three. You find out that Alma Chastain had been virulent in her assertions to members of CIT-GIM that she'd taken steps to make it impossible for developers to get hold of any more Chastain land."

"Well, the deal was brought up at lunch and a couple of the guys wives were involved with CIT-GIM. Hey, you told me yourself that Alma was reluctant to sell any land that was to be used for development." He nodded.

"Anomaly four. Dent Billie and his family die in a fire just after he talks to you concerning the deal."

"Aha!" I said. "The next thing was Linda Wong's death. By accident, I might add."

"That was the next thing you learned about but we now know that the trailer fire preceded that event." I had to admit he was right. "Linda Wong's death was anomaly five." I tried to follow his reasoning.

"Yeah. Then there was the light bulb thing, the next anomaly." He shook his head.

"That was an anomaly within an anomaly, if you will. It served only to highlight anomaly five, Linda's death." I thought about the chain of events for a moment, seeing the logic of Ollie's trail of anomalies but not able to connect the dots.

"But what does it mean?" I asked him. "It's a series of coincidences and I can't see any obvious connection, even though it feels like there should be."

"That's anomaly six," Ollie said.

"How's that?"

"A series of unexplained and seemingly unconnected coincidences which nevertheless seem to be pointing toward, indeed facilitating, a certain conclusion. In this case, a sale of real estate involving a large sum of money." He sipped at his drink and I thought about the word picture that he'd just painted.

"Do you think it means anything?"

"I don't know," he said.

We talked a few moments more, looking for a way to make sense of all the 'anomalies,' but failed to reach any conclusions. Eventually, I finished my drink and stood to go. Ollie rose and accompanied me to the door.

"You know," he said. "It could mean that someone is killing people and making it look like accidents in order to make a multi-million dollar deal go through that shouldn't." He looked very solemn.

"I know. It's very farfetched, but possible." He just nodded. We stood a moment more before Ollie reached for the handle of the door.

"Well, um, I'll see you later."

"Yes," he said. I headed for the outer door and exited.

Before leaving the parking lot of the strip mall that housed Ollie's office I punched up the number of the Sheriff's office on my cell phone. I asked for Detective Servais and was immediately put through.

"Hello?"

"Hello, this is Roy Dixon. I have some information that may prove interesting. And I wanted to talk to you about Linda Wong," I began. "Have you received anything from the Medical Examiner yet on her death?"

"Yes, yes I have. I received the Official Report on Friday. Death by Misadventure. An accident. No foul play suspected. Why? Have you learned anything to indicate something different?"

"I'm not sure."

"What's that mean?"

I told him that I'd gone to see Alma Chastain's chauffer in an effort to verify her last will and testament. He brushed that aside somewhat impatiently.

"Yes, yes, that's what led you to ask Linda Wong to check the records of her deceased boss, what's his name?"

"Ralph Rennegar," I provided.

"Yes. So what else?"

"Tell me, what exactly did the ME's report say."

"Her neck was broken. Not inconsistent with her particular fall. In fact, the ME seems to think that the broken neck was the cause of death, not that it matters."

"Oh, it matters, alright." I was surer than ever that foul play was involved with Linda Wong's death. And Dent Billie's. And his wife's. And grandbabies. I was convinced we were dealing with a homicidal maniac.

"What are you talking about?"

"Well, there's a lot more than you know about!" I filled him in on the facts surrounding the trailer fire. Then I led him through the litany that Ollie had outlined for me.

"And what do you think all of that means?"

"I think someone is killing people connected to the Chastain will and trying to make the deaths appear accidental!"

"Let's look at this from a detective's perspective. A detective looks for certain things when evaluating whether a crime has been committed. Motive is the first of them. Why would someone commit these murders, if indeed that is what they are?"

"CIT-GIM," I said. "Or, more accurately, to free the land from constraints placed upon it by the real will so that it could be sold for a large sum of money. Several people swear that Alma Chastain was adamant about protecting her land from development. The people who are now dead could possibly testify to the existence of another will."

"What about the kids?"

"Collateral damage." Just using that unfeeling term caused a fluttering in my stomach. "They were in the wrong place at the wrong time."

"You said that the Indian, what was his name?"

"Dent Billie."

"Yes, Dent Billie. You said that you spoke with him and he couldn't remember another will?"

"He couldn't when I talked to him. Maybe after he spoke with his wife he did. Donna, my friend's wife, said that she was more likely to know something anyway."

"Hmm." I thought maybe I was making some headway toward convincing him.

"Maybe neither one of them remembered anything but the killer knew that they MIGHT and couldn't take a chance," I said. He was quiet a moment.

"Alright, what about means? Or opportunity? Just who do you suspect is responsible for these deaths?" It was my turn to think for a while.

"Toby Chastain. Or Jack Muncie. Maybe both of them.

"Toby Chastain is the scion of a local family of prominence and Jack Muncie is a respected attorney. You want me to believe that they, singly, or working in concert, are somehow responsible for these deaths? That they committed serial murder for monetary gain? When the will was deemed authentic and entered into Probate and you, yourself, could find no evidence that another will ever existed?" His calm and analytical manner dampened my fervor.

"There could have been another will in Rennegar's files," I said, a little less confidently. "That's why Linda had to be done away with. Or another will had been prepared by Muncie and he's now suppressing it. Either scenario may be the reason that Dent and Lontine had to go. I don't know, you're the detective. I just think something's wrong with this picture. Don't you?" I ended on a feeble note. Another silence.

"I think you have an active imagination, Roy. But I promise you that I will think about the situation. Maybe check into the fire at the Billies'. Do some detecting. If I find that there is anything to detect, I'll give you a call." I caught no hint that he was patronizing me. That made me feel somewhat better and I let out the air that I'd been holding in my lungs.

"I appreciate it. I hope I didn't sound too hysterical but I didn't know what to do, what to say. I don't have any experience with this kind of thing, although in my job I sometimes feel like a detective, you know, tracking down documents and past actions by people who are just faded signatures to me, but never anything this real, or deadly before." I was rambling and audibly snapped my jaw shut. I could feel myself reddening.

Oh well, I thought, the worst that could happen was that I'd end up feeling like a colossal fool and the best that could happen was that a killer or killers would be brought to justice. Unfortunately, nothing could restore life to Linda, Dent, Lontine, Burke and Cremona.

As I headed back to the office I had the feeling that someone was watching me.

Chapter Twenty-Seven

He had pulled off the narrow country road onto the sandy shoulder where he sat, truck running, as he watched the long dirt lane that led to the old cracker house. He had to devise some way to accomplish what he had come here for but for the life of him he couldn't come up with a plan. He drummed his fingers on the steering wheel as a hot breeze tinged with the smell of smoke blew through the open windows.

He was in the shade of some tall gumbo-limbo trees and, though he could see the house, he thought that anyone up there would have difficulty seeing him. Which was a good thing. It might take some time to figure this out.

There was no traffic, though he stayed alert for any sound or movement, as he thought furiously in a vain attempt to come up with a plan. He was aware almost immediately of the figure coming around the corner of the house and shuffling down the drive with a labored gait, toward the road. Toward him!

He ducked low in the seat, maintaining his view through the spokes of the steering wheel, as the figure came slowly closer, head down, moving painfully. He stiffened a bit as recognition set in. He whipped his head around and surveyed the road, first in one direction, then the other. Not a vehicle in sight. There wasn't another house for at least a half a mile in either direction.

He returned his eyes to the figure of the elderly woman and watched as she finally reached the road and went to the mailbox. She struggled a bit with the door and he took one more look around. Up the road, down the road, along the drive to the house – he could see nothing moving, no sign of any other people about to witness what he had suddenly decided to do.

He sat up straighter and eased the shift lever into gear. He let the truck roll slowly onto the pavement; he didn't want to leave tire tracks. He watched CSI like everybody else. A quiet chuckling burbled from his throat and it was all he could do to keep from screaming his delight that the fates had favored him on this day.

On the pavement, still nearly a hundred feet from the woman who had her back to him as she fumbled with the mail, he mashed the accelerator to the floor and held the wheel tightly with both hands, the old ten and two position, as taught in driver's ed. The truck lurched forward and picked up speed as he threw his head back and let out with a squeal of sheer pleasure.

She took a step backward into the road and closed the mailbox door before turning to make the long trip back to the house. As she looked up the truck was upon her and she had a second of recognition. Her eyes widened and her mouth opened but she didn't have time for anything else.

He saw the sudden panic in her eyes and felt the crunching thud as the truck collided with her frail body. She was driven in a high arc, end over end, much the same as a football kicked for a field goal, and he removed his foot from the gas to allow her to fall to the road in front of him. He needed to be sure.

She came down hard, rolling and bouncing along the narrow blacktop, a storm of mail fluttering about. He accelerated again and felt first the front tires and then the rear bounce over her mangled form. As he roared away he looked in the mirror and watched as she rolled to a stop, head crushed, limbs askew, blood everywhere, and he laughed with the joy of it. He thought himself to be one lucky fellow; not everyone enjoyed his work so thoroughly.

Chapter Twenty-Eight

Sigrid was clacking furiously at her keyboard, the telephone receiver gripped between her jaw and shoulder, and she was shouting at whomever was on the other end that she needed a payoff figure NOW, the closing was already in PROGESS! She lifted her eyes in my direction and nodded as much as the arrangement with the phone would allow. Then she rolled her eyes in frustration and returned her attention to said instrument.

"NO, I do NOT want to hold for Mr. Vaughn! He couldn't help me before when I talked with him last." Even in my agitated state I admired her forcefulness, and felt a bit sorry for the person on the other end. I had no doubt whatsoever that she'd end up getting the info she wanted. I headed down the hallway to the right of Sigrid's desk, intending to tell Jenna everything about my talks with Ollie and Detective Servais.

As I approached the closing room on that side of the building I heard elevated voices coming from within. I stopped so I could see through the glass of the door. Jenna was standing at the head of the closing table with several people seated around her. One man was waving his hands about and bellowing at her, his florid face contorted into a mask of hate. The others looked at their clasped hands on the table or at the sheaf of papers before them, anywhere but at the wildly gesticulating fellow who seemed to be on the verge of apoplexy. Jenna stood, back erect, face molded into a mask of pleasantry, as the fellow vented his anger and frustration. I wanted to barge into the closing room and let the man know that he couldn't speak to my wife, er, ex-wife, in that fashion, no matter how upset he was. I quickly canned that impulse. I knew from vast experience that Jenna would deal with the situation expertly and professionally, politely yet firmly deflecting the anger and damping his temper. She could charm a whole roomful of disgruntled buyers, sellers, and prima donna real estate types, defusing any possibly explosive situation, leaving all participants thankful that they'd closed their real estate deal at Mason Dixon. I kicked myself mentally for even coming this way. Sigrid had said that a closing was in progress. I'd been so eager to tell my tale to Jenna that I'd missed that. I continued on to my corner office.

I sat at my desk, fidgeting, waiting for Jenna to be done. About twenty minutes later I heard Jenna enter the room just up the hall and the copier started its whirring ways a few seconds later. I knew that she was making copies of all the pertinent papers for each of the participants in the closing and decided that I should wait to speak to her until the closing was completely, well, closed. The copier whirred for a while and then I heard Jenna's footsteps receding. I leaned forward over the big desk and riffled through the assorted piles of paper, not looking for anything in particular, just needing to do something. Talking to Jenna is what I really wanted to do.

I began looking through the various scraps of paper scattered about the broad desk top, the notes I'd written to myself, the notes from Jenna about pending files, from Sigrid asking for direction on several files. Several slips of paper were protruding from the edges of the desk calendar that covered a large portion of my desktop, and I lifted it in an attempt to corral all of them. To my surprise, there were several phone message slips that had become entrapped beneath the blotter.

I gathered them all to me and began leafing through them. There was a message concerning a file that I'd successfully dealt with a month before. There were several others that were related to pending deals, all of which I was aware. There were several cryptic messages in pencil from Sigrid that I could not assign to any particular deal, but which I was sure had been dealt with. Likewise a handful from Jenna. But there was one that shook me from head to toe. A message from Dent Billie, dated two days after I'd first driven to the Emporium and spoken to him, two days after I'd witnessed him, full of life, attaching chicken parts to cane poles so that the tourists could experience the thrill of a snapping gator up close and personal. One that simply informed me that he and his wife wished to speak to me because he'd mentioned my visit to her and they remembered something that might help me.

I was stunned. How had I missed that particular message? And what did it mean? What had Dent and Lontine remembered? Did they remember a will different from the one that was being probated? Had that remembrance caused their deaths? And that of the children? I was chilled even though my feverish imagination was working overtime. WAS a mass murderer at work here? If so, it was only a short mental step to the conclusion that I, and subsequently my family, was also in danger. I fetched up short of outright panic and reminded myself that all was speculation to this point. Sure, there were a number of coincidences that one could interpret any way one wished, but there was a dearth of proven facts to support such suspicions. With that thought I was able to calm myself down a bit. I leaned back in the big chair and tried to hurry the closing by sheer strength of will. Then it struck me. The message was dated two days after I'd talked with Dent at the Emporium! But the Indian kid had told me that the fire had occurred the night of the day I'd visited Dent. What was going on? I quickly stifled the irrational thought that Dent Billie had reached out to me from beyond the grave. Sigrid had filled out the message slip. I gathered it up and hurried to her desk where, I was relieved to see, she was off the phone and straightening the items on her desktop. I laid the slip on the desk before her and tried to keep my voice calm.

"Sigrid, do you remember taking this message?" She looked at it and wrinkled her brow a moment as she tried to recall. Then her face cleared and she pushed the slip back toward me.

"Yah." I waited but she didn't elaborate.

"And?" I prompted.

"And what?" She looked sharply at me.

"And when did you take this message?" I struggled to remain calm.

"Well, I really didn't take it, not really."

"But you just said you remembered it!"

"Yah. But I wrote it down for you after listening to it on the machine." I was uncomprehending.

"What?"

"It was on the answering machine on..." she looked at the slip again and then at her desk calendar. "Mmm, a Monday, so the message was left on the machine sometime over that weekend. I listened to it and then I wrote it down for you. That is why you have it now. Are you just now seeing it?" Her look said that she didn't approve of work habits that would allow that to happen.

"No. No, I just wondered when it was received, that's all." I picked up the pink slip, turned and walked slowly toward my office.

"Yah, it came from the machine. You can ask me anytime for something I can tell you."

So, Dent must have gone home and told Lontine of my visit and one or both of them thought of something that they felt was important enough to call me about right away. A few hours later they were dead. I sat in my chair and pondered the situation until I finally heard the closing breaking up. Voices in the lobby were polite, exchanging pleasantries, all hints of animus gone. The closing party slowly dissolved and at last there were only the voices of Jenna and Sigrid, congratulating each other for a job well done and bitching about the unreasonable demands of the demented.

I hurried to the lobby and hustled Jenna toward my office, shushing her objections and motioning for Sigrid to remain behind her desk. I gently pulled Jenna down the hallway to my office where I closed the door after us.

"Goodness!" she exclaimed, totally misreading my actions. A small, sexy smile played about the corners of her mouth. "What's going on, He-man?" He-man was her love-play name for me.

"Listen," I hissed at her, anxious for her to understand me. "I think that a killer is at work in the Chastain deal." I knew what I must have sounded like but I was sure that I could convince her when I started explaining what I knew and what I believed.

"What?" she said, still in a horseplay mode. "What do you mean?" She giggled, a bit of uncertainty creeping into her voice. I crossed my arms and tried to present a calm and reasoned argument.

"There are too many anomalies," I began.

"What?" she said.

"Anomalies, you know, things out of the ordinary." I reminded her of the problem with the light bulb that Detective Servais had pointed out and then recited to her the list that Ollie had led me through. When she'd digested those, I introduced her to the fact of Linda's broken neck. Then I showed her the message slip and explained how Dent had tried to reach me just hours before he died. When I'd finished Jenna sat in my chair with a look of stunned surprise on her face.

"Well?" I asked. She stared at the hands folded in her lap a moment before lifting her eyes to mine.

"Well, what?"

"Well, what do you think now?" I was sure that she'd see the same pattern that I had. Namely, that there was a killer on the rampage.

"I don't know." She said. "I suppose someone could be behind the deaths." She looked uncertainly at me. "A killer."

"What else could it be?" She sucked her lower lip into her mouth and my heart melted.

"I don't know. Maybe a coincidence?"

"Do you really think all of this is due to a coincidence?" She looked me in the eyes.

"I don't know," was all she said. I stood up and paced back and forth in front of the desk. "There are too many coincidences."

"We got the check today."

"What check?"

"The check for the Chastain deal." I yanked myself out of the gruesome reverie I'd been engaged in.

"We got the check?"

"Yeah. Rita Muncie dropped it off about lunchtime. Along with the paperwork." I winced. I hoped Jenna hadn't noticed. She continued as if she hadn't.

"She said the deal was closed and they'd appreciate it if we could send out the policy as soon as possible." She paused but seemed as if she wanted to say more.

"Yeah?" I prodded.

"And I told her we would. Send out the policy, that is. And I sent it." Usually there was a lag time of two or three weeks after a closing before we executed a policy. We generally did policies in batches, once or twice a month, depending on how busy we were.

"That was quick," I noted. Jenna looked at me with an almost pleading attitude.

"Look," she began. I gave her my full attention and she hesitated briefly, lowering her eyes from mine.

"What?" I asked, trying to help her with whatever she had to say.

"Can't we just take the money and let the other stuff go? Besides, what else can you do? Where do you want to take it from here?"

"Well, I can check out the other witness on Alma's will, the one that was entered into probate. And maybe warn them."

"Who was that? Didn't you already check them out?" I shook my head.

"No. I checked out Dent because I thought I knew something about him."

"So, who was the other witness?"

"I don't remember." I walked behind the desk and retrieved a photocopy of the Chastain will from a drawer. I flipped to the last page and laid it on the desk in front of us. I used a forefinger to track down the page to the acknowledgements and, skipping over Dent's signature line, placed my fingertip just below the signature of the other witness. Jenna and I looked at each other.

"Iselda Driggers," Jenna said. "Do you know her?" I shook my head.

"No, no, I don't think so." Jenna reached for the phone book I kept in a bottom desk drawer and flipped through the white pages before stopping at one and running her finger slowly down the page. She removed her finger and closed the book.

"No Driggers. Not in Mangrove Springs, anyway. Could be anywhere in Lee County. Or Collier County, for that matter."

Chapter Twenty-Nine

When the afternoon crawled to a close we locked the place up for the day. I didn't feel much like marketing so I followed the Taurus home. Jenna was going to throw together a chicken and noodle and something casserole for dinner. Thank God for condensed cream soups: mushroom, chicken, celery, asparagus, whatever. You could whip up some mighty fine meals with any of those. I decided, after being shooed from the kitchen and shushed in the living room, to take a walk around the camp. The sun was still up but low in the western sky over the bay.

I circled the camp in a counter clockwise direction. Several Dixon children were playing, waiting to be called for dinner, and a couple of cousins waved a greeting as they laid fires in their grills. Soon the smells and sounds of sizzling meat would tease and tantalize those who waited. The eastern end of the compound, near where the chicken pit had existed briefly, was home to the young singles of the clan. Here among scattered singlewide trailers were shirtless and shoeless young males and t-shirted and shoeless young females lounging in lawn chairs and at picnic tables under sheet metal carports drinking beer and swapping lies. A few had drug out their grills as well. As I circled by them on the main shell road running around the camp some waved and called my name or offered beer. I smiled and waved and declined. Several dogs stretched out among the weeds surrounding the trailers couldn't quite bring themselves to get up to investigate the intruder and instead snuffled and growled half-heartedly to let everyone know they were on the job.

Twenty minutes or so of leisurely walking brought me back around to the bay and I found myself in front of Lemuel and Chili's house. The veranda was in deep shadow from the wide overhang but I thought I could see some movement there. I moved closer and was able to make out Aunt Chili rocking serenely in her chair. Lemuel's rocker was still and empty beside her. I waved.

"Hi, Aunt Chili." She slowed to a stop and peered at me from the gloom of the porch.

"I can see ya but not good enough to know ya," she said. I stepped closer.

"It's me, Aunt Chili. Roy."

"Callie's boy. Shoulda knowed by the voice. Gettin' old, I reckon." She started her rocker up again. "Come on up and sit a spell. Right time a day for it." She was right. The sun was more interested in the horizon than in torturing us, and a cooling breeze was skipping in from over the bay. I climbed the stairs to the veranda and stepped around Chili to drop my bulk in Lem's chair.

"Where's Uncle Lem?"

"He's come to prefer a nap about this time a day." We rocked in silence for a while, watching as the sun started sinking like he had urgent business elsewhere.

"I always felt a mite sorry for ya, boy." Startled, I looked at Chili.

"Why?" She rocked a moment more before answering.

"Seems every boy ought to know who his daddy is, even if he can't know him personal." She looked at me. "I always thought that somebody ought to tell ya."

"You know who he was, er, is?"

"Naw, Callie wouldn't tell nobody. Real pig headed that way." She looked my way again. I blew out a breath and relaxed.

"It doesn't matter, Aunt Chili. I'm not sure she even knows."

"A woman always knows the daddy of her children. Less, of course, she, your Momma I mean, was messed up on those Hippie drugs they were always talkin' bout then." I laughed gently at the confusion in her old voice.

"Now, that could be from what I hear. They say Callie was a real wild child in her day." She smiled and rocked.

"Now, what's botherin' ya, son?" I was caught off guard by that one.

"What do you mean?"

"Somethin's botherin' ya, I can hear it in your voice. What is it?"

With a sigh I started my tale of woe, beginning with the divorce, at which she frowned a bit, then Jenna's relationship with Vern. I told her about the unusual lunch meeting.

"Ya say she had lunch with him?"

"Yes'm."

"And she don't usually?"

"Yes'm, I mean no Ma'am."

"Don't think ya be needin' to worry about that problem no more." I asked her what she meant, but she wouldn't say. I continued my tale. I told her about the lack of cash flow with Mason Dixon and the seeming salvation of the Chastain deal. She frowned some more at the news that Chastain land was being sold for development. Then I got into the suspicious deaths, including those of the children, and my current efforts to track down the other witness, Iselda Driggers.

"Iselda Driggers? Haven't heard that name in a spell." I perked up at that.

"You know her?"

"Lord, yes. She was a Marchand. Married a Driggers from Tampa, there were a mess of 'em, used to come here on fishin' trips and raise Cain. Iselda always handled the charter reservations for 'em. Course, none of the Marchand's ever come down here." My interest was piqued.

"Well, can you tell me where she is? It could be important," I said.

"Zel moved away," she said.

"Moved? Where? Do you know where she moved to?" I thought I'd found her and now I may have lost her again. My head began to ache with futility.

"Up around La Belle somewhere."

"Why did she move up there?"

"Danny Driggers, that was Zel's husband, brought her to Mangrove Springs in the fifties. He met her in La Belle when he was workin' on a road buildin' project up there and they was married. Then he came here to work for the Southwest Florida Quarries drivin' a dump truck haulin' crushed rock. They bought a place over on Hidalgo Street and lived there right until he died. He'd been retired for quite a while, of course, and he had his hobbies and she had hers." I just listened as Chili related the whole story to me. There probably wasn't anything I could have done to speed her up anyway.

"Well, she got to know Alma early on, they belonged to the same garden club, and she agreed with Alma 'bout developers ruinin' the place. Course, she and Alma didn't think that way the whole time, they just got tired of seein' what was happenin' round here. They started that club or whatever it was."

"CIT-GIM?" I asked.

"Yeah, that's it."

"When did she move back to La Belle?"

"Well, after Danny died, his heart ya know, he had a triple bypass a few years back. Zel was real active in her garden club and that other thing, CIT-GIM?"

"Yes'm."

"It seemed as if they were all she had. What with Danny's family up around Tampa and her relatives all secluded up there around La Belle, she was real lonely, had a lot of time each day to eat up."

"What do you mean, secluded," I asked.

"What?" Chili sounded a bit confused at being interrupted.

"You said that the Marchand family was secluded up around La Belle. What did you mean?" I asked as gently as I could manage. There was a pause before she continued.

"Oh. Her family was in some Fundamentalist Religion, real Central Florida, if ya know what I mean. Didn't believe in the comforts of modern life. Thought they were the work of the Devil, don't ya know? Sort of like them Amish up north. Zel said she'd rather die than live that way."

"So how did she end up going back there if she disliked it so much?"

"She got cancer. She didn't have nobody else to look after her in her sickness so one day an uncle or somethin', along with a couple of young kids to help with the movin', drove a flatbed truck and a farm trailer down to get her. She'd been writin' back and forth with them since Danny had died. They loaded her and her stuff up and headed back for La Belle. Some Realtor," Chili looked at me. "Ya probably know who, handled the sale of her home and I haven't heard from her since, though she promised to write."

"How long ago was that?"

"That was, let's see, bout 6 months, now."

"You haven't heard from her since?"

"No."

"The Marchand's are farmers?"

"Yep, real basic, back to the land types. Zel told me that besides truck farmin' they were beekeepers. They said that was the most natural way they could earn money. To pay taxes, buy the things they couldn't make or grow."

"Beekeepers?"

"Yep. For the honey. They harvest it and sell it to some honey company in La Belle. It's big business around there. They say La Belle bees make real good honey." We spoke a while longer about the Drigger's and the Marchand's but I didn't learn any more of consequence. When the conversation wound down we just sat there in the gathering gloom.

"Did ya mean what ya said?" Aunt Chili finally offered.

"What was that?" She cast a plaintive look in my direction.

"Ya know, 'bout not sellin' the family land?"

"I meant it," I said with some conviction. "I'll never agree to sell Dixon land!"

"Good, good. I thought I could count on ya." We sat a few more minutes watching as the sun disappeared beyond the rim of the horizon with a spectacular showing of fiery reds, golds, purples, yellows and blues. A screen door creaked and Uncle Lemuel appeared yawning and scratching on the veranda.

"What, we got comp'ny?" he wanted to know. I hastily stood from his chair and came around to the other side of Aunt Chili.

"It's Roy, Callie's boy. Came by to say hello." She gave me an elaborate wink that was as safe as could be because Lem's vision was as bad as her own. After the pleasantries I headed toward home. The last of the sun's rays were sparkling across the bay, leaving trails of shining iridescence lingering in the deepening purple. When I reached our house the savory aroma of chicken, noodles and whatever wafted across the twilight and tickled my nose.

Chapter Thirty

The morning television news was full of the wildfire story, reporting that the fires had broadened across the Everglades and spread westward until they were dangerously close to developed areas. Several thousand acres were now charred in southwest Florida and smoke was becoming a problem along the interstate. Fire fighters were working frantically to cut firebreaks. Water and fire retardants were being dropped on the fast moving flames by the helicopters and airplanes usually used to deliver mosquito control chemicals. The fires were spreading up and down the peninsula and additional firefighting assets were coming in from at least four neighboring states.

At the office I said a brief hello to Sigrid and went directly to the title plant where I logged onto the Internet. La Belle was the County Seat of Hendry County. I did a Google search and found a web site for the Hendry County Clerk of the Circuit Court. I clicked on the link and after a few moments the site came up. It was an animated work crew, hammering and sweeping, beneath a banner that read 'Under Construction.' A blurb at the bottom of the screen noted that the site was projected to be up and running in three weeks. So much for my bright idea of finding Marchand property via public records. Long distance, at any rate.

"What's that mean?" Jenna had come into the plant to see what I was doing.

"Means I have to go to La Belle to find Zel Driggers." I'd told her of the conversation with Chili.

"Aren't there phone listings on the internet somewhere?" I nodded, feeling like a dummy, and ran a search for the La Belle telephone directory. When I had it I searched for Marchand's. Nothing.

"Still means I have to go to La Belle." Neither Jenna nor I could think of any other possibility so I shut the computer down, waiting until Bill Gates told me it was safe before I cut the power.

It was about sixty miles to La Belle and I figured an hour and a half one way, tops. I stood and looked Jenna in the eye.

"You sure you're okay with this?" She nodded bravely, with that simple gesture giving me her full support. I wanted to take her in my arms and hold her close.

There was an accident or something on Sunset and traffic was backed up from the east almost to new 41. I cut through the side streets that wound through old Mangrove Springs, crossed old 41 at the park, and turned south on Dutch street hoping that whatever had backed up Sunset wasn't this far east. I crossed the Royal River on the easternmost bridge before I-75 and saw the entrance to the Chastain homestead on my left. The drive was partially hidden by unkempt cabbage palms, palmetto bushes and towering pine trees, but the single width asphalt track seemed in good repair. The Chastain land straddled the river and ran east for about half a mile from Dutch street. The river curved through it, abruptly narrowing halfway, and there was little boat traffic to speak of. Walker Chastain had been worried about hurricanes. That's why he'd chosen property so far inland to build his home on. I slowed to see if I could catch a glimpse of the main house through the tangled foliage when an idea struck me. I wondered if Toby was home? I wondered if Toby knew where Iselda Driggers could be reached? I wondered how I could get him to tell me without arousing his suspicions? Hmmm.

I slowed and, with no clear plan in place, but confident that something would come to me, I turned into the lane. On the other side of the dense plantings the drive traversed several hundred feet of majestic live oaks and tall pines. Air plants were perched in the crotches of the live oaks and suspended in the upper reaches of the pine trees, and reminded me of my childhood, when the weird, un-rooted plants had been everywhere. Now, like so much of the Florida I'd grown up with, they were disappearing.

Around a last curve the house came in sight, a pillared three story antebellum concoction that evoked thoughts of New Orleans or a Mississippi plantation. Not the typical cracker house but not unknown to the area either.

The great house sat near the bank of the river amid pines and live oaks. In the front yard was a multi-trunked Banyan tree that was seventy-five feet tall and at least as big around at the base. A

Johnny-come-lately aluminum pool enclosure could be seen off to one side at the rear and hewn cypress slabs set in the ground made a walking path that led to a small boat dock. No boats were in sight. A Jaguar convertible was parked at a covered portico to the east end of the structure. A vintage Mercedes was pulled into the circular drive at the foot of the steps that led to the front entrance. I parked behind the Mercedes and got out of my car. I still had no clear idea of what I'd say to Toby Chastain. It didn't matter. There was no one home.

I knocked, using the big brass doorknocker cast in the shape of a lion's head. I peered in windows. I walked around the property, even down to the deserted dock, where I saw a seven-foot alligator sunning on the far bank of the river. Nothing. I was getting into the Caddy when the distant sound of a rumbling diesel engine came to me and I stopped in mid plop and looked around. The sound was coming from the east, where a dirt lane wandered past several out buildings and a small cottage, Dent and Lontine's former home, I guessed, and disappeared into the woods. I could see slow to and fro movement in the distance through the trees and bushes.

I pulled around the Mercedes and followed the drive to where I'd come in. Instead of taking the paved lane that would lead to Dutch street, I turned east onto the dirt path and bumped my way past the out buildings. Another hundred yards and the Caddy rocked into a clearing near a bend in the river, which flowed sluggishly some ten or twelve feet below the banks. A white pickup was parked off to the right. To the left, Toby Chastain sat upon a small tractor with a box blade on the front and a backhoe at the other end. He was shirtless, wearing shorts and sunglasses, and busily engaged in pushing large limestone rocks over the bank of the river. I stopped the car and cut the engine. The benzene-sweetened odor of burning diesel fuel overrode the smell of wood-smoke. It blanketed the clearing with a blue haze that could be traced to the stack protruding from the engine compartment of the little tractor, which had been new during the Seminole Wars, from the looks of it. I got out and leaned against the hood of the car, content for the moment to watch him at work.

The limestone rocks were in a pile a few yards from the bank and Toby would back and fill, nudging a rock until he had it cut from the herd, so to speak. Then he'd push it along the ground with the box blade until it tipped, slowly, over the embankment. Each one went over at a different spot and it was easy to see the left to right pattern Toby was using. I watched, fascinated, until there were no more rocks left and Toby shut the tractor down. He stood and removed the sunglasses, which he placed in the bare steel bucket seat of the tractor. He wiped his dripping, diesel stained face with a red and white bandana and jumped with cat-like grace to the ground. Then he saw me.

There was no hesitation, no hitch to his movements, as might be expected from someone who thought they were alone and suddenly found they were being watched. He came toward me, using the bandana to towel the sweat from his lean and muscled torso, and I felt a chill overcome me as he grinned coldly.

"Well, hello there," he said. "What a pleasant surprise." He continued toward me and I straightened up from the hood of the car. He walked to within eighteen inches of me, still grinning, severely invading my personal space, before he stopped. The blue-black tattoo of a scorpions tail ran from beneath his khaki shorts and over his flat stomach. Each calf bore a stylized tattoo of a red-eyed serpent and a grinning devils head was etched into his left breast. I could smell the dark sweatiness of him and I had to beat back an atavistic urge to flex and grimace. He was two inches shorter and forty, all right, fifty pounds lighter than me, and my high school wrestling training told me that I could take him, though it would be a squeaker. He was younger and in better shape while I was bigger and more experienced. And I wasn't really sure about that last one.

"Hi there!" I decided to play it light and airy. "Congratulations! Your deal has closed and I'm here to make sure that all loose ends are tied up." He kept grinning that cold grin.

"What loose ends?" He was finished with the bandana and crumpled it into a ball and put it into a hip pocket. For some reason I noticed he was wearing red topped crew style athletic socks and sand brown desert boots.

"Well, you know, just paperwork odds and ends. Like getting affidavits from the witnessing parties." I was winging it, hoping he'd know little or nothing about closing procedures and requirements.

"Witnessing parties?" I lowered my voice and tried to make him feel like we were sharing great confidences.

"Yeah, the witnessing parties to all the pertinent documents relative to the closing and all related matters, both pre and post recording, must sign an affidavit testifying as to their cognizance of the officiousness of their signatory acts before such matters may become a part of the public records." I spread my hands and hoped he didn't read the gobble-de-gook. "Of course, you know about Dent Billie?" I asked with a feigned air of solicitousness. He drew back a bit and squinched his eyes.

"No, what about him."

"He's dead. So's his wife. And two of their grandchildren. You didn't hear anything about it?" He snorted through pursed lips.

"No. How could I?" I shrugged.

"Doesn't matter, I can clear his signature by the legal claim of a writ of performance, that is, a long history of performing similar witnessings for the decedent." I was deep into bull doo-doo here, making it up as I went along. "After all, it was an accident, that's what the cops say." I watched for any sign of anxiety or discomfiture on his part. I must say he reacted with polite shock.

"Dent and his family are dead?" He sounded genuinely surprised.

"Yeah, trailer fire. Awful."

"That's a real shame."

"Yeah, well it's the other one that I'm worried about." He frowned.

"What other one?" he practically demanded. I shook my head again, thoroughly enjoying this.

"Iselda Driggers. Evidently, sometime after witnessing your Grandmother's will she became ill and rejoined her family in another part of the state. Did you know her?" The question caught him off guard.

"Uh, yeah, I think so. But I don't know where she went." He recovered quickly.

"That's all right, I think I've got a line on her." This had an effect on him that I hadn't anticipated. His face darkened and his body tensed as he leaned in close to me. I recoiled as far as the hood of the Caddy would let me where I prepared to make my stand. Just then the rumbling of another diesel engine and the squeal of air brakes got our attention. A dump truck was making its way along the unpaved road toward us. The truck was filled with large limestone rocks. The driver pulled up behind the Caddy, unable to go any farther. He leaned out the driver's window and waved a sheaf of papers about.

"Riprap for the Chastain's! Is this the right place?" Riprap is what they call a seawall made from just such limestone rocks. Toby had been shoring up his riverbank and here was a fresh load of material. Just in the nick of time, as they say. I made quick use of the interruption.

"Well, I'll just be moving on," I said, and in an over the top display of macho, I placed a hand on the driver's door and vaulted into the Caddies driver's seat. I started the car and quickly circled around the dump truck and sped off down the lane. I refused to exhibit any effect from the collision of my right knee with the steering column until I was sure I was out of sight. Then I rubbed my knee and bounced up and down in the seat. Boy that hurt!

Chapter Thirty-One

What the hell was wrong with me? I'd practically alerted my number one suspect to the fact that I was on to him, spewing some easy to see through malarkey, and nearly having to physically defend myself against a man I was willing to consider as a psychopathic murderer. I also might have endangered Iselda Driggers. And my knee hurt like hell! What was that all about? Something about Toby just seemed to bring out my worst instincts. '…their cognizance of the officiousness of their signatory acts?' A moron could see through my antics.

I stopped for a light at Sunset and put the top up because the smoke was beginning to sting my eyes. I headed east, where I jumped on I 75 north. I settled into a steady speed of seventy-five miles an hour, just slightly higher than the posted limit, and weaved my way through moderate traffic. A pall of smoke hung over all, obliterating the sun. The big engine hummed smoothly, exhibiting no strain at being asked to propel two and a half tons of steel at highway speeds. As I traveled north the smoke thickened and, around Estero, I began to see the reddish yellow of flames dancing in the near distance to the east and traffic slowed. In several places there were fire trucks and emergency vehicles parked near the tree line. Fire fighters were off-loading equipment and heading into the trees. To the north I could make out some wispy tendrils of smoke where the fires started up again. I exited at Route 80 on the north side of Fort Myers, well past the airport. I turned east on the state road and headed for La Belle. The fires were now north and south of me.

I passed through Alva and then the signs of civilization thinned out and the highway narrowed to a bucolic two-lane country road, widening occasionally to provide a passing lane for one side or the other. Country stores and lonely looking churches appeared infrequently on the south side and narrow lanes with billboards advertising riverfront lots were spaced out on the north side, interspersed with orange groves and an odd RV park or two. The Caloosahatchee River wasn't too far north of the road. Finally, the speed limit dropped and the road widened to four lanes and began winding through a commercial district that was the beginnings of La Belle proper.

A little more than two hours later I left the Courthouse, walking much slower than when I'd entered, head reeling with images of all the documents I'd viewed, going back as far as Nineteen-eleven. First, I'd looked at the current tax rolls but had not found any mention of a Marchand who owned property in the county. Next, I started looking at recorded deeds. I'd found but two mentions of a Marchand and both of those were for the sale of property, and the Marchand's were not likely to live on property they'd already sold.

Back in the parking lot I slowly made my way to my car. I closed the door, cranked up the air-conditioning and just sat, too numb to decide what to do next. I finally realized that I was hungry and I was in La Belle. That could only mean one thing: Flora and Ella's.

As I pulled into the graveled parking lot of the restaurant I could feel my spirits rebounding. I climbed the stairs and crossed the wide veranda, past the row of rocking chairs conveniently placed for patron's use, as in years past. The rockers were empty now and I glanced at my watch, noting that it was just after two, past the traditional lunch hour. No wonder I was hungry. I pushed open the door and entered the cool interior of the building. I was in a sort of anteroom, a store really, with racks of cards, candies, novelties, canned and bagged specialty foods and stuffed toys for sale. A cash register stood sentinel at a counter to the left and straight ahead was a doorway that led into the dining room proper. A sign requested that diners wait to be seated and I stopped at it and made a line of one. Within seconds a young girl approached with a menu and asked me to follow her. I did and sat at the table she led me to. I took the menu and told the waitress that I'd like a sweet iced tea.

I opened the plastic clad menu. Pork chops, country fried steak, fried chicken, chicken and dumplings, meat loaf, sausage gravy and biscuits. All tempting, all sounding delicious, but I was quick to settle on one of my favorites: Hoppin' John. Black-eyed peas in their own gravy served over rice with scrambled ground beef, chopped fresh sweet onions and diced tomatoes. Salt and pepper to taste, a goodly splash of hot sauce and corn bread on the side rounded out the feast that I ordered as soon as the waitress returned.

I sopped up the last of the gravy and washed it down with the last of my second glass of tea. I leaned back and surveyed the empty dishes before me. That's the way I liked to leave 'em, empty. The waitress appeared with the check in her hand. She remembered to ask if I desired a slice of one of their heavenly pies. I couldn't conceive of taking another bite and told her so. She smiled prettily and set the bill before me.

"Thanks for visitin' with us today. Hope everything was satisfyin'?" I patted my stomach and rolled my eyes.

I reached for the bill and studied it. $7.95 and I could hardly breathe. No complaints there. On my way out I headed for the restroom. As I washed my hands, I noticed a poster hanging on the wall that proclaimed the health enhancing benefits of all natural, organically farmed Belle Honey, sweetest in the land. It sweetened foods, fought allergies and softened skin. It was, the poster proclaimed, totally unprocessed and sold in the natural comb. And it was produced locally, though it was sold worldwide!

At the register I waited as an elderly gentleman shuffled from the dining area to the counter. He wore one of those old-time green shaded things on his head that wasn't really a hat because there was nothing on the top. He wore a long sleeved white shirt, buttoned at the throat, and a polka dot bow tie. His pants were cotton twill with a neat crease, blue, held up by a wide leather belt AND suspenders. Can't be too careful. He was shod with brown leather lace up work boots, well worn but freshly polished. His costume was completed by a bright red arm band about his spindly left bicep and a gleaming pair of half glasses, the kind used for reading, perched low on the bridge of his nose. All in all he looked as if he might have been Flora and Ella's grandfather. I immediately assumed this was a bit of theatre to emphasize the country charm and history of the place, but after he spoke, and by the way he operated the register, I wasn't so sure. Maybe he WAS Flora and Ella's grandfather. I laid my check on the counter.

The old gentleman peered through the half lenses and pecked at the register one key at a time. Look, peck. Look, peck. I asked him if he carried Belle Honey and he pointed to a display behind me where pint jars of cloudy, unfiltered, honey were arranged in a pyramid. I plucked a jar from the top. The label was obviously produced on a computer printer and the jar had a home canning type lid on it. Sold worldwide, huh? The sign hanging from the display table indicated that the pint jars cost $5.95. I told the old man to add it to my total.

"Thank ya, sir. We surely enjoyed your company. Please come and visit with us agin." I had the feeling that he meant what he said. Too bad his world was vanishing. As was mine.

I took my change and my honey and exited onto the veranda. I eased my black-eyed pea swollen bulk into a rocking chair and studied the label on the jar.

Belle Honey had been produced continuously, according to the label, since nineteen fifty-one in beautiful La Belle, Florida, and was guaranteed to be the most tasteful, most nutritious, most pure and natural of any honey found anywhere in the world today. It was harvested by a combine of beekeepers committed to the production of natural, organic honey in the finest of natural traditions. Belle Honey could be purchased at many fine retail outlets, ordered from the web site, by toll free number, by mail or in person at the worldwide headquarters located in La Belle, FL, USA. Furthermore, 10% of the proceeds from the sale of Belle Honey went to the Church of the Divine and Preordained Ascension. Aunt Chili had said that Zel's family kept bees. I had a notion that the good folks at Belle Honey's worldwide headquarters might know the Marchand family.

I got in the car and drove back toward the courthouse, looking carefully at street signs as I went. One block past where I'd turned earlier for the courthouse I encountered Main Street. I waited for the light and when it turned green I turned left. After several blocks the street crossed over the Caloosahatchee and entered North La Belle. I found it on the second block over the river and pulled into the graveled parking lot that butted up to the side of the two story brick structure that looked as if it had been built at least fifty years earlier, maybe more. There were two cars, a van and a pick-up in the parking lot. The side of the brick building was windowless and painted with a faded two-story version of the Belle Honey label. The plate glass windows that fronted the street were darkened by a peeling window tinting substance and plastered, from the inside, with posters proclaiming the beneficial properties of Belle Honey.

I got out and went to the front door. It opened easily and I entered into sudden dimness. I took off my sunglasses and let my eyes adjust to the gloom. The place was laid out like a general store from the early nineteen hundreds. There were several rows of shoulder high shelves placed across the scuffed dark wood floors. The shelves were filled with various sizes of containers holding cloudy honey and natural wax comb. The air was cool, conditioned, and forced from vents in exposed ductwork running along the high ceiling. The air conditioning had obviously been added to the building long after the original edifice had been built. A wall separated the front of the building from approximately the rear two thirds, according to my recollection of the depth of the building, as viewed from the parking lot. A door was evident in the wall and muted mechanical sounds could be heard coming from the other side. Two men stood together behind a counter toward the rear of the room. They were both in their middle thirties, rustically dressed in what could be termed farm attire, though the clothes were clean and neatly pressed. They both wore baseball style caps with Belle Honey emblazoned across them, above the bill. Their shirts bore names stitched over the left pocket and I could make out 'Tim' on one breast and 'Roger' on the other. Their faces were pleasant and slightly expectant at the sight of me, and Roger ventured a 'hi!'

"Hi," I replied, in my best good 'ole country boy voice.

"Can we help you?" Tim offered with a smile. "Have you come for some famous Belle Honey?" I grinned sheepishly.

"Well, actually, I just bought some down at Flora and Ella's. I'm from out of town."

"So, you from out of town, huh!" he exclaimed. "Where at?" I lowered my eyes and reluctantly admitted I was from Mangrove Springs, not too far to the south and west.

"But I ain't never tasted anything like Belle Honey and I just wanted to stop in and let you folks know how highly I thought of your product. It's entirely natural, huh?" Roger appeared to be ready to pop out of his Dickees.

"That's right," Tim said. "Our harvesters don't treat with any chemicals and we don't process the honey at all. All our honey is just pure, natural, unfiltered, on the comb goodness!" These guys were really into their product.

"I think the thing that's as important to me as the all natural nature of the honey is the fact that y'all tithe ten percent of proceeds to the church." I could see a gleam in their eyes at the mention of the church.

"Yep, ten percent of everything goes to The Church of the Divine and Preordained Ascension," Roger volunteered. "We have a purpose here at Belle Honey, and that is to further the works of Jehovah, God of Gods, and Master of the Universe. There is no other!"

"You know," I said. "I believe I have family in the area, dedicated church people, and the reason I've come, aside from getting some of the honey of life, is to meet my relations that I'm told are doing the Lord's work, harvesting honey for the Lord!" I hoped that I was believable. I'd be extremely embarrassed if found out by these Fundamentalists. Especially since I didn't intend for my actions to be in any way disrespectful. I didn't share the beliefs of the earnestly religious of Central Florida, but I respected and admired their attempt to live their lives in a righteous manner. Sure, some of them went overboard from time to time and a few were downright tyrannical and pigheaded when it came to their religion and other people. But most were decent folk, fervent in their beliefs but slightly prone to having their faith abused by leaders engaged in extreme demagoguery for personal gain. In short, some of them were butt-heads, just as some in any group are. I'd made no conscious effort to try the tactic of assuming a good-ole boy religious fervor instead of asking outright about the Marchand's, Iselda in particular. It just felt like the right approach to take. I felt like an honest to God sleuth.

"Oh? And who might those good folk be?"

"Well, I'm not really related, only just by marriage, you see." Roger squinted in bafflement.

"I'm actually a Driggers, originally of the Hillsborough County Driggers, up by Tampa. My cousin married into the Marchand clan, who are known to be beekeepers in this area. Now, I've never met any of the Marchand family but I'm hoping to. I thought you fellas might know them, being in the honey business and all."

"There is a family by the name of Marchand tending bees in this county, one of the oldest families in the area. They've been here since before the Civil War, I think," Roger said.

"Yes," Tim continued for him. "A couple of the Marchand family are members of our combine and the rest of them are good folk, as well." I grinned at them both.

"Could you tell me how I might find any of them? I assume any Marchand family member will be able to direct me from there."

Chapter Thirty-Two

I headed north, mentally reciting the directions as I searched for the landmarks Roger had mentioned. About eight miles out of town, past the Indian General Store and Trading Post, and after making a couple of turns onto smaller and smaller roads, I spied the turnoff that Roger had said would lead me to the Marchand property. There was a sign announcing the Farm of the Fundamentalist Sect of Christian Devouts. That explained why a search of the County land records yielded no results for the Marchand name; all of their property was vested in the church. The lane made its way through the thick pines and scrub oak for about a half a mile before opening onto a pasture. I headed for a pole barn that seemed to be at the center of things.

Rusted trucks and tractors and all sorts of farm implements were haphazardly scattered about. Weeds grew tall around some of them, indicating that they'd been there for a while. There were several primitive sheds and lean-tos and the one large pole barn that I was pulling up to. Several men were engaged in various tasks in and around the barn and most paid no attention to the stranger in the big car. Several dogs were more inquisitive and came running to the driver's side door as I came to a stop. As I got out, one Labrador stood on hind paws and thrust a wet nose in my direction. I recoiled just a bit and a man who had noticed my arrival called to the dogs before assuring me that I was in no danger.

"Them uns ain't gonna trouble ya none," is what he actually said. The dogs obeyed the man's call but pranced just behind him, still very curious.

"Hi," I said brightly. It had suddenly occurred to me that I couldn't pretend to be part of the family, by marriage or otherwise, as I'd led the honey guys to believe. I'd have to tell the truth. The fact that I'd prevaricated at the honey store would probably find its way back to the Marchand clan. Roger and Tim would almost certainly mention it the next time they talked to a Marchand. 'Hey, some relative by marriage was in here looking for y'all. Did he find you? Big fellow in an old Caddy convertible.' I guess I wasn't such a great sleuth after all.

"Aft' noon." He looked at me with the same level of curiosity as the dogs, which he was keeping behind him with a hand that patted the air just in front of their noses. One, however, the Labrador from before, ventured forward and sniffed at my dangling left hand. When the dog had satisfied himself as to my non-threatening nature I gently rubbed his head and ruffled his ears. Mistake. Each time I tried to stop he pushed his nose forcefully into my hand until I rewarded him with some more petting. I decided to get right to it.

"My name is Roy Dixon and I'm from Mangrove Springs, down below Fort Myers." He nodded but said nothing. One of the men from the barn climbed up on one of the rusted tractors and I was surprised when it started right up and moved off with a puff of blue smoke. The Marchand's were different from the Amish in that they didn't mind employing labor saving devices. "I'm a title examiner. I check out the legal history of a piece of property before a sale of that property can take place. See if there's any reason the property shouldn't, or can't, be sold." He nodded at me.

"Deeds and notes and sech." He kept his level gaze on my face. "How can we hep a title zaminer from Mangrove Springs?"

"I'm working on a sale that involves a large parcel of land that is in probate. That is, the previous owner passed away and I need to determine who is in title now. There's a will offered but I suspect there may be a later will, one that is very different from the will in probate." He nodded some more.

"I reckon that could be a problem. But, us Marchand's don't have nothin to do with no property in Mangrove Springs. Grow five or six cash crops and harvest some mighty fine eatin' honey. Land's in the Church's name. So, like I said, how can we hep ya?"

"I'm trying to locate an Iselda Driggers who used to live in Mangrove Springs. I've been told that after her husband passed away and she became ill herself she moved up this way to be with her family. Her maiden name was Marchand. I thought you might be related." He was nodding his head solemnly and ran a calloused and grease stained hand over the gray stubble on his chin.

"Ah, now I see. Zel." He dropped his hand and looked solemnly at me. "It's Zel you're wantin'. She was married to a man name a Driggers. Came back to us last year. Had a cancer and her husband died so she needed her fam'ly. Didn't have no children."

"Then she's here? Can I speak with her?" I felt a rush of hope that I might finally be getting somewhere. The Labrador mistook my sudden excitement for a desire to do more petting and he pranced and nudged my hand to let me know that it was all right with him. I absently fondled his ears.

"What might ya be wantin' with Zel?"

"Well, I, uh, that is…" I found it difficult to articulate why I wanted to speak with her in just a few words. I took a deep breath and launched into the tale of Alma Chastain's land and the confusion over the veracity of the will in probate. I didn't mention my suspicion that someone was killing those people possibly able to discredit the will. Nor did I mention that the confusion of which I spoke seemed to be mine alone. He stood and listened politely to me as the men in the barn behind him hurried to and fro, carrying some things and working on others. Another one left in, rather, on, a truck that was stripped of its body. It had a seat bolted to its exposed chassis but no roof, doors, windshield or other unnecessary parts. The steering column protruded through the firewall, which was the only thing between the engine and the driver. It appeared from its engineering and design to be quite old. The gentleman I was speaking with took note of everything with his quickly darting eyes but appeared to hear everything I said. He waited patiently for me to finish and took a moment to digest everything before speaking.

"I'm 'fraid Zel died last week." His words hit me like a hammer blow. I suddenly found it difficult to breathe.

"We'd prepared for her passin', what with her cancer and all. Sometimes it seemed as if it would ease off and then it would begin tormentin' her again. She gave it a good tussle." My breathing evened out and the roaring in my head that was probably my blood pressure abated. Of course! Iselda, Zel, had been ill for some time. Nothing sinister here. A mixture of emotions swirled through me as I feebly thanked the man for his time and offered condolences to his family for their loss. He nodded and watched as I gave the dog one last rub and then opened the car door and collapsed onto the front seat. As I started the throaty engine he said something that I couldn't make out.

"What's that?" I said when the engine had revved down.

"I said twas strange, that's all. Like a sad joke. But the Good Lord works in mysterious ways." I lowered the window and closed the door.

"What do you mean?"

"A sick lady, one like Zel, sick near unto death. Her getting runned over like that while checkin' the mail at the end of her sister's lane. She had fought the cancer and fought the cancer and that walk down the lane was a victory each day that she could make it. Hit and run driver. They ain't never found the swine." I broke into a cold sweat at his words. Another person connected to Alma Chastain's will had died violently within the past two weeks. That made six. That I knew of. And I might be a good candidate for number seven. That was definitely a sobering thought.

I thanked the man for his time and hurriedly left the way I'd come in. I went faster and faster, eager to be on the move, resisting the impulse to look over my shoulder to see if something was gaining on me.

Chapter Thirty-Three

When I got back to the interstate, smoke lay over the landscape like a dirty cotton ball and traffic was snarled north and south. I crept into the southbound lanes and moved toward Mangrove Springs at a steady fifteen miles per hour. Eventually all southbound traffic was herded into the right lane and made to exit at Alico Road. I could see the interstate was empty beyond in all four lanes, save for emergency vehicles rumbling to and fro. Smoke hung thick and noxious in the air and I could make out flames ahead where the fire had jumped the highway.

For every vehicle exiting southbound, one was entering northbound. We idled along Alico Road, start and stop, horns honking and lights flashing, tempers flaring. It took twenty-five minutes to reach 41 where traffic sped up a good bit as we entered the six-lane artery headed south.

I rolled into Mangrove Springs about seven. I tried calling Ollie. Three rings and the answering machine picked up. I hung up. Then I tried his cell phone. Three rings and I reached his voice mail. I left a message for him to call me as soon as possible. Then I tried the Sheriff's sub-station and asked for Detective Servais. I was told that it was his day off and was asked if someone else could be of assistance. I told the pleasant sounding female voice on the other end of the line that no, I'd try tomorrow. I pondered my next move. I really needed to talk to someone. Not just anyone, but someone familiar with the events of the past few days.

I called Jenna's cell phone number. I was amazed that we had ever gotten along without the personal communication devices. Three rings and I reached her voice mail. Likewise, no answer at the house number. I hung up in disgust. I hadn't been able to reach anyone! Land line or cell phone. I headed for The Grouper Hole.

When I entered I saw an empty barstool that seemed to beckon to me. I made my way toward it. Dan, busy at the far end of the bar, nodded to let me know that he was aware of my presence.

I surveyed the place and saw several people that I knew, including Mayoral candidate Dottie Springbridge and her grandson. They were sharing a small table with a couple I didn't know, and were engaged in animated conversation. Evan Muster was jawboning with several ex-tomato growers, standing in a knot near the hallway that led to the restrooms. Cousin Lonzo was seated at the bar and seemed to be singing to no one in particular.

Dan appeared and asked if I'd have the usual and I nodded. Rick Palomino was working the crowd, which included a number of Realtors, no doubt pushing the services and products of his various companies. At a table in a far corner, hovered over by a couple of young men obviously hopeful of achieving carnal knowledge of the attractive young woman, sat Rita Muncie. I recoiled a bit at the sight of her, our failed interlude painfully fresh in my mind. Dan brought my drink and I turned my face away from her, hoping that she had not seen me.

The free food was a tray of crab balls. No, not that, silly. Breaded balls of faux crab meat and spices, deep-fried and served with containers of tartar sauce and cocktail sauce. The line-up for the table of free food was long and growing longer. I felt a tapping at my left shoulder. It was Evan.

"Hey, Roy! How's it goin'?" He slid onto the empty stool next to me. I kept my head low as I acknowledged him.

"Hey, Evan." I snuck a peek in Rita's direction. She was thoroughly engaged in conversation by the young men hanging about her table. Evan motioned for Dan to refill his glass and I drained my drink and asked Dan for a refill as well.

"Well, the big day draws near! How do you think it'll turn out? Will we 'Muster The Vote For Muster" as it says on my bumper stickers?" I shrugged.

"I don't know. We've never had anything like this in Mangrove Springs before." I was giving him about fifty percent of my attention. I was fidgeting, nervous and preoccupied, and not only because of the presence of Rita Muncie. I glanced at her table, much as one probes with a tongue at a painful tooth, and was surprised to see that she was no longer there. I quickly looked over the room, right to left and then left to right, but there was no sign of her. I settled my gaze upon the hallway that led to the restrooms and waited for her to appear. She never did. In the meantime, Evan continued to pump me for my feelings about the election. I tried my best to reassure him while keeping an eye out for Rita. After a bit he evidently felt the need to move on and said he'd see me later, and don't forget to vote Muster. He took his drink and waded into the thickening crowd, shaking hands and smiling his greetings to those he met, whether he knew them or not, in the best tradition of a politician.

I was well into my third drink when my cell phone chirped. I unclipped it from my belt and peered at the caller I.D.: The Law Offices Of... I punched a button and placed it to my ear.

"Hello?"

"Roy, is that you?" I didn't quite recognize the voice.

"Yes. Who's this?"

"This is Jack. Jack Muncie." I never would have guessed. Gone were the unctuous tones, the intonations of a snake oil salesman.

"Jack? Is that really you? You sound so different. Is something wrong?"

"Look, a real problem has come up, one I need your help with."

"Problem?"

"Yes, well, nothing we can't work out, but I need to get together with you soon."

"Sure, Jack, just say when."

"I'd, uh, I'd really appreciate it if you could see me tonight."

"Tonight? Jack, the day's over, I'm relaxing at my favorite watering hole." I didn't tell him that his wife had been relaxing here also, with a couple of men friends, until just a little while before.

"I really think we should get together tonight."

"All right, Jack. I'm at The Grouper Hole enjoying an icy one. Why don't you come over here and we can discuss whatever it is that's troubling you and down a few of our favorite libations."

"No, I think it would be better if you came here. I'm at my office. Everyone else has gone for the day and we won't be interrupted. There are, uh, some things that I need to show you."

"Jack, I…"

"Please." Within that one word was enough anguish and pathos to sway even the flintiest soul. I gave in.

"Okay, okay, Jack. I'll be there in thirty minutes or so." He was only ten minutes away but I wanted to give myself a little breathing room. He almost blubbered his thanks.

After I'd hung up, or, whatever you say when you end a cell phone call, I motioned to Dan and when he came I asked for coffee, the hotter the better. I wanted to clear any cobwebs from my mind that may have been deposited there by three martinis and a full day. Dan didn't flinch or comment, taking the order in stride, and soon I was cupping a pale blue china mug between my hands, blowing across the black liquid to cool it a bit. My cell phone chirped again. The Caller I.D. said Private Caller.

"Hello?"

"Roy, it's Ollie. I got your message. You sounded a bit excited. What's going on?" I was glad to hear his voice; glad for the opportunity to lay out my fears and suppositions for someone who wouldn't think I was crazy.

"Ollie! Have I got some things to tell you? First off, I found another of the witnesses to Alma Chastain's will, at least the one in probate, and guess what? She's dead! Oh, she had a cancer too and was expected to die, like Linda Wong, but that didn't stop someone from running her down at the mailbox and now Jack Muncie wants me to meet him at his office right away so he can show me something that's a problem, no, er, there's a problem and he needs to show me something, and…"

"Hold on, hold on a minute. You're not making any sense. Now just slow down and give it to me slowly, rationally." I sucked in some air and looked around to see if anyone had noticed my animated discourse.

"Look, I've found another anomaly and now Jack Muncie insists on seeing me right away!" With patient questioning on Ollie's part I was able to relate all that I'd found out about the Marchand's, Zel Driggers and Belle Honey. I also remembered to tell him that we had received the Chastain check.

"So, why do you suppose Jack Muncie needs to meet with you in person, and immediately?" he asked. "After all, the deal is already closed and we, that is, Mason Dixon Title, has already received payment in full. What do you think the man wants?" I had no answer for that.

"Well, I am a bit suspicious and it would behoove you to act with extreme caution. Do you think that you should see him this evening?"

"I offered to meet him here, at The Grouper Hole, but he insisted that I come to his office."

"Hmm."

"What's that mean?"

"What?"

"Hmm."

"Oh. Nothing. I was just thinking. There may be some hanky panky going on here, maybe even, God forbid, murder, or multiple murders. But I don't think that Jack Muncie is the one responsible, if anyone is, for the deaths."

"God, Ollie. You sound like a damn lawyer."

"Yes, I do, don't I? Where was I?"

"Something about the murderer probably not being Muncie."

"Oh yes. It sounds more like Jack has stumbled onto something about the deal that he didn't know before which makes him nervous."

"Well, why call me, for crying out loud?"

"Because," Ollie said in that exaggeratedly patient voice he used when explaining things to the less intellectually endowed among us. "He knows that the source of whatever he's found that is troubling him can't be you and therefore he can trust you."

"Oh." It sounded so reasonable when put like that.

"Whatever's spooked him has caused him to seek an ally, and you're the most likely candidate." I thought about that for a moment.

"Should I go see him or not?" I wasn't a deep thinker, not in the Machiavellian way, and I wanted Ollie to advise me, not confuse me.

"Yes, I think you should. A meeting at his office should be all right and you, we, definitely are interested in finding out what he has to say. And, if it seems appropriate to do so, you can fill him in on what you've discovered and the suspicions arising out of those findings."

"It may be," Ollie continued," that what he's discovered is another will. That would be enough to give any competent attorney nightmares."

"Competent is the operative term here."

"It would only be natural to call you, as the underwriter's agent, to discuss the possibilities and ramifications." I wasn't sure I bought that, though I decided not to tell Ollie, because I really wanted to buy it, I really did.

"I called Detective Servais."

"Oh? And what did he say."

"I didn't reach him. It's his day off."

"Hmm." There was that Hmm again.

"What's that mean?"

"Nothing. Look, you go see Muncie and I'll wait here at home for your call. Call me as soon as you get through with him. If I don't hear from you within a reasonable time I'll take the appropriate steps."

"What?" I quickly looked around again to see if anyone had noticed my raised voice. I continued in a more subdued fashion. "You think there's real danger involved, don't you?"

"No, no, no. I just wanted to reassure you that if there were any hint of trouble, any at all, that I'd be there for you, immediately. Just trying to bolster your self-confidence. I really don't think there is anything to be concerned about. Not as far as physical danger goes, at any rate." That somewhat mollified me.

"Well. Okay. If you really think seeing him is the best thing to do."

"I do." Ollie spent another minute or so attempting to put me at ease and, when he was reasonably sure that I'd be all right, he ended the conversation on a cheery note. Sort of.

"At least we already have the money. As Martha Stewart used to say, 'That's a good thing.' Right?"

I hadn't quite finished my coffee and, upon raising it to my lips, discovered that it had gone unpleasantly cold. When I was able to catch Dan's eye, I motioned for another. He brought a fresh cup and I told him to ring me up, placing my check/debit card on the bar. He took it and by the time he returned with a receipt for me to sign I was halfway through the new cup of java. I signed the tab and made my way to the door. Under a lamp in the parking lot I paused to look at my watch and was surprised to note that it was but eight-thirty.

Chapter Thirty-Four

Once in the Caddy I put the top down. Smoke was drifting by, hugging the bay and the roads, and it tickled my eyes and throat. That was better than the claustrophobia I had suddenly felt in the closed car. I placed my cell phone on the passenger seat and plugged it into the cigarette lighter. I didn't want to be without my phone under any circumstances, whether I could reach anyone or not. I could always call 911, I reasoned. They were sure to answer. Weren't they?

Jack Muncie's law offices were located in a two story, hundred-year-old frame cracker style building in the old downtown section of Mangrove Springs. A civic improvement group, the Mangrove Springs Old 41 Commercial Re-Development League, had fought for years for County, State and Federal funds to preserve and return the area to it's historical appearance. The retro improvements included nineteenth century lampposts, brick sidewalks and the cobble stoning of the main thoroughfare. The place looked older than it ever had.

The building had been refurbished from a rundown, ramshackle former residence, housing, during its last incarnation, rooms full of illegal immigrants here for the paid-cash-daily work. Jack Muncie had purchased it for a song and, taking advantage of tax credits and grants, he'd restored it to its original state. I parked in the side lot under a sign that advised that walking tours of Historic Downtown Mangrove Springs started here. There was only one car other than mine, a Lexus. I recognized it as the vehicle, or, at least, the same make and model vehicle, that Rita Muncie drove. I heard sirens in the distance.

Several lights were burning on the first floor, visible through the tufts of smoke. The second floor was dark. I climbed the stairs to the porch level and tried the knob of the front door. It turned easily and I entered into a foyer paneled in knotty pine and floored with random width pine planking.

"Hello," I called out, not wanting to surprise anyone." "Hello," I repeated. Silence. I saw a light at the far end of the hallway and cautiously made my way toward it, passing a small lobby-like area. The light was spilling into the hallway through a door to the left that appeared to open into Jack's outer office. His secretary's desk stood sentinel in the middle of the room surrounded by office equipment, bookshelves and side chairs. Behind the desk and to the left was another door, slightly ajar, that looked as if it led into Jack's private office. A thin band of weak yellow light was cast through the crack in the door.

"Hello," I called out again. No response was forthcoming and I wasn't sure what I should do. Finally I moved to the door and slowly pushed it open. It swung inward without a sound and I could see the source of the yellowish light: a brass Banker's lamp sitting on a broad oak desk. The lamp provided the only illumination in the room and more was in shadow than not. I could make out the form of a man seated behind the desk, leaning forward, head on the desk like a first grader taking a time out. One arm was curled under his head, acting as a pillow, and the other was hanging down at his side.

"Jack? Is that you?" It looked as though he'd gotten tired while waiting for me and had fallen asleep at his desk. I moved closer to him. "Jack." I was about to speak his name again when I caught sight of a stain on his desk blotter spreading outward from where his head rested. A big stain. A dark stain, almost black in the dim light. I stepped around the left end of the desk and looked at the arm hanging at his side. Just below it, on the deep pile of the expensive carpet, was a pistol. I looked closer at the head and saw the entrance wound at the right temple. I saw that it was, indeed, Jack Muncie. I quickly felt for a pulse though I knew before I reached that I wouldn't find one.

I felt a wave of panic trying to claw its way from the pit of my stomach and I beat it back with rapid breathing and much clenching and unclenching of fists. I had to stop finding dead bodies like this, I thought. I desperately needed to think and I slowly backed away from the desk. What should I do, I wondered, casting frantically about for ideas. Call Ollie was the one I seized upon and I spent a few moments debating whether I should return to the car to use my cell phone, or go to the secretary's desk to use the phone. I did not, I repeat, not, want to stand there next to Jack Muncie's corpse and try to make a call from the phone on his desk. I wasn't sure I could do that and remain coherent.

I retreated to the secretary's office and sat down at her desk. My legs were weak and rubbery and I actually collapsed into the chair. My heart was racing and I was still fighting panic. I closed my eyes and attempted to make the pounding in my temples go away. I practiced some deep breathing exercises that Jenna and I had learned from watching a fitness show that was the craze in the nineties and it seemed to help. My pulse slowed some and the pounding decreased. I contemplated how good it would feel to just sit there, eyes closed, and think nothing but pleasant thoughts. No thoughts of a dead Jack Muncie in the next room, no need to call Ollie or the Sheriff's Office. No thoughts of Zel Driggers or Linda Wong. No thoughts of Dent Billie and his wife and grandchildren. No thoughts of Jenna in Vern Otto's embrace, no thoughts of Mason Dixon Title being crowded out of business by the big developers and their title insurance divisions. No thoughts of Dixon family problems such as the loss of livelihood due to the net ban or the loss of Dixon land due to rising taxes and encroaching civilization. No thoughts of a father I'd never known. No thoughts of fire, or drought, or red tide, or hurricanes. No thoughts of the thousand and one problems, little and big, that had beset my life. Just pleasant thoughts would entertain my mind. Thoughts of a young Jenna and the wonder in her eyes when I told her I loved her. Thoughts of Jenna today and how, despite the divorce, I loved her even more than before. Thoughts of our children and the different stages we had seen them through. Thoughts of the good times spent with my mother and endless cousins growing up in a semi-tropical paradise before civilization had found us and hemmed us in with miles and miles of blacktop, strip malls and horrendous traffic. Thoughts of all that was good and right with the world and the exhilaration that can come from just being alive. Not like poor Jack Muncie. I wondered what had been so bad, so unbearable as to cause a man like Jack Muncie to cease his desire to live. Could have been his money problems. Or maybe he'd found out about his wife's philandering ways. Maybe he really hadn't known and just found out. But why would he summon me to bear witness to his act of despair? Oh! I'd been tempted by her charms and perhaps he'd wanted to make a statement of sorts to one of those guilty of the cuckold. I mentally shrugged off the pain and confusion, deciding that it was well beyond my feeble reasoning power to make sense of it all. Besides, there was undoubtedly a large body of facts surrounding the situation that I was totally unaware of. It's hard to make an informed judgment when one isn't really informed.

I opened my eyes and reached for the ATT Multi-Line System Telephone Station on the Secretary's desk, punched a button and, when the line lit up and I heard a dial tone, I pecked in Ollie's number. As I waited for a connection to be made, I heard a slight rustling noise behind me. Just as the number I'd dialed began ringing I turned my head to look back toward Jack Muncie's inner office. The door leading to the inner office was wide open and something was coming toward me at an alarming rate of speed. I heard a whooshing noise. Blinding white light and searing pain engulfed me. I descended into a pit of darkness studded with thorns and barbs that scratched and grabbed at my flesh as I fell. Ollie's voice was the last thing I was aware of.

"Hello?"

Chapter Thirty-Five

The world was black. The world was red. The world was pain. Over and over again, the world was black, the world was red, and the world was pain. When the world was black I'd watch in fear for the coming red haze because I knew that right behind it would be soul-searing pain. Over and over again in a rhythm that matched my heartbeat. Gradually I realized that there was more to life than the pain. Like the steel bands wrapped around my chest, pinning my arms to my sides, making it somewhat difficult to breath. Like the numbness of my hands and feet and the smell of damp soil and vegetation mixed with wood smoke. Like the buzzing echo that filled my ears. I came to realize that the throbbing pain was located primarily in my head and the left side of my face. I expended great effort in an attempt to open my eyes though I couldn't for the life of me think of a reason for doing so.

After several attempts I succeeded. With multiple dots swimming in front of me and the pain in my head causing copious tears, I gradually began to make out my surroundings.

"Wo ho! I think he may be coming around!" I'd never expected the voice of God to sound so, well, human. Surely I was dead and arrived at my heavenly reward.

"Yeah, I think he's waking up." Mrs. God? The voice was definitely feminine. Did God morph between male and female, man and woman, as a way of expressing universality?

"Good, good! I thought I was going to miss the opportunity to explain just why he had to die." God again. I followed the sound of the voice upward and to the left, where it receded into a blazing white light. Somehow, God sounded like Toby Chastain. And Mrs. God sounded suspiciously like Rita Muncie. What the hell was going on? I squeezed my eyes shut and tried to dredge up any recollection or knowledge of what was happening. Images came into my mind, slowly at first, then at full flood, and I suddenly recalled it all. The will, the suspicious deaths, the visit to Jack Muncie's office, and the white heat of the pain before blacking out.

"Hey, Roy! Roy Dixon! Wake up!" I opened my eyes again, blinking away the moisture. This time I could make out that it was indeed the voice of Toby Chastain, who was directly in front of what appeared to be a headlight on some sort of tractor. Tractor? And why was it suspended above me? How long had I been out? And where was I? The horizon was bathed in red.

Toby was above me. Directly in front of me was a vertical wall of damp, sandy soil with a few broken roots indicating that a dig of some sort had recently taken place. Lowering my eyes a bit more I found myself looking through a windshield and across the broad expanse of the hood of the Caddy. My gaze traveled farther down, past the steering wheel to my legs, partially covered with soil. A look at my chest revealed a silvery expanse of what could only be duct tape wrapped around the split bench seat and me: The steel bands. Moving my head as far as I could to first the left and then the right I could see only vertical walls of sandy soil. A glance in the rear view mirror showed a sloping ramp gouged into the soil, and down which, I presumed, the car had been pushed or driven.

A small avalanche of dirt clods and sand rained down from above and one clod struck me in the forehead, causing the throbbing pain to ratchet up. I closed my eyes and shook my head feebly, trying to dislodge any loose soil. Mistake. Big time. It felt like there was a rock loose inside my skull, banging back and forth. Above me, Toby Chastain laughed as gleefully as a naughty child finding new ways to torment the family pet. I looked up and he was sitting a few feet from the rim of the hole that the caddy and I were in, perched on the blade of the tractor I'd seen him using earlier in the day. Earlier in the day? Seemed like weeks. At least I knew where I was. That was good and that was bad. I knew which way to run if I somehow managed to get free. But I also knew that no one would hear me no matter how loudly I screamed. If I could scream at all.

Rita Muncie stood closer to the edge of the hole, which was about eight or nine feet deep. Her arms were crossed and, though she faced me with her back toward Toby, she kept throwing knowing little looks over her shoulder at him. Toby had seated himself sort of sideways on the blade with his left arm dangling behind.

"Well, Roy, what do you think? Have you figured everything out yet?" I longed to be able to move from my duct-taped position to relieve the cramping that was occurring in most places in my body. I'd figured out enough of it so that I didn't want to figure out any more. I didn't tell him that. I wasn't sure that I could coax any sound from my parched and constricted throat. When I didn't answer, Toby sent a shower of dirt and sand my way with a flick of his booted foot. I grunted.

"I asked you a question, Roy. You must be polite and answer me," he said in a patient voice that one would reserve for the learning impaired. "Have you figured everything out yet?" My left eye felt swollen and gritty. Tears flowed freely from it, across my cheek, where they dripped onto the field of duct tape below. I nodded my head.

"You want the money," I croaked, causing a tickling in my throat that started me on a coughing jag that lasted for what seemed an eternity. Toby erupted with amused laughter.

"Ah, yes, the money. You would think of that, would think it the only obvious motivation for recent events." I looked up with my still functioning right eye and saw that Rita was looking with bafflement at Toby. He just glared at her. Slowly, Toby returned his attention to me and his face brightened a bit at the resumption of whatever sick game he was playing. Rita turned uncertainly my way as well.

"There is more to life than money, my friend. I can call you friend, can't I?" He sounded by turns like a college professor, a willful child and a peevish teen. His rapid shifts kept me off balance as I tried to deal with his nuttiness, the life-or-death situation that I obviously was in, and the horrendous pain and hideous physical discomfort. Rita looked once more over her shoulder at Toby.

"The money's why we did it, right? I mean, killed people, Jack, for God's sake, for the money, right?" Her voice dropped an octave and softened, as she turned more fully to face Toby. "And each other, right? Cause we love each other." She was practically oozing sensuousness and sexiness, trying to exert the control over him that she felt was naturally hers. Her greedy nature surfaced once more, though, at the end. "And the money, right?" She turned all the way toward him, giving him the full benefit of her hip shot, lip-pouting seductiveness, the alluring arch of her breasts and the inviting view of her taut body encased in form fitting navy slacks.

Toby laughed and raised his left arm, which had been hidden behind the blade of the front-end loader, and I could make out, through my one good eye, that he held an automatic pistol in his hand. He raised it to her head level and she only had time to register a bit of surprise on her face before he squeezed off two rounds. Somewhere in the back of my consciousness I labeled the flat crack of the report as being from a .22 caliber weapon. Rita's head snapped back and she stumbled rearward toward the pit that held the Caddy and me, stumbling over a pile of dirt mixed with some limestone rocks, turning toward the hole as she fell head first into the void. I saw her approaching and involuntarily flinched as she crashed onto the hood of the car, her head slamming into the windshield with force enough to create spidery cracks in the safety glass, radiating outward from the center of impact. She bounced once, twice, and then came to rest with her wide, staring, unfocused hazel eyes not more than three feet from my own damaged orbs. Her nose appeared to have broken on impact and was trickling blood onto the windshield, as were the two black-tipped holes caused by the bullets. The flow from her wounds was minimal, I surmised, because her heart had already stopped beating.

That was the last rational thought to cross my mind before a high-pitched keening noise began to issue from my damaged throat. I was thoroughly and forever tired of violently dead people and I thought that my bladder had emptied, though it was hard to tell, what with the numbness and the cramping caused by the duct tape. I was afloat in a surreal environment where nothing made sense when measured against my previous life, a life where senseless violence and torture and murder were not everyday occurrences. Not even every other day, for that matter. I slowly came to the realization that Toby was tossing sand and pebbles at me in an effort to get my attention. He'd moved from his spot on the box blade and stood directly over me at the rim to the pit, as I was coming to think of it. The pit, I thought, was a good name for it, as in the pit of hell. Toby tossed dirt with his right hand while waving the pistol with his left hand. In the back of my mind, far from the pain and insanity of my physical world, a reasonable and rational thought surfaced: Was Toby Chastain ambidextrous? He seemed rather adept at performing varied tasks with either hand.

"Hey! Do you still think that the desire for money is motivating me? Can you really believe that?" He crouched and looked at Rita's remains and frowned. He began slowly shaking his head from side to side. Though I was paralyzed with fear and duct tape, I began to appreciate the depth of his insanity.

"No, no, that will never do!" he shouted. He tucked the pistol into his waistband, after carefully engaging the safety, and then startled me even further by leaping from the rim of the pit onto the hood of the Caddy, where he crouched like Spiderman for a moment, before stepping over the windshield into the passenger side of the front seat. One part of me sadly noted the dents this maneuver had created in the hood of my gallant steed. I wished with all my being that I could free myself enough from the duct tape to reach out and grasp him to me. I briefly reveled in the thought of what I'd do to him, of the sensations that I'd deliver to him, if only I could reach him. But, the duct tape held.

He turned and reached over the windshield, grabbing Rita by the shoulders and turning her over. When he had a good grip, he proceeded to hoist her inert mass over the windshield, stepping carefully into the back seat, and hauling her limp body into the soft leather of the passenger side of the front seat. He sat her up neatly and, from his position in the back of the car, guided the nose of the seat belt into the locking mechanism.

"There, that's better. Did you know that you and Rita ran off together? Left old Jack behind, cleaned out their bank accounts and he committed suicide? She knew before I did that Jack was using you to write the insurance. She told me about the evening of sin at that motel." He grinned wickedly. "Grrr, tiger!" He snorted a laugh. "Oh, yeah, she told me. 'Bout your little soldier that couldn't come to attention. Didn't matter. Some people saw you together and the foundation was laid. Pardon my pun. Or lack of one." He chortled merrily and I felt flames of embarrassment licking at my face.

"Of course, she thought we were setting up a slightly different scenario. But what I envisioned all along was that you and she had a thing, took all the money available to you, and drove to Mexico." He was making less and less sense as he rattled on. He sprang over the front seat and the windshield where he crouched upon the hood facing me. His piercing gaze made me uncomfortable, made me feel that, whatever was going on, it was almost over. He looked at me with a gleam in his eye and a bemused grin upon his face.

"Control, Roy. That's what it's about. Control. Whatever the game, whatever the stakes, control is the goal. The way I controlled Jack tonight. Rita saw you at The Grouper Hole and we, I, sprang into action. After our talk this morning I knew I had speed up the schedule. Jack really thought that I would let him live if he could lure you to his office. Was willing to give you up to secure his own safety. Even though all the rules of logic dictated that I had to do away with him, even if he cooperated." He kneeled on the hood and rested his arms upon the upper rim of the windshield. He leaned his head upon his forearms and studied me, face just above the smear of blood that Rita had left on the glass. He giggled somewhat shrilly.

"The goal is control. Control is the goal. Get it?" I didn't have any idea what the maniac was talking about but I didn't think it would be wise to let him know that. I nodded my head. Immediately his face clouded and he frowned and pursed his lips in a pout. He waggled a finger at me.

"Ah, ah, ah, ah!" he admonished. He was making no sense. My hands were numb, useless blocks at the end of throbbing arms that were immobilized by duct tape that was too strong for me to escape, and my head and eyes and many other things ached and throbbed and I could see no way out of the mess I was in. Rita Muncie had been killed and was strapped into the seat next to me in a car that was to be buried and I was powerless to stop any of it. I did the only thing that I could think to do in the situation. I gathered what saliva I could and spit it as hard as I could in his direction. The gob of spittle fell short of its mark and landed harmlessly on my side of the windshield where it slowly began to drip toward the dashboard. I drooped in my duct tape cocoon. Toby recoiled and then, when he saw that I'd come up short, relaxed and chided me in almost fatherly tones.

"Roy. Roy, Roy, Roy." He pursed his lips and thought a moment before continuing.

"It's a game, Roy. Or, rather, a series of games. All variations on a theme, and one must master the games in all their permutations. One can enjoy baseball, a team sport where individual achievement is recognized, played before many spectators, and still get a kick out of chess, a one on one contest of a more private nature. But they're both games of control. See what I mean?" I scrubbed my hands against the cloth tape again and again, hoping for a slight lessening of the tension, a sign that I might be loosening my bonds. No go.

"What do you want from me?" I managed.

"Why, Roy, I want you to understand. I believe, after the tenacity and originality you have exhibited in your dogged pursuit since that idiot, Muncie, farmed out the title work on this deal, that you may be the one, the only one that it has been my pleasure to meet, who will be able to grasp my genius." I stared at him, recognizing him for the monster he was. "Oh, I understand you, all right," I said. "I understand that you're a sick puppy, something to be scraped off my shoe like the shit you are!" Not eloquent, but heartfelt. I was almost spitting with anger and frustration and pain.

"Why, Roy? Why do you insist on getting yourself all worked up? It can't do you any good and it must be awfully frustrating." He was looking at me almost tenderly. I was too tired and hurt to say any more and he evidently took that for some sort of acquiescence. He leaned again on the windshield.

"When I first came to live here I wasn't sure exactly who I was. What I was. I knew that I had these feelings, these urges. I'd played a bit with some animals in Maryland and it felt good." I remembered Dent Billie commenting about tortured animals.

"I guess my coming of age, so to speak, really began with my parents and continued after I arrived here." I gaped at him.

"You killed your parents?" I croaked. "How? Why?"

"Oh, the how was easy. I studied a Chilton's Repair Manual for their make and model of car. I found the book in the Public Library, of all places." He grinned at me. "I just made a few adjustments to the car when I knew they were going out alone, adjustments that would be hard to detect after the fact, and voila! I was a poor widdle orphan!" He laughed, a banshee wail, for several moments. I thought he'd left reality completely. When he at last composed himself, he resumed his tale.

"The why was something I had to figure out. Over there," he pointed behind me, "is what I call my Pet Cemetery, with apologies to Stephen King. Many hours of experimentation, of growing self-knowledge, are there among the bones buried deep under the sand. Dogs and cats were good but I found that a much greater thrill was to be enjoyed when I worked with wild creatures. Armadillos, egrets, raccoons. There was more danger to me, hence, more satisfaction in a job well done. Do you know what I mean, Roy?" He looked earnestly at me over the plate glass. I closed my eyes and tiredly shook my head a bit, too sickened to try to comment.

"There were several small alligators and a bobcat, rare even in those days. Listen to me, I sound like a silly old man reminiscing about decades past when it was only about nine years ago. I had to teach myself how to trap the animals. It was fun! The library helped again." He shifted around and leaned his back against the windshield, careful not to get any of Rita's blood on his clothing.

"After several fortunately minor injuries I learned to be careful with the creatures, to treat them with the respect they deserved. And the task wasn't always easy. Have you ever tried to be creative in killing an alligator? Took some real effort, some real artistry." The bright lights and the muffled rumble of the tractor were insufficient to distract me and I listened with disgust and fascination.

"Over there," he pointed, "is where I located what I call my Migrant Garden. As I got older I became more confident, stronger, more needy. I'd experienced what it felt like to work with humans, in a way, and wanted to try again with a more hands on approach, so to speak." The pun caused him to look coyly at me from lowered lids. He giggled.

"The tomato packing houses, the farms, the labor camps, all provided me with excellent hunting." He sighed a bit wistfully. "All but gone, now. I'd ride my bike about dusk, cruising one or another of those areas, looking for little brown kids in shabby clothes, ones that looked as if they might be hungry. I'd look for loners." I stared at him, anger boiling anew inside me. "An offer of candy, a promise of more to come and they'd climb onto the bike with the nice gringo kid. Their parents were usually working in the fields or the packinghouses and it might be days before they were missed, I really don't know. I do know that very little fuss was made about the kids gone missing and I always thought that it was because they were migrants. In fact, I'm sure of it. The only time there was a stink and I feared being found out was when I worked with that Kelly boy." He chuckled and shook his head. "Boy, did the ship hit the sand, if you know what I mean. Almost a little too much thrill!"

"You bastard!" He smiled at me, like he was glad to be acknowledged. I ground my teeth together, not willing to let him know the pain and suffering he'd brought to Bobby Jane, to my family.

"Oh, you know that girl I was with at the After Hours? The little blonde waif?" When I didn't respond, he continued. "She's over there." He pointed toward the Immigrant Garden. Then he pointed toward the Pet Cemetery. "And over there." He giggled again. "I felt the need to separate her head, arms and legs from her torso. It just seemed so right, somehow." I wasn't sure how much more of this I could take.

"I picked her up in Miami that afternoon. She was a hooker with a weakness for cash and coke, not necessarily in that order. That's where I've found the bulk of my work recently, among the ladies of the evening of Miami or Tampa or Orlando." He leaned close and whispered. "I've taken a few from Fort Myers when I've felt pressed for time but I really don't like to do that. Big cities are better. More of a selection and less risk for me. I flash money and powder at them and bring them back here for fun and games, which I really do provide," he hastened to assure me. "Then, when they've had their fun I get down to work." I realized that all along he'd been referring to his penchant for butchery as his 'work'. Like a plumber. I guessed that he had to call it anything but what it really was.

"Then, after I worked with Gram, I..."

"You killed your Grandmother, too?" I was stunned but he just gave me a quizzical look.

"Why the surprise? I come to love all my jobs but I loved her most of all. I couldn't let her continue to suffer. The Hospice left a number of vials of morphine and syringes to administer it with if the pain, *when* the pain became unbearable. Their nurses kept talking about aggressive pain management and the end of life scenario. I believe they were telling me to help Gram make the transition. I didn't really want to but it was the right thing to do and I was finally able to help her escape the pain. There was no autopsy. She was known to be a terminal patient, and she was cremated almost immediately." His voice had turned a bit glum and I believed that, in his own, twisted way, he'd cared for his grandmother. Suddenly, he perked up a bit.

"Then this whole estate thing began to develop and after that idiot, Muncie, decided to have you do the title work there was suddenly any number of jobs to be done."

"Was there another will?" I asked him.

"Sure, there was the one that Muncie had prepared for her, the one that left it all but the house to some conservancy that was to be set up upon her death. I hadn't really given that end of things any real thought but Jack approached me, very carefully, circumspect, like, and eventually we stopped our verbal dancing and made a plan whereby he and I'd share in the diverted wealth. He was desperate as it turned out. He had made some really stupid investments. Hmm, I guess I should have taken that for a warning sign that he would muck this up, too. And then he wanted to keep our little friend here," he looked at Rita, "in the fine manner to which she was accustomed. He never tumbled to the fact that she did the nasty with every eligible man in town and about eighty-five percent of ineligibles, too. Of course, I never really planned to honor the agreement, that's why I initiated an affair with our little Miss Rita." He swept his arm in the direction of the cooling corpse in the passenger seat of my car. I didn't need to look, having seen her killed. "She was more than happy at the prospect of a much bigger cut of the pie." He shook his head.

"I mean was there another will, one that Linda or Dent or Lontine or Zel Driggers could have led me to?" I needed to know whether their lives, and their deaths, had meant anything in the end. Toby just shrugged his shoulders.

"Don't know. Muncie didn't know. He said that Gram had told him that the will he'd entered into probate, the will you were given, was the last one that Rennegar had prepared for her but, by the time she'd instructed him to draw up the new one, he was unsure of her mental capacity. We, I, just couldn't take the chance. When Jack took over her legal affairs she provided him with a copy of the will that you are familiar with. It was a couple of years later that she instructed him to prepare the new one."

"So you just killed them, not knowing whether it was necessary or not?" I listened in amazement to my own words. This creep had me describing murder as necessary! He shrugged again.

"It didn't really matter. It's not like I couldn't or wouldn't do the work. Those jobs were a windfall, that's the way I look at it. And I needed to make them look like accidents. That was interesting. I hadn't done that since my parents."

"But, old people? And babies? You know that Dent and Lontine's grandchildren were killed in that fire?" He grunted before answering.

"Yeah, I know. One of them, the oldest, I believe, woke up and tried to get out of the trailer. It's a good thing I stayed around to see that everything went all right instead of just leaving after the fire was started. The kid came flying out the door, screaming and carrying on, and I had to scoop it up and squeeze it's neck hard enough to cut off the breath but not to do any more than that. When it blacked out, I tossed it back into the trailer and watched until I was sure that they all were dead." I guess I'd finally had enough. A thin gruel of vomit spilled through my parted teeth and made its way over my chin and onto the gray expanse of duct tape. My throat burned and the nasty tasting bile continued to be pumped by my churning stomach. The flow increased and bubbled into my nasal passages to exit, burning, from my nostrils. A fit of coughing seized me as I aspirated the vile stuff. Toby watched in amusement. Slowly the coughing abated. He waited until I was finished before speaking again.

"You all right?" he asked. I was breathing better but decided against pointing out the inanity of the question. He took my silence for a yes. Eventually, I was able to speak.

"Why did Muncie have me research the deal?"

"I'm not sure. Rita thought it was because he was trying to cover his rear end in case another will surfaced." He turned to look at me. "You know this was only the first parcel? There's a good deal of acreage left to sell. To the same buyers, probably. Rita said

Jack wanted a prior policy to refer to for any future sales. That would remove the onus from him. The reason he supposedly chose you, my friend, is because you were known to be a bit sloppy in your work and hungry for income."

I recalled the comment that I hadn't understood at the time, hadn't even been sure I'd heard correctly. Rita Muncie had muttered something like 'no wonder it was you' and I hadn't known what she'd meant. Now I did.

"I had a couple of claims in the past," I admitted. "Though, they weren't for the reasons people may have thought. I didn't miss anything!"

"Well, you might have been hungry for the income, but I'll attest to the fact that you were anything but sloppy." His voice softened and I felt some sympathy emanating from him. "Not that it matters." I let my chin loll onto my chest as I contemplated the untenable position I was in. I frantically cast about for some avenue of escape but my addled mind could not seize upon a way to extricate myself from this predicament. A sudden, crushing realization struck home with all the force of a collapsing building; I was going to die here, wrapped in duct tape, after exchanging pleasantries and heart felt revelations with my murderer. The whole affair was absurd and insane but real, nonetheless. As if to punctuate what I was feeling, Toby sprang to his feet upon the hood of my beloved Caddy.

"Well, coffee break's over!" He looked down at me. "Time to move on, Roy," he said, his voice taking on the warm tone one usually reserves for a lover or intimate friend. "It's been real. I mean real!" He reached out and grabbed my left ear, the damaged one, and shook it like a hand, laughing all the while. It hurt like hell! I recoiled but was unable to escape his grip. Instead, I tried spitting again. The glob of bile-tinged spittle fell straight to the field of duct tape. Toby laughed and bounded over the windshield, all the way to the back seat, before leaping onto the trunk lid. I watched in the rear view mirror as he jumped from the car onto the ramp that he'd dug with his machine and raced off toward the top of the pit.

My eyes dropped and I found myself staring at the dash of the Caddy. At a cord hanging from the dash. The phone charger! My cell phone! Irrational exuberance engulfed me. I followed the cord with my eyes and was dismayed to see that the phone itself was nowhere in sight. It was probably under Rita. My heart dropped seven stories back into my chest.

Toby circled around toward the tractor and climbed into the operator's seat where he began manipulating the levers. I could just see him over the rim of the pit in front of me as he began to maneuver the machine back and forth, pushing dirt and limestone rocks as big as microwave ovens into the pit. He made every effort to be even in his approach, moving around the rim and pushing dirt and rock in from all directions equally. I watched in horror as the pit slowly filled in. The little tractors diesel engine thrummed and each time he switched direction I could hear the grinding of gears. The pit was filled up to the door handles on the Caddy and I couldn't escape, no matter how I struggled. So I screamed. I knew it would do no good but I had nothing else, nothing to alleviate the frustration and anger that I felt, no other way to channel my fear-produced and adrenalin-fed panic. So I screamed.

As I screamed I thought that my head or my heart might explode at any moment from the force of my efforts, saving me a ghastly death by asphyxiation. I thought of my family. I wished I'd been better about telling them that I loved them and how much, how very much that I cared. Now, I'd never have a chance to remedy that. Jenna, Cleve, Rae, Bobbie Jane, Mom, Aunt Chili and Uncle Lem, all the aunts and uncles, in fact.

I thought of all the people I knew. I'd never see them again. Or would I? I professed a faith in God and the Hereafter. Did I really mean it? I hoped so. Soon I'd find out.

Smoke and ash filled the air, making it hard to see. Toby steadily maneuvered the small tractor about the rim of the pit and the hood and trunk of the car disappeared under sandy soil and limestone rocks, which thudded more hollowly now, as they no longer struck bare metal when they landed. The interior of the car began to fill, covering my legs and, I noted by slightly turning my head, the lower portion of Rita's body. She didn't seem to mind, her expression never changing, as a rock bounced off the other side of her head, pushing her over toward me as far as the seatbelt would let her fall.

I wondered if my life insurance payments were current. Jenna took care of that kind of thing. Though we were divorced, I still named her as beneficiary. Then I realized that with no body to be found and all evidence indicating that I'd run off with Rita, it would be at least seven years before Jenna could have me declared legally dead and collect on the policies. More, she and everyone, kids included, would think that I'd taken off with Rita and abandoned my family and my home. I couldn't even die right!

My throat finally lost all ability to create sound and I gasped for air and tried to clear the mud that had been created in my mouth. As I panted painfully I realized that my life was sort of flashing before me as had been reported by others who had had near death experiences. Mostly, my life seemed to be regrets for all the things I didn't do or didn't say to those I most cared about. I needed more time!

Toby was working to the front of the car and a great mass of dirt cascaded into what was left of the pit. As I looked up at him I could see that he was sweating. Sweating and smiling. He was backlit by the flames in the distance and appeared demonic. He seemed to be enjoying his work.

As he backed the tractor in preparation for another run I thought that I heard voices. The Angels preparing to welcome me to another world? Then I heard popping noises and pinging noises and Toby stood on the tractor and, while he raised his pistol with his left hand, his other hand swung the wheel of the tractor to his right. There were suddenly flashes of quicksilver cascading through the beams of headlights and his face seemed to glisten. I felt cool dampness on my face and lips.

Toby began firing his gun at an unseen target and, as the tractor neared the pit at an angle, I saw him fall or jump from the machine, disappearing from my view. The tractor continued its forward motion until its left front tire collapsed the rim of the pit and it tipped over, falling into the now shallow hole in the ground. I was sure that the thing would crush me as it toppled, seemingly in slow motion, but the blade on the front end dug into the earth and stopped it half on and half off the rim of the pit. Its rear tires, neither of which was touching the ground, were spinning as the forward gear was still engaged. I had but a moment to heave a breath of relief before I saw the rock tumbling over the edge and heading straight for me. I ducked, but, with limited mobility, there was no way to get out of its path. It struck my head and I thought I heard a crunching noise just before the world exploded in another burst of white, hot pain.

...The End of the Beginning

And so my recovery proceeded. I'd wake for intervals that slowly increased in length and spent the rest of the time in oblivion. When the periods of wakefulness became often enough and long enough, the intra-venous contraption was removed from my wrist. Food, real blessed food, was given to me in increasing quantities as I became stronger.

At first my visitors consisted of only Jenna, Mom, aunt Chili, and a baffling assortment of doctors and nurses. I'd had a number of medical procedures done. Each one required a different team to perform and sometimes a whole new team to do the follow up. Jenna explained everything to me while feeding me lukewarm and flavorless chicken soup, which tasted better than anything that I'd ever eaten, save, possibly, the green gelatinous mass that followed as dessert. I was famished and couldn't get enough of the bland hospital food. All my visitors agreed that this was a good sign.

The room was filled with flowers and Jenna read all of the cards to me. She told me that Ollie and Cleon Servais had come upon the scene where Toby was trying to bury me alive and that they'd stopped him. She said that it had started raining as I was being buried and the wildfires had been put out in the torrential downpour that had followed. I had many questions but she insisted that I find out the details from Ollie and Detective Servais. They would be visiting me soon, she said.

I found out that the doctors had punched a hole in my skull to relieve the pressure from a badly swollen meninges, or brain sac. I wanted to feel the hole but Jenna assured me that it had been plugged sometime before I awoke. I asked for a mirror and when Jenna held one up I was able to see for myself why I mispronounced the simplest of words and had to have excess spittle wiped from the left side of my face every few moments. The top of my head was wrapped, turban-like, with yards of white bandages that the nurses changed daily. The entire left hemisphere of my face was basically purplish black, with a mottle of orange and yellow where the bruising was beginning to heal. There were two lines of stitches across my left cheek where the doctors had *entered and pinned and wired my facial bones together. The left orbit, the bony eye socket, had been shattered and they'd rebuilt it using plastic and stainless steel. I hadn't noticed it before, but my nose was bent. Jenna said that was one of the things they would fix later, after the worst of the damage had healed.*

Each day I slept less, ate and bitched more. The food began tasting as bland and as rancid as I'd known all along that it was, and I celebrated my achievement when I convinced Jenna to allow my mother to smuggle me in a bag of burgers, real grease bombs. Jenna helped me to the toilet where I spent the next half hour, but I didn't care. They were that good. Over the course of this time, Jenna never seemed to leave me, showering in the rooms bathroom, changing into clothes that Mom brought for her from home, and crawling into the hospital bed beside me when I slept.

The kids were finally allowed to visit and my room became quite a raucous place as befits the hospital room of a man who has cheated death. Cleve, Rae and Bobbie Jane were a comfort to me, and a source of much pride. They told of how they were dealing with the home front in Jenna's and my absence and how they were looking forward to school closing for the year. Rae told me that Mrs. Benz sent her meows. Each time I looked at them my eyes got wet, they meant so much to me. I found that I wanted to cry more in general. The deaths of Dent and Lontine and their grandchildren, Linda, Zel, and Jack and Rita Muncie, seemed such a waste. Well, maybe not Jack and Rita.

Jenna explained that the office, under the guidance of Sigrid, was doing okay. Our Underwriter had been gracious enough to send down a closer and all property searches were being done at the Underwriter's main office. Everything was working smoothly in our absence, according to the ever-cheerful Jenna.

The special Mangrove Springs election had taken place sometime while I was in never-never land. Delbert Hinley had been elected Mayor. I was pleased. Evan Muster had easily won a seat on the City Council. The remaining four seats were split between two good-ole-boys and two retired corporate types who lived in expensive condos out on the beach.

Rain had finally come to SW Florida, starting as Toby was trying to bury me in the pit. I remembered the slanting silver streaks I'd seen just before blacking out. Jenna told me that a number of trailer homes east of town had burned down, as well as the Red S. I was going to miss the country-fried steak. No one had been injured or killed, thank goodness. Fires were still burning in other parts of the state.

One afternoon, as I awoke from a nap, fully aware of the pins and screws in my face, Jenna told me that I was about to have some visitors. I perked up a bit and was awake enough to observe Cleon Servais push Ollie Mason into the hospital room. Ollie was slumped in a wheelchair.

"What the hell happened to you?" I wanted to know. Cleon pushed Ollie's chair right up to the foot of the hospital bed and engaged the wheel locks. Ollie just grinned at me. Cleon actually answered.

"He took a couple of bullets from Chastain's gun before he went down. Those 22s tend to ricochet around inside a person. There was some internal damage and they performed surgery to repair it and stop the bleeding." Cleon looked down at Ollie with something like pride. "He'll be okay. Needs to stay off his feet a while longer." Ollie was grinning a simpleton's grin. I hoped that the wounds hadn't affected his mind. I should have known better.

"I plugged that bastard. From forty feet and at a full gallop. In the rain. Hit him foursquare in the chest. He just got lucky and hit me a couple of times. But I nailed his carcass!"

"What about Toby?" Ollie just grinned and looked at Cleon.

"Dead," Detective Servais said. "Two bullets from my 9mm and one from Ollie's .380 took him out. I didn't even know that Ollie had a gun."

"I have a permit to carry a concealed weapon," Ollie blustered. "Had it for years. Because, in my daily business, I sometimes carry large amounts of cash." Detective Servais scrutinized my patchwork face.

"You spent some time alone with Chastain." I nodded solemnly and he continued. "What happened?" I took a deep breath.

"Well, he basically confessed to me that he'd killed all the people involved with the Chastain will." I paused and looked Detective Servais in the eye. I proceeded to tell him about the Pet

Cemetery and the Migrant Garden, where he could probably find the remains of all those missing children from a few years back, Patrick Kelly included. Jenna groaned. Then I told him about the hookers who had provided fodder for his insatiable blood lust in recent times, including the tale of the dismembered, cocaine sniffing blonde who had accompanied Toby to the After Hours. Jenna audibly gulped at that.

"Why was Rita Chastain strapped into your car?" I collected my thoughts before relating the whole chain of events; from the call I received from Jack Muncie, to the end, everything that I could remember, even the unfruitful night with Rita. Jenna calmly patted my shoulder.

"He said he was trying to create a scenario in which it would be assumed that Rita Muncie and I had run off together. I believe he engineered the emptying of Muncie's bank accounts and several other factors to make his point."

"You're okay, Roy. That's what's important." Ollie said. "You're alive and so are we and that creep is dead. He'll never hurt anyone again!" Cleon looked at him briefly before turning his attention back to me.

"Ollie called me at my home number."

"He gave it to me during the time that he was investigating that break-in of my property," Ollie said.

"He told me someone had called. From Muncie's. But when he answered, no one spoke."

"I heard some strange sounds and then nothing."

"He told me what you were up to. I picked him up and we went to Muncie's. We found Jack Muncie bent over his desk, dead, and you were not in evidence. We didn't know where to look for you, but we got lucky. Ollie's phone rang and your cell number showed on the caller id. When he answered, we heard Toby ranting. Kinda' muffled, but clear enough." I guessed Rita's corpse had hit the speed dial button for Ollie.

"We figured you must be on the Chastain property. So, we drove up by the main house, but it was dark," Ollie said. "We saw lights through the trees. Cleon turned off the car lights and we followed a dirt road toward the back of the property."

"The light was from the back hoe. Ollie saw the tail end of your car at the bottom of the ramp into the pit. And your head sticking up. Most everything else was already buried." The Detective paused for a moment to clear his throat. "I'll have lots more questions, but we can get together later." He nodded toward Ollie. "Your Caddy was dragged out and hauled to the Sheriff's impound lot. There was extreme damage but Ollie owns a piece of a repair shop and his mechanics and body men told him that they can restore it. As soon as it's released from evidence." I just stared at them. Ollie knew what that car meant to me, had been with me when I bought it. He knew that to me it represented a time gone by, a simpler, maybe better time. Ollie bowed his head a bit and grinned.

After they left I talked to Jenna as she straightened the bed-clothes and cleaned up the room a bit. I watched her as she prepared for bed. When she'd crawled in beside me she said that more of my friends would be visiting tomorrow, Don Stone, Pete and Repeat and the rest of the gang. She also said that Sigrid had expressed an interest in visiting. And of course there would be family. Lots of aunts, uncles and cousins.

I cogitated on the current state of affairs and, after much deliberation, asked Jenna what she'd thought of Ollie's effort to save me from Toby's mad scheme to bury me alive.

"I don't know. He was doing what he could to save your life?" She lay next to me and pulled the crisp covers over her.

"Did you ever notice that Ollie is a big man?" Jenna nodded.

"Uh huh."

"So, I'm big. You know?"

"Uh huh. So what?" I thought about the actions of Ollie Mason, both in the present, when he'd risked his life to save mine, and in the past, when he'd sponsored a bowling team, backed me as I learned to play pool, counseled me about my travels, supported me financially in the title insurance business, and, just generally been there when I needed him.

"I don't know. I'll have to think about it." Jenna snuggled closer to me, wiggling deep into the bedding.

"Jenna?" I whispered.

"Hmm?" she murmured. I gathered my courage and finally said what I'd wanted to say ever since the divorce.

"Will you marry me?"